FOR WHERE THERE ARE HARPS

ANGELS HAVE TREAD TRILOGY
BOOK 3

ALYCE ELMORE

Copyright © 2025 by Alyce Elmore

All rights reserved.

No part of this publication may be reproduced, distributed, or transmitted in any form or by any means, including photocopying, recording, or other electronic or mechanical methods, without the prior written permission of the publisher, except as permitted by U.S. copyright law. For permission requests, contact [include publisher/author contact info].

The story, all names, characters, and incidents portrayed in this production are fictitious. No identification with actual persons (living or deceased), places, buildings, and products is intended or should be inferred.

Book Cover by Aaesha Zhara

First edition 2025

ISBN Softcopy 978-1-7638502-0-0

eBook 978-1-7638502-1-7

Published by Fanciful Flights

www.alyceelmore.com

For Yvonne, Sharon, Judy and Peter

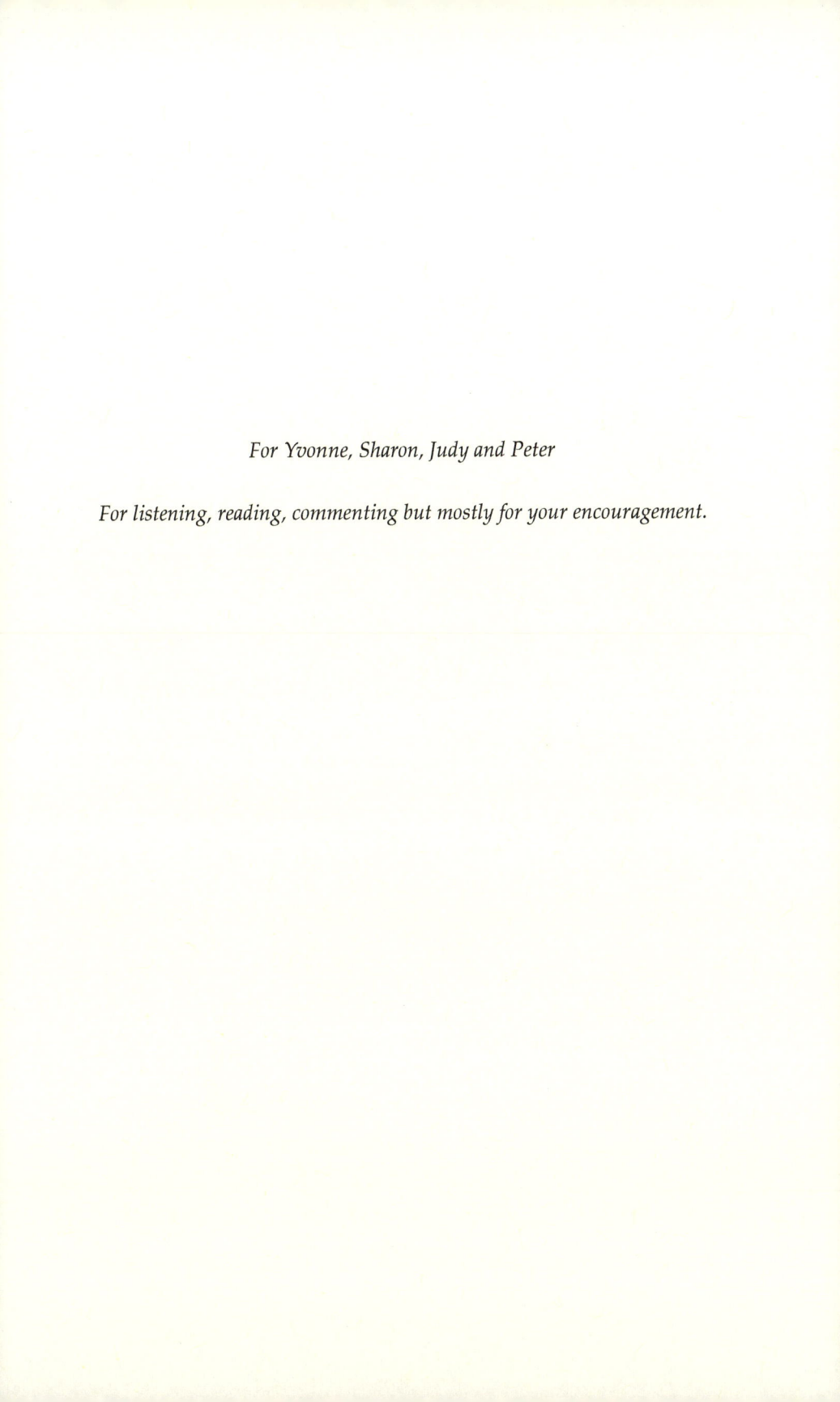

For listening, reading, commenting but mostly for your encouragement.

CONTENTS

THE SERIES SO FAR...

When All Hope Is Lost: Book One	3
Pray To The Dead: Book Two	5
Glossary of Terms	7
Character List	9
1. The Old One's Cabin	11
2. The Old One's Cabin	16
Carla	18
3. The Old One's Cabin	27
Patricia	28
4. The Old One's Cabin	38
Inverloch	41
5. The Old One's Cabin	51
Catherine	54
Monika	62
6. The Old One's Cabin	68
Sofia	70
7. The Old One's Cabin	82
Inverloch	83
8. The Old One's Cabin	92
Monika	94
Catherine	97
9. The Old One's Cabin	105
Dr Harris	106
10. Josh	113
11. Karen	119
12. The Old One's Cabin	128
Patricia	131
13. Patricia	141
14. Monika	147
15. The Old One's Cabin	153
Inverloch	155
16. The Old One's Cabin	163
Monika	164
17. Thomasina	171

Geraldine	176
Jenny	180
Monika	182
18. The Old One's Cabin	184
Dr Harris	186
19. The Old One's Cabin	196
Monika	197
20. Patricia	207
21. Inverloch	211
22. The Old One's Cabin	217
Evelyn	219
23. Josh	224
24. Dr Harris	234
25. Catherine	242
26. Dr Harris	248
27. The Old One's Cabin	254
Steve	256
Benny	260
28. The Old One's Cabin	263
About the Author	267

THE SERIES SO FAR...

WHEN ALL HOPE IS LOST: BOOK ONE

When did his story become hers?

A young girl, hoping to gain entrance to the prestigious Melbourne Institute of Historical Studies is told to interview someone who has lived through the pandemic of 2029, known as the Desolation, she discovers that history books don't always tell the whole story. As the interview progresses, the girl encounters another, more sinister version of the events proceeding the elections of 2050. According to the Old One, the Desolation did not kill all adult males. A few survived. And the defect that makes boys die by the time they turn twenty also has some exceptions. Two of these individuals escape from their prison on French Island but during that escape, they encounter a woman and her young lover. One of the males, Matt, kills the woman but as they flee, they decide to split up. Matt is killed but the younger man, Steve escapes. Evelyn Perkins, the woman credited with saving the Greater Republic of Melbourne covers up the existence of the survivors even as her security officer Davina Warren hunts for them. To keep her inner circle from finding out about the survivors, Evelyn Perkins orchestrates a rivalry between her long-time protégé Monika Thomas and the newcomer Catherine Williams. Patricia Bishop, an investigative reporter is assigned to look into the murders of a string of boys instead of the Premier's murder. As she looks into these deaths she puts the pieces together and in the process meets the researcher, Dr Bonnie Harris. They both get sucked into the political intrigue and find themselves running from Evelyn Perkins' secret police. Caught up in the events are four young friends, Karen, Josh, Benny and Zane, who call themselves the four musketeers. Looking to escape the restrictions imposed on males in the Republic, they plan to escape to the free colony of Warragul but their plans get waylaid when Zane is found dead. The Subversives, a clandestine anti-government group, smuggles Benny out of Melbourne along with the survivor Steve. Karen is also smuggled out but Josh, his mother Dr Harris and Patricia Bishop seek refuge in a deserted apartment building in the Old CBD.

PRAY TO THE DEAD: BOOK TWO

By the year 2049, women rule and men no longer grow old.

The Old One continues the tale of the events that led up to the civil war of 2050, called the Great Upheaval.

The survivor Steve and Benny are met at Venus Bay by a red haired girl, Cherry and two lancers, Bulldog and Jack Russel. They are to take the escapees to Warragul but land pirates attack them and take Cherry prisoner. As the lancers go in search of Cherry, Steve and Benny make their way towards Warragul. Encountering a group of boys, they learn that Warragul is no longer 'male friendly' so Steve and Benny join the group and head for the lancer colony at San Remo. Karen wakes to find herself at the Warragul co-op where she is given a new identity and the new name of Tanya. Patricia Bishop and Dr Bonnie Harris need to escape Melbourne so they go in search of Patricia's links to the Subversives, Penny and her sister Carla. Penny takes Patricia to meet the Subversive leadership who it turns out include several of Evelyn Perkins' inner circle. They want Patricia to expose Evelyn's cover-up of Premier Anderson's murder but not the existence of the survivor because they fear that the public, knowing of a potential cure, will indict them along with Evelyn. Meanwhile, Dr Harris meets with her boss Geraldine Williams. Geraldine tells her that for years she has been smuggling lab supplies to her contacts in Warragul. If Dr Harris can get to Warragul she is to contact Sofia Vargas and give her the code word Genesis. Dr Harris refuses to leave without her son Josh so Carla guides the doctor back to the Old CBD but when they arrive the area is on fire. Dr Harris tries to enter the fire zone and is tranquillized by a paramedic. In Warragul, Sofia has her own problems. Her close friend Jocelyn, who is pregnant is accused of murdering her boyfriend and must stand trial. Back in Melbourne, the meeting of the Subversives is interrupted by orders to evacuate because of the fires. Patricia sees them lead away a girl with red hair and a young boy. The boys from Warragul, along with Benny and Steve enter the coastal town of Inverloch and find themselves surrounded by lancers.

GLOSSARY OF TERMS

Collapse - heart failure among Cusp- aged males
Cusp - the last year's of a young man's life.
Cuspers - young men between eighteen and twenty
Floorboys - derogatory term for young men working in retail
Grunts - derogatory term for young men and boys working as labourers
Lancers - homeless cusp- aged males
Lost boys - young boys deserted by their mothers
No-gos - derogatory term for young men attending university
Studs - derogatory term for young male sex workers
Subversives - underground male's rights group
Survivors - men who didn't die in the pandemic
The Desolation - the pandemic that killed adult males 2029-2032
The Transition - the period immediately after the pandemic 2033-2048
The Interim - the period between the first democratic elections and the Civil War 2050
The Great Upheaval - the Civil War 2050-2053

CHARACTER LIST

Melbourne
Members of New Order Party

Evelyn Perkins - Founder of New Order Party
Monika Thomas - Deputy Premier, formerly minister of for infrastructure
Catherine Williams - Minister for infrastructure
Jenny Connors - staffer
Dorothy Anderson - Premier
Gloria Fenton - Party secretary
Rose Walsh - Party treasurer
Davina Warren - Head of Evelyn Perkins's security

Daily News Feed

Joan Simonds - Editor in chief
Patricia Bishop - Political journalist
Tiffany Prosz - Junior reporter
Amanda - Reporter

Gentech

Bonnie Harris - Head of research
Geraldine Williams - Administrator
Mark Connors - Head of research (deceased)

Four Musketeers

Karen Jacobs - a.k.a. D'Artagnan — Jenny Connors's ward
Josh Harris - a.k.a. Athol — Dr Bonnie Harris's son
Zane Greyson - a.k.a. Porthos — floorboy
Benny Tyler - a.k.a. Artemis – Monika Thomas's toy boy

Melbourne Residents

Penny Zan Soeng - Computer security analyst
Carla Zan Soeng - Restauranteur
Helen Cutter - Coroner
Jaime - Karen's deceased brother
Madelyn Jacobs - Karen's mother
Mike - Patricia's deceased brother

10 ALYCE ELMORE

Nick - Thomasina's cusp-aged brother
Thomasina - Catherine Williams' wife

Survivors

Matt Stevens - ex- SAS soldier
Steven Baker - French Island resident

Warragul

Colony Political Leaders
Jocelyn - Council chair
Sofia Vargas - Council moderator
Kerry - Bailiff
May - Head of police
Alicia - CFA commander
Ginger - Head of health services
Terry - Head of education
Ernestine - Treasurer
Claudia - Secretary
Juanita - Head of housing

Residents
Sara Lang - professor of history
Tanya Baker - name used by Karen Jacobs
Florence - Fish market owner
Philippa - Worker at Heart House
Ingrid - Naturopath and masseuse
Georgina - Owner market co-op
Ursula - Manager of the Sunday market
Cheryl - Former worker at the market co-op
Lauren - Truck driver
Jackson - Trader

Inverloch

Craig - Uni student from Warragul
Jai - Uni student from Warragul
Malcolm - Uni student from Warragul
TJ - lancer twin from eastern colony
Vaz - lancer twin from eastern colonu
Bulldog - lancer from Imverloch
Jack Russel - lancer from Inverloch, Cherry's boyfriend
Cherry - runaway from Melbourne

CHAPTER 1
THE OLD ONE'S CABIN

SEPTEMBER 2069

The cachinnation of a kookaburra shattered the silence of the bush and brought the girl to a halt. Running might take her away from Warragul. It might take her to places she'd dreamt of going. But it wasn't the solution. Much as she wanted to escape the questions that the Old One had raised, she knew that now it was too late. They'd taken up residence. Another laugh from the kookaburra.

The whole point of leaving Warragul was to learn new ways of thinking and encounter new experiences but now that she was confronted with a new way of seeing past events, it frightened her. And with good reason. The views expressed by the Old One were as dangerous today as they were twenty years ago and the stories, true or not, raised doubts that were no less treacherous. Like the women of the post-transition period, everything the girl had accepted as normal was under question and no matter how fast or how far she ran, she couldn't escape the fact that what the Old One told her might be true.

Leaning on her knees to catch her breath, the girl closed her eyes and listened to the quiet of the Gippsland bush. At dinner the night before last, the Old One had said, "Determining the truth requires patience which is why young people have trouble finding it and old people have trouble hanging onto it."

It was another one of the Old One's sayings that didn't make sense. Ancient history required patience because you had to dig through layers of sediment to find enough pieces on which to build a credible story. But the events the Old One recounted were part of the modern world. They were events that occurred in the Old One's lifetime. Events that had been documented and were therefore irrefutable.

A small branch toppled through the canopy of leaves brushing past her head and landing at her feet. She looked up to see the kookaburra, high up in the tree. This time its laugh seemed to be mocking her. Picking up the branch she was tempted to throw it back at the bird but instead tossed it into the scrub. The bird had gravity on its side.

At school, both history and science were taught as facts. History using events and science using laws. Unlike philosophy, they were not up for conjecture. Like Newton's laws of motion. The first said that an object could not change its motion unless something acted on it. She threw the stick and gravity pulled it to earth. It was a fact. The second law stated that force is equal to its mass times its acceleration. The harder she threw the stick, the farther it went. It was measurable, reliable. Until she encountered the Old One, she'd thought that modern history, like science, was based on facts and those facts, like the laws of nature, were something you could rely on.

She continued along the path arguing with herself. The Old One would say that the forces of nature existed but our ability to understand them changed. It was a valid point. She thought of Newton and his apple. His understanding of gravity replaced Descartes' theory of ethers and vortices. That new understanding hadn't changed gravity but it had altered the understanding of it. Then Newton's understanding of gravity, a law that was seen as incontrovertible, was replaced by Einstein's theory of space-time valleys. Einstein didn't alter gravity. The old equations still worked but the understanding of gravity changed. Perhaps the same was true with the Old One's stories. They didn't change the events. Only the understanding of them.

That, however, raised another question. Could the laws of motion be applied to history? Once put in motion were ideas about the past not likely to change without an equally strong force acting on them. And that thought reminded the girl of Newton's third law of motion. For every action, there is an equal and opposite reaction. Airing the Old One's stories were likely to have severe consequences.

Thinking back over the last few days, the girl wished they hadn't wasted their first couple of days together. The girl, as the Old One pointed out, had been as impatient to complete her assignment as the Old One had been reluctant to begin. It was only now, having listened to the Old One's version of events that the girl understood that reluctance. She might be rejected by the Institute for capturing this information but the consequences for the Old One spreading them were far more severe, especially now that Warragul was part of the Republic. Under the Republic's sedition laws, undermining the state was treason. That would explain why the Old One was hiding in this cabin in the bush but it didn't explain why the Old One was now divulging those secrets.

But beyond the secrets and the sedition, the stories brought the world of 2049 to life. The girl especially liked hearing about the four teens who, like herself, were facing an uncertain future. They'd grown up together, calling themselves the four musketeers. But they were also the Desolation babies. Conceived during the pandemic, but born after the last adult died, they were thought to be uninfected.

And they certainly appeared healthy. By the time they were ten, it was obvious that the disease had changed something in the male genome. Josh, Benny and Zane were required to take the Selection test while Karen, being female, was exempt. The laws of nature had changed and each of those friends had, in their own way, rebelled against them. In the last twenty years, the Republic had grown and the laws had changed but young people, like herself, were still required to live by rules thrust upon them by an older generation. No wonder she identified with those teens from a previous generation. At the same time, it was sobering to think that they were the generation she was rebelling against.

Perhaps the Old One was right. She was impatient. Impatient to get on with her life. Impatient to make her mark on the world. Impatient to explore what those worlds had to offer her. Like the four musketeers who wanted to escape the repressive Republic, the girl wanted to escape the provincialism of the former Free Colony of Warragul. The Old One might be satisfied with a cabin in the bush but the girl wanted to see the world beyond it and the Melbourne Institute of Historical Studies was her ticket out. Much as she would like to stay and listen to more of the Old One's stories, it was imperative that she finish today because tomorrow morning, she had to either leave or lose that chance forever.

So why had Tanya suggested the girl interview the Old One when she could have chosen any number of others in the Colony? She could understand why Florence and Georgina weren't good choices. They'd been labelled as rebels during the Great Upheaval. But Ingrid, now mayor and formerly a Melbourne resident, would have been an excellent choice, except that Tanya didn't like her. Still, anyone would have been a better choice than the Old One. Or maybe Tanya thought no one was going to listen to the recordings. After all, the letter from the admissions council said the interview was only a formality.

Part of your curriculum will be learning how to do a proper interview. This entrance requirement will be used as a baseline by which you can judge your progress. Think of it as something you'll look back on and smile.

They made it sound so pleasant. Like one of those warm summer days when everything slumbers through the heat; an afternoon of quiet meditation before the intoxicating vitality of the big city. Obviously, they hadn't met the Old One.

And the start hadn't been that controversial. It began with descriptions of life before the pandemic. Her history books painted a picture of a world on the verge of collapse while the Old One maintained a more nostalgic view. Otherwise, the Old One's account differed from her history book the same way a colouring-in book differed from one that had been coloured. The historical record created the outline while the Old One's stories added the colour. It was when the colouring began to go outside the lines that the girl became concerned.

The kookaburra laughed and another answered. Philippa told her that the kookaburras' laugh was meant to keep other birds away from their territory. Was that what Tanya was doing? Did Tanya think that these stories would dissuade her from going to Melbourne? Or maybe Tanya knew that this interview would get her rejected. Either by persuasion or deterrence, Tanya seemed intent on destroying the girl's chances of leaving Warragul. If that was the case, then the girl was even more determined to leave.

The path took a steep dip and the earth, swollen from the rain, grabbed at the girl's boots, refusing to let go one minute, then recalcitrantly pushing her away the next. Slipping and sliding, she made her way down to the lake. There at the water's edge, she picked up a stone and tossed it as hard as she could. It skimmed the surface, creating tiny ripples until it ran out of energy and sank. Last night, the Old One said that every life was like a stone tossed into the vast waters of the universe. It wasn't the stone that made an impact. It was the waves it left behind. While her history book only talked about the big events, the tsunamis, there were an infinite number of smaller waves that went unnoticed and ignored, but they too, shaped the shore.

Sitting on a branch that hung out over the water, sat a kookaburra. She had no idea if it was the one that had mocked her or the one that had warned her to stay away but in the end, it flew away.

Returning to the cabin, the girl saw the Old One sitting at the table, hands wrapped around an empty cup. The recorder, turned off, waited patiently and next to it, sat the girl's history book.

"Are you ready to continue?" said the Old One not bothering to look up.

Sara removed her boots but left them sitting on the porch. Tomorrow she would decide whether to slip back into them and stay or switch to her running shoes and leave. For now, her priority was to complete this interview. Sitting down at the table she said, "I'm ready."

CHAPTER 2
THE OLD ONE'S CABIN

SEPTEMBER 2069

"Are you sure you want to record this?"

Sara considered the question. Before she took her break the Old One had been talking about the night the old CBD burned down. Earlier in the day, Dr Bonnie Harris and her friend Dr Geraldine Williams held a clandestine meeting in the Women's Peace Park. Bonnie confided that researchers in San Francisco had figured out the cause of the disease. It was a viral-influenced genetic mutation but unfortunately, she didn't know which genes were affected. Geraldine told her that after she was ordered to shut down Bonnie's lab, she was given a new genetic defect to screen for. They both agreed that there was a strong connection between the two. Geraldine then informed Bonnie that there was a backup lab she could use to continue her work but she needed to get to Warragul and give Sofia Vargas the code word, Genesis. Geraldine said she would organise transport for Bonnie but that Bonnie had to leave her son Josh behind. Bonnie, refused. But, as the Old One explained, fate stepped in.

Before leaving for her meeting, Bonnie had told Josh to wait in the apartment building that the reporter Patricia Bishop had taken them to. The unit they were hiding in had once belonged to Patricia's family and they thought it was safe because it was in a derelict part of town that was inhabited by homeless males referred to as lancers. Decent women and even police and firefighters avoided that area. While it was an excellent place to hide, what they hadn't expected was a fire.

The girl knew, even before the Old One continued, that this story was going to be edited out but for some reason, she pressed the record button anyway.

The Old One hmphed and then continued.

"I believe we left off with Carla in charge of keeping Dr Harris safe. Not that she volunteered for the job. Carla had only joined the Subversives so that she could save boys from the labour camps. Her sister Penny was the one with political motives but as Penny pointed out, without Dr Harris, there was no cure and without a cure, there would be no boys to save. Bonnie, however, was adamant that Josh come with her. She hadn't spent twenty years researching a cure for other boys. She was looking to cure Josh."

"So Carla took Bonnie to find Josh because she empathised with her as a mother?"

"That and because Bonnie refused to be reasoned with. Carla thought if she took Bonnie to Josh, then Josh would talk sense into her."

"You said earlier that the paramedics sedated Dr Harris. Is that how Carla was able to get her to a safe place?"

The scarred hand tapped on the table. "The sedative allowed Carla to get Bonnie away from the fire zone but it was Carla's ingenuity that got Bonnie out of Melbourne and on her way to Warragul."

CARLA

FRIDAY 10 DECEMBER 2049 - 6:00 A.M.

Carla sat up, pushing back her hood. During the night, the wind had died down, but it was still blowing from the south, giving the early morning air an unseasonable chill. Briskly, she rubbed her arms to warm them then stood up and stretched. After spending the night curled up in one of the empty storefronts along the old Princess Highway, she needed to get some feeling back into her legs. She stepped out of her shelter and looked in the direction of the Old CBD. The lack of traffic on the road didn't surprise her. Not only were a number of roads closed because of the fires but all businesses throughout the Greater Republic of Melbourne were closed for the memorial service of Premier Dorothy Anderson. In a few hours, news crews that had been covering the conflagration would be relocating to the cathedral. They'd be staking out new vantage points, hoping to get a few sound bites from Monika Thomas, the Acting Premier and to snap pictures of the new infrastructure minister, Catherine Williams. While both women belonged to the NOP, they spoke to different generations. Monika Thomas came from the pre-pandemic world and like many women her age, had strong ties to the past. She'd worked alongside Evelyn Perkins during the Transition and was assumed to be the NOP's candidate. Catherine Williams, however, was the candidate of the future. Along with her wife, Thomasina, she represented the modern nuclear family that consisted of a guardian and a carer but she also lobbied for carers to be allowed to work. Just as Monika was considered to be next in line after Dorothy Anderson, Catherine appeared to be next in line after Monika. As for the opposition, the Progressives, they had yet to produce a candidate or an agenda so the elections weren't shaping up to be much of a race.

That was why Carla didn't have much interest in politics. She left that to her sister, Penny. Penny believed the Subversives could make a difference, whereas Carla's interests were more pedestrian, and right now, getting out of town topped the list. Self-drives would have been the most expedient form of transport to get where she was going but rentals were too easily tracked. Hitch-hiking was another option but traders didn't only transport goods. They traded in information, as well and Carla valued her anonymity. That left public transport. Driverless, and fairly empty at this hour, it was her best option. Stepping onto the highway, she checked again for signs that a bus was headed her way. Last night, there'd been a few busses, but by the time she arrived at the highway, they'd stopped running, and the road had been clogged with army trucks heading south. Around dawn, the trucks came less often and the busy road was deathly quiet. Businesses were closed out of respect for the former Premier but Carla hoped the busses were still operating. If not, it was a long walk to Hastings Pier.

The walk from the Old CBD to St Kilda last night hadn't been long but it had been arduous. Even with the help of her boys, it had been a struggle to get Dr Harris as far as the deserted amusement park by the beach. Then when the doctor passed out, Carla thought she'd run out of options. She was tempted to leave the unconscious woman on the bench and keep walking because as far as she was concerned, she'd done as much as she could. Not that she didn't feel for the woman wanting to get to her son. Risking everything to save the ones you loved was something Carla understood. What she found hard to accept was having responsibility for this woman shoved onto her. She baulked when Penny told her that the Subversive leadership wanted her to protect Dr Harris.

'Political refugees are your domain," she'd told her sister. "I have my boys to look after."

That's when Penny erupted. She'd pushed Carla up against the wall, making her message very clear.

"Without Dr Harris, there'll be no cure and without a cure you won't have any boys to protect."

What scared Carla in that moment wasn't so much the message but the vehemence of its delivery. Penny was the controlled one, the one who never showed her emotions. Whatever Penny's Subversive friends were up to, it was big. It was something so big that individuals were only as important as the role they played and Dr Harris apparently had the lead. As a bit player, Carla accepted that she only had to do her small part and then she was free to leave. Her little task was to arrange a meeting between Dr Harris and Dr Williams, the administrative head of Gentech. Penny said, "Get her safely to her meeting and then hide her back at the safe house and await further instructions." That was all Carla had to do but after the meeting, Bonnie, as Dr Harris insisted on being called, told Carla that she needed to get to Warragul. That was difficult enough but she also stipulated that her son Josh had to come with her.

"Stupid woman," Carla said under her breath. Every border guard in the Greater Melbourne Republic was looking for a mother and son trying to escape. But this woman was stubborn. Exasperatingly stubborn. There was no reasoning with her so Carla improvised. She figured they could head for the apartment in the Old CBD where Josh was hiding, find the boy and then get him to reason with his mother. Carla'd met Josh and knew he was a reasonable lad, so it was worth a shot. Worst case, Carla could bring both of them back to the safe house and let Penny figure out how to get them out. As they headed for the Old CBD, Carla's biggest concern was how to get to the apartment without being spotted. That's where the fires came in. They provided Carla and Dr Harris with a diversion. Moving on foot, they stuck to small streets and laneways, skirting past road closures. Then as they neared the area, they got lost among the melange of emergency workers, reporters and onlookers. Carla, seeing the police cordon, nearly panicked, but then she realised that they were more interested in lancers fleeing the blaze than two women moving towards it. The nearer they got to their destination, however, the more apparent it became that there was a bigger issue. Whereas Dr Harris was panicking over her son being trapped by the fire, Carla was worried about him escaping. If he got picked up by the police he was likely to be recognised and handed over to Evelyn Perkins' personal police force. When they interrogated him about the whereabouts of his mother, he might not be able to tell them where his mother was but he did know the location of Carla's safe house. That's when Carla realised the word 'safe' no longer applied.

And the fire. It had sounded bad on the news but no words could possibly describe what they encountered as they neared the apartment building. It was a raging inferno and Carla knew that if Josh was still in the building, then he didn't stand a chance. Dr Harris, however, refused to accept that her son might be dead and tried to force her way past the barriers. Carla tried holding her back, but the woman went crazy. Even the police had trouble controlling her and that's when the paramedic arrived. In hindsight, tranquilising the doctor was the best thing that could have happened. Carla's boys, who'd been tagging along, helped her move Dr Harris away from the fires and Carla got her to the beach before the woman collapsed on the bench.

Despite sitting apart from the clusters of others who'd come to watch this historic event, Carla and Dr Harris, simply blended in. Groups formed. Disengaged. Wandered apart. Came together. Locals emerging from their homes mingled with non-residents who'd travelled in for a closer look. Some were dressed for an evening out. Others for a jog. Even some in pyjamas. Carla thought it was reminiscent of the intermission at a theatrical event her brother had taken her and Penny to see. Well-dressed attendees from the prized box seats intermingled with those from the cheaper seats in the rafters. Like instruments warming up in the orchestra pit, everyone was talking around and over each other, as they sipped their drinks and anticipated what was going to happen in the next act. Carla had been only five when the pandemic struck. She'd grown up amid the chaos of the meal stations where her mother worked. Often left unattended, she learned to expect the unexpected. Emergency workers grabbed food before rushing off. Some broke down. Some sat down and stared into space and were later carried off. It was no wonder that in the midst of cacophony, Carla found peace. In the food tents, at the theatre and now surrounded by spectators, she felt a sense of calm underpinned by that sense of anticipation. That anything might happen and that's exactly what had happened.

Stomping her feet to get the blood flowing, Carla chuckled at the thought that in a few hours, Dr Harris would be coming out of her drug-induced sleep.

When she wakes up, she'll be furious but at least she'll be on her way to Warragul. And best of all, she's no longer my problem.

Staring at the deserted highway, Carla wasn't sure but she thought she could see headlights heading in her direction. She pressed the signal for the bus hoping that all she had to do now was wait.

And it was waiting that had paid off last night at St Kilda beach. While Carla sat next to the snoring doctor, she'd overheard a couple arguing. They were standing next to a brightly painted van in the parking lot adjacent to the Palais Theater. One was a large woman, in a flamboyant outfit. She was poking her finger into the chest of a much younger, scrawnier woman in plain trousers and an off-white blouse. The poking continued until suddenly, the young one slapped the offending finger aside. The bigger woman responded with a resounding slap to the girl's face that knocked the girl to her knees. Getting back on her feet, the girl screamed, "Bitch", then angrily picked up her bag and storming away from her adversary, headed towards Carla.

"Know where the nearest bus stop is?"

"Where do you want to go?"

"Anywhere that's away from here."

Pointing towards the large white building on the other side of the road, Carla had said, "There's a stop opposite The Esplanade but roads into the CBD will be blocked. You won't get past the Junction, but if you cross the road in front of the building, there's a stop that will take you towards Brighton."

The girl cursed softly, looking towards the fire, and then glanced back at the woman standing by the van.

"That was quite a row you had," said Carla.

The girl was breathing hard as she jammed her hand into her bag.

"Bertha thinks she can call all the shots but not this time. We were supposed to do two more shows at the Palais, but now, all of a sudden, there's this big rush to get out of town." The girl continued searching for something in her bag as she talked.

Carla nodded towards the Old CBD where flames were still shooting up into the night sky. "She might have a point. I think the city's going to be preoccupied with that for a while."

The girl pulled a sucker out of her bag and ripped the paper off.

"Even if she's right, I'm not going back. Them and their rewrite of Shakespeare. Imagine playing Hamlet as a princess. It doesn't make any sense." The girl waved the sucker in Carla's face. "I was good as a male Hamlet. There was no reason to change. Anyway, they're expecting to put on the new, all-female Hamlet this weekend in Warragul. Well, I want to see them pull that off without me."

She stuck the candy in her mouth.

"You're an actress," inquired Carla as a plan started to take shape.

"Actor," growled the furious girl, keeping the sucker's stick gripped between her teeth.

"My mistake," apologized Carla. "We don't get many acting companies."

Removing the sucker and waving it like a wand, the girl continued. "Well, after tonight there'll be one less. Bertha says it's time to move on, but I heard Melbourne's looking for talented artists. They say there's plans to reopen the arts centre."

"And you'd like to get in on the ground floor, I suppose."

Holding the sucker in front of her eye, staring through it like a rose-coloured monocle, the girl replied, "You bet."

"Still, it must be nice to be a travelling actor," continued Carla. "You probably have a border pass similar to the traders and relays."

"Of course, we can come and go pretty much when we want. We travelled through the northern colonies last week. They've got some nice theatres up that way. In that regard they're ahead of Melbourne but that'll change, you'll see and I'll be a part of it."

She bit into the sucker and Carla paused as the girl crunched on the bits. The sugar seemed to be working because the girl's breathing became steadier.

That was Carla's queue.

"Well if you're staying in Melbourne, you probably won't need your pass?"

"I sure hope not, iron fist back there wouldn't let me have it. Said she needed it for my replacement. Hey, is that a bus coming?"

Carla, had gotten the information she needed, and eager to move the girl on, said, "Yes, that's your bus but you'd better run because it's probably the last one tonight."

The girl dropped the stick on the ground. "Sounds like my ticket out of here."

Your not alone in that regard, thought Carla as the girl ran to the bus stop. Looking over her shoulder, Carla saw the smiling moon face of the giant head guarding the entrance to the amusement park and smiled back. "Well Dr Harris, it appears fortune is smiling on both of us tonight."

That had been last night's lucky break, but watching the approaching vehicle, Carla realised it was going too fast for a bus, so she pulled her hood up and stepped back into the shadows. The vehicle became a truck and as it flew past, Carla could see its back was full of lancers. She'd seen them travelling in convoys of five or more during the night and had wondered where they were heading.

At least she knew where Bonnie was headed. The transaction with the fat lady by the van had been straightforward. Carla'd walked up to her as the woman lit a cigarette.

"I hear you're leaving town tonight."

"Yep, as soon as these army trucks get off the roads, I'm heading for Warragul."

"What a coincidence. My friend over there needs to get to Warragul, but public transport's a problem because of the fires. She's a friend of Sofia Vargas. I don't suppose to know Sofia?"

"Sofia? Everyone knows Sofia. You wouldn't be looking for me to give her a ride would you?"

"I might need more than that," said Carla, "See, she lost her bag when we were escaping from the fire, and well, she's got no ID and no pass."

Inhaling, the light from the burning cigarette highlighted a glint in the woman's eye which Carla interpreted as a good sign.

"I might be able to help but there's risks."

"Sofia would be quite disappointed if her friend were unable to make her appointment so if you could deliver her, I know that she'd be happy to compensate you."

Smoke filled the air as the woman exhaled.

"What's she doin' layin' on the bench?"

"She got hit in the head and I think she's got a bit of a concussion."

"Hmm. Concussions cost extra."

"Like I said, Sofia will look after you, once you deliver her friend to her."

The woman stomped out her cigarette.

"Alright, but you gotta help me get her in the van."

After that, Carla was free. She'd done her part and passed the doctor onto Bertha's Traveling Shakespeare Company. What happened now to Dr Harris was up to fate. It was with a virtuous heart that Carla walked from the beach to the highway where she found a place to sleep and expected to sleep the deep and resounding sleep of the just. But with every truck that rumbled past, she thought of Josh. She'd only met him once which was how she knew he was a friend of Zane's. Poor Zane. He'd been mistaken for his friend Benny, who had information the Subversives wanted revealed and the secret police wanted kept secret. Carla didn't know Benny or what had happened to him but she knew that Zane's friendship had cost him his life. And now Josh was either dead or on his way somewhere, and everyone knew that boys on their way somewhere usually wished they were dead.

Another set of lights headed towards her. This time, it was a bus, so she pulled down her hood and stepped into the light.

They were nice boys, Zane and Josh, but there were other nice boys.

Too many to save them all, she thought, but that didn't mean that she wasn't determined to save the ones she could.

CHAPTER 3
THE OLD ONE'S CABIN

SEPTEMBER 2069

"So no one knows what's happened to Josh and Carla has managed to find a way for Dr Harris to get out of Melbourne but what about Patricia Bishop? Wasn't she also wanted by the secret police?"

"So Josh is dead, too!"

The girl was visibly upset. Does Dr Harris tell her when she gets to Warragul? And Benny—"

"Slow down," said the Old One. "Before we get to Warragul we need to talk about Patricia."

"Well, I know she survives because she wrote a book about the war."

"And we'll get to that soon enough, but first, we have to get her out of her current predicament. As you recall, she was meeting with the Subversive leadership, Rose Walsh, Gloria Fenton, Jenny Connors and her editor-in-chief Joan Symonds, when they had to evacuate because of the fires.

PATRICIA

FRIDAY 10 DECEMBER 2049 - 6:00 A.M.

Patricia pulled the latest version of her article off the printer and slammed it as hard as she could on the desk where Joan slept. Her editor, head pillowed on her arms, opened her eyes and stared at it wearily before she straightened up, and, stifling a yawn, picked up her red pen. All night Patricia'd made changes to her words. Deletions. Additions. Move this to the top, that farther down, no, no, no, you can't put that in. What she wanted to report and what the Subversive leadership wanted the public to know might not be totally aligned but surely this version had found that common ground. Besides, she was exhausted from a night of hassling over words and wanted nothing more than to finish this article and go home and sleep.

Feeling like a caged animal, Patricia paced around the room. Something important was annoying her but she couldn't put her finger on it. That nagging feeling had hounded her all night which was probably why every little thing from Penny's whistling snores to Joan's staccato pen and the drum beat of water dripping from a tap somewhere in the house, all conspired to intensify that itch in her head. Even now, seeing Penny blissfully asleep next to the back door frustrated and angered her so that she was tempted to step on her or trip over her, but then she heard the scratch of Joan's pen on paper. Not another change! Infuriated, she stormed past Penny and kicked the door instead. It flew open then ricocheted back at her so that she had to put out her hand to defend herself.

Swearing, she stepped outside where the cool morning air confronted her. Some of the houses, like this one, had been finished before they were abandoned, while others had been left in varying stages of completion. No noisy neighbours with their barking dogs or meowing cats. No birds welcoming the day with their warbles. It was an entire suburb of deserted dwellings huddled together as the encroaching bush surrounded it like marauding barbarians.

To the east, the city skyline, that might once have enticed the intended inhabitants of this place to venture in for entertainment or shopping, lay hidden behind the invading trees. Last night, they'd been invisible because the thick black clouds from the fires had shrouded out the moon and erased the stars but this morning the sun was smeared across the sky in a brilliant streak of orange and all was laid bare. In the still air, the smell of smoke lingered the way a woman's perfume hung around long after she'd left. A sign, not only that she'd been there, but that now she was gone. That orange haze and the wisp of a smell were the only reminders of last night's frantic race from the townhouse in North Melbourne to this derelict house in the western suburbs.

Navigating the tiny deck, Patricia stepped onto the first of two steps that led into the backyard. The space separating house from yard was barely big enough to allow for a small BBQ and one person to tend it. It was incongruous for a suburb this far from the city to consist of oversized houses whose outdoor areas were no bigger than the balcony of her family's old apartment in the city. At least from her family's apartment, she could look out on the city, but here, the narrow decks and postage stamp-sized backyards looked inward. The place felt claustrophobic. Where were the children supposed to play? Where were the clothes to be hung out to dry? Not that it mattered now. This suburb had not survived. Dead on arrival. How many times as an ambulance driver during the Desolation had she heard –

No, she wouldn't let her mind go there. Instead, she directed her thoughts to her grandparent's house in the city's inner suburbs. Unlike this suburban backyard that had barely enough room to swing a cat, the house she now shared with her mother, had a massive green lawn with flowers that magically re-emerged every spring. It was a place large enough to accommodate a game of tag and tranquil enough to enjoy reading under a tree. There, fences defined the extent of the backyard while here, they jostled against each other as if struggling to garner more room for themselves. Like a child dressed in clothes two sizes too small these houses were squeezed up against each other and what greenery existed was wild and uninviting. Instead of pretty butterflies flitting around or bees humming as they moved from flower to flower, swarms of orange and brown beetles scurried from place to place, their rear ends stuck together. As she watched them, she wondered if one always led while the other followed or if they exchanged roles from time to time. Like so many neighbourhoods in the outer west, this had been under construction when the Desolation hit and now neither Melbourne nor the wilding colony of Melton claimed it. Half-formed, what little beauty it might have generated had been abandoned. It was no man's land. As the term popped into her head, lassitude overwhelmed her and she sank down on the step. She wanted to leave this place and return to her own world but there was no leaving until Joan was satisfied.

The sound of footsteps interrupted her thoughts. Then a hot mug appeared in front of her as Penny sat down next to her.

"It's been a long night. Are we done yet?"

Penny's question, innocent as it was, only served to pique Patricia further. She resisted the urge to hurl the mug as hard as she could into the forest of weeds. Oh, to be a child again and throw a tantrum. Kick something. Scream. Instead, she wrapped her hands tight around the mug and stretching out her foot, squished a beetle couple. She wanted to blame Penny for getting her involved with these people but she couldn't because it was Penny who had tried to warn her off. She wanted to blame Joan for assigning her to this story but she couldn't because it was her curiosity that had led her down the rabbit hole of disappeared boys. No, she had no one to blame but herself and that infuriated her even more. Raising the mug to her lips, she took a sip. The coffee was bitter and too hot to drink but she swallowed it anyway. Why did she subject herself to things that felt uncomfortable?

When the evacuation orders brought last night's meeting to an abrupt end, Patricia thought she'd received a reprieve. At least she was no longer the centre of anyone's attention and felt free to observe. She'd observed a plain white van as it pulled up in front of the townhouse and blocked the narrow street. She'd observed hands carrying boxes. Observed them being passed, baton-like, into waiting hands that shoved them into the van. It was a frenetic moving day scene but off in the corner, away from the mayhem, Patricia observed Jenny. She was staffer to both Monika Thomas and Catherine Williams, and yet, here she was, talking in hushed tones with the secretary of the NOP, Rose. Could there be any more incongruous people joined together under the Subversive banner? But still, Patricia stood quietly observing. She observed how the more Jenny talked, the more Rose's face darkened. If only she was observant enough to read lips. Then, she'd been distracted by a ruckus in the hall. The closed room that Joan had escorted her past, the one that held back harsh whispered voices, was thrown open. She watched as a couple of teenagers, a boy and a girl were hustled past her and shoved into the van. Their eyes had momentarily connected, and in that brief exchange, Patricia saw a kindred spirit. There was a fierce defiance that Patricia had had but lost along with so much else during the Desolation. Then the van door was slammed shut and it moved away to be replaced by another white van. And all the while Patricia continued to observe until she too was grabbed and shoved into a van. And now, here she was doing the same thing to Penny, passively observing her friend pensively drinking her coffee and staring intently towards the CBD. Passive on the outside but like the girl in the van, seething on the inside.

"What does forced silence mean?"

Penny, about to take a sip, stopped. Stretching out her arms so that they settled on her long athletic legs, she took a deep breath.

"Where did you pick up that term?'

"I heard Jenny mention it to Rose as they rushed out the door. I heard her say, "She's been picked up", and then something about "forced silence".

Penny emptied the remnants of her coffee onto the long grass and watched the coupling beetles scatter.

"Subversives work in small, semi-autonomous cells. When someone in the group gets picked up, all the links in that cell are at risk. If those links can't be taken to safety, we have to make sure the incarcerated link doesn't talk."

"And how do you do that?"

Penny stood up and without answering, walked back inside.

Patricia's thoughts turned to the young girl, Karen, who'd publicly announced that the government had closed down Dr Harris' lab. Was she the person who'd been picked up? Did she know that her guardian, Jenny, was a Subversive? Was that the thought that was nagging at her? She replayed yesterday morning when she'd learned that the girl was missing – but no, it couldn't be Karen that Jenny was talking about because Karen had turned up at the morgue very much alive and surely that trader had gotten Dr Cutter and Karen safely out of Melbourne. So who had been picked up and who were they likely to betray? Carla? No, Penny wouldn't be here if her sister had been picked up. Was it Dr Harris? She was supposed to be safely in Carla's custody. Josh? He was supposed to be safe in her family's old apartment in the Old CBD. She looked at the orange glow to the east and her hand went automatically to her neck but the chain was gone. She'd given Josh her good luck charm and now she could only hope that it had served him well. These were the people she cared about and they had all been accounted for so why was she so concerned about someone whose identity she didn't even know?

"Joan wants to see you."

Penny was standing in the doorway but Patricia didn't bother to look over her shoulder. Using the handrail she pulled herself up with one hand and poured out the remaining coffee with the other. The hot liquid sent more beetles scurrying out from their hiding places.

Joan might not have been the best editor the Daily News Feed ever had, thought Patricia as she headed back inside, but the woman knew what the Subversive leadership wanted and she wasn't going to let

Patricia leave until she got it. The story Patricia wanted to write, the one she wasn't allowed to write, was about the survivors. Their existence meant there was hope. It also gave meaning to those boys whose already short lives had been cut even shorter. The fact that someone was killing them to make sure the existence of survivors remained a secret, meant only one thing. Someone knew that a cure was possible and they were intent on making sure that the public didn't know. The Subversive leadership insisted that Evelyn Perkins was the culprit. They stated that Evelyn had lied to them about the Premier's death which meant that she knew all along that the murderers were adult males and not lancers. But did that mean that Evelyn knew that a cure was possible? The woman was as close to sainthood as a human could get so accusing her required more than assumptions. It required undeniable proof.

And that was at the crux of Patricia and Joan's arguments last night. The Subversive leadership wanted to disclose Evelyn's cover-up of the Premier's murder but they didn't want the public to know about the survivors. At least, not yet. They argued that they needed to distance themselves from Evelyn before they could denounce her fully. "What do you think would happen," Joan said, "if all those mothers whose sons died thought Evelyn held back a cure? Do you think they will discriminate between Evelyn and the others in her inner circle?" She hadn't waited for Patricia's response. Instead, she continued with, "And what if she doesn't have a cure? We only know that two adult males have survived. That fact alone doesn't mean there's a cure but if you mention survivors that's exactly the conclusion the public will draw. These public protests against the new restrictions on cuspers already have a growing base of supporters. Do you want to be responsible for what happens next? Are you willing to take that chance?"

Patricia, unconvinced, asked Joan why the Subversive leadership thought they had the right to decide what the public should or should not know. Didn't that make them as guilty as Evelyn when it came to making decisions about what was good for society?

"Why not tell the public what we know? Let the election become a referendum."

"And who would we run in opposition?" asked Joan.

So was that the real issue wondered Patricia. Were they buying time to find a candidate?

As Patricia walked back inside, she saw Joan standing next to the desk, packing up her things with one hand while the other held her phone up against her ear. She signalled for Patricia to come closer then looked at Penny and nodded towards the front door. As Joan turned her back on both of them to finish her conversation, Patricia had the uncomfortable feeling that something had changed. The shift was subtle but that only served to make it all the more concerning.

Joan ended her call. Picking up her bag, she said to Patricia, "You've done an excellent job. It's the best article you've ever written so I'll make sure it carries your by-line."

"What? No, that was not part of the deal. You put my name on that article and my life won't be worth anything."

"Which should make it easier for you to remember who your friends are. Now Penny will keep you company while I'm gone. Don't worry, you're safe here."

Those words weren't that comforting and even less so when Joan whispered something to Penny as she walked out. As Penny locked the door, Patricia felt her nagging feeling take shape.

"How did you get involved with these people?" Patricia lashed out.

"The same way you did. I started asking questions."

"Do you trust them?"

"Some of them." She hesitated, then added, "Sometimes."

Patricia probed further. "Rose was once a rival of Evelyn's, wasn't she?"

"That was a long time ago. They settled those differences."

"But, they haven't always agreed, have they?"

"That has nothing to do with why Rose and Gloria are Subversives. Rose has close ties with elements that benefit from boy labourers. Gloria, on the other hand, would like to see boys treated more fairly. What they have in common is their opposition to Evelyn's long-term agenda."

"So the Subversives are not a cohesive little group."

"Political parties rarely are," replied Penny.

"And what about you? Where do you stand in all of this, you and your sister Carla?"

Penny lounged against the door, but Patricia knew she'd hit a nerve because Penny was biting her lip. As chess opponents, they were not well-matched. Penny was far superior but Patricia had learned that Penny only bit her lip when she'd made a bad move. That tell-tale sign was Patricia's signal to look for the blunder. The question now was what weakness had she stumbled upon?

"You said Rose and Gloria had different agendas but found a common goal. Is that the same with you and Carla?"

Penny bit on her lip but didn't respond.

Patricia realised she'd been unconsciously aware of a conflict between the sisters.

"Did you recruit your sister or did she recruit you?"

Penny considered her next move and decided to open up.

"Our brother was sequestered like other men deemed important. He was in the SAS and was sent to a secret location. After things settled down, my mother went looking for him. She never returned. Carla wanted to go looking for her but I said there were better and faster ways to find information. But Carla couldn't sit around. She had this drive to do something. One day, she came home and said she knew what she had to do. She'd gone to some male rights meetings and met people. When they learned who I was, they said they wanted to meet me as well."

"Because of your computer skills?"

"It seemed like an equitable exchange. They needed my skills and, in return, offered me greater access to the internet where I was free to search for the men who were unaccounted for."

"And Carla?"

"She frees boys from labour camps and they help to smuggle them to the free colonies."

"So some of the Subversives want to keep boys alive so they can provide cheap labour and others want to free them. How does that work?"

"The business end of town finances Subversive operations and turns a blind eye to the smuggling operations because the colonies don't take older boys, and they're the ones that are most in demand. What they both have in common is a desire to take control away from Evelyn Perkins."

That's when Patricia realised what had been nagging at her. It wasn't about the boys. Not directly anyway. And it wasn't about the election.

"Without a cure," she said, "the slavers—"

"Businesswomen," restated Penny.

"No," said Patricia firmly, "let's call them what they are, slavers." Then continuing, she said, "Without a cure, they have a steady supply of throw-away workers, which ends if Evelyn gets her way. On the other hand, if there's a cure, they also lose because boys are no longer a commodity. They're as opposed to finding a cure as Evelyn but they buy the loyalty of males' rights activists like Carla. What the factions within the Subversives have in common is that they both need to keep boys alive. And that's why they covertly support the smuggling trade. Even if Evelyn manages to get rid of males in the Republic, people like Carla have managed to keep some in reserve. All they have to do is retrieve them from the colonies.

Turning on her friend she asked, "So what are these boys in the colonies, future labourers or breeding stock?"

Patricia could see that Penny knew she'd been trapped, but she was ready to admit defeat.

"I'm not sure," she said. Then she quickly added, "And I don't want Carla to know about any of this. She risks her life to save these boys."

Standing to attention, so that she looked down on Patricia, Penny took back control. Speaking with calm determination, she added, "A cure changes everything. It disrupts Evelyn's plans for a lasting matriarchy and—"

"It also upsets the delicate balance in the Subversive group," said Patricia, finishing Penny's sentence.

The two eyed each other. Was this checkmate or was there another move?

"That's why you tried to warn me off this story. You were afraid I might discover that the Subversives are as opposed to finding a cure as Evelyn."

"Only some of them," clarified Penny. "I knew that certain individuals wanted to get their hands on the survivor, so I made special arrangements for him to take a different route than we normally used, but even my plans were interrupted, and I must admit, I'm glad he's disappeared. Now, no one can take advantage of him."

Patricia considered this, then said, "Your survivor, the one you rescued said that there were more men imprisoned on French Island. Why don't the Subversives try to free them? I mean, they went so far as to risk kidnapping Davina Warren's kids to find out if Evelyn's researchers had a cure—"

"They didn't kidnap her children. Davina put out a bounty on them. Rose found out that they'd been found and offered the pirates a better deal."

"But why?" asked Patricia. "Why get involved in kidnapping kids when they could go to French Island and find out for themselves? It doesn't add up and you know it."

When Penny didn't respond she continued, "Why hasn't anyone gone down to French Island?"

"Because it's too dangerous," replied Penny.

"No, I think," mused Patricia, "that they don't care about the prisoners or the boys for that matter. They only want to know if there's a cure because then they can make a deal with Evelyn to keep their labour supply."

Penny remained silent but Patricia knew what her next move was going to be.

"We need to go there. We need to go to French Island," she said. Even as Penny shook her head, Patricia nodded. "You know that too, don't you?"

CHAPTER 4
THE OLD ONE'S CABIN

SEPTEMBER 2069

"But while we're talking about everyone's agendas, let's not forget Evelyn's protégés; Monika and Catherine. They were both so desperate to get Evelyn's endorsement that they never stopped to think about what it was going to cost."

"But I thought it didn't matter. That the election of 2050 was between—"

"Forget what that textbook says. Yes, the election created a new party that rivalled the NOP, and the votes were close, but the real issue in 2050 wasn't about who would or would not become Premier. That election was nothing more than a sideshow orchestrated by Evelyn to distract the public from the real issue - a male's right to exist."

The Old One spread the pile of photos that sat on the table.

"Monika and Catherine weren't the only ones who fell for it."

Waving gnarled fingers over the scattered pictures, the Old One said, "We all fell for it, but fooling the public into thinking the election was important was one thing. Fooling the contestants into believing they were important was an even greater tragedy.

In their short time together, the girl had seen many sides to the Old

One but for some reason, seeing a single tear shocked her even more than the scandalous stories.

Seeing that lone drop wind its way among the wrinkles like a weary traveller, the girl wasn't sure if it expressed anger or sadness because the Old One's voice registered both.

"Despite the lives of millions of boys hanging in the balance, Monika and Catherine were so distracted with each other that they failed to see how Evelyn's fear-mongering, her rumours and misinformation, were polarizing communities within Melbourne and even the surrounding colonies. Those two may not have caused the Great Upheaval, but as leaders, they failed to prevent it."

"So," the girl hesitated, not sure what to say. Meanwhile, the tape whirred. Taking a breath, she asked, "Are you saying that the election led to the Great Upheaval?"

"You're not listening!"

The Old One banged the table and tea splashed onto the girl's history book

The girl was taken aback but before she could say anything, the Old One calmed down and said in a voice devoid of emotion, "Neither Monika nor Catherine gave a second thought to the boys who were being rounded up and transported out of the city. No one paid attention to that. And it wasn't only lancers in the Old CBD who were being taken away. It was any male who was out during the curfew. Even boys harbouring in their homes were picked up over the coming weeks. Registered or unregistered, they were all picked up and taken away."

"But surely boys with –"

"What? Families? Who were those families going to contact? There was no hotline to call, no Red Cross to match lost boys with their families, and no police station that noted the names and faces of the missing. For the families of those boys who disappeared, there was simply a wall of silence."

The girl considered this. Her textbook had mentioned the Conflagration of '49 as having rid the city of some deserted high rises. Their destruction, it said, made way for new communities. Ones with broad boulevards, elegant townhouses and new infrastructure. It spoke of urban renewal but failed to mention how it made the area's previous inhabitants homeless. Was it because the lancers, like their homes, stood in the way of progress? Could people have been so oblivious to the plight of those boys that they never questioned where they were being taken? Or maybe there was another reason.

"You said that the gender laws in the Republic were becoming more and more oppressive before the elections so maybe being sent out of Melbourne was a way of protecting them. Weren't both Karen and Josh planning to escape to the Free Colony of Warragul? And when Benny needed to get out of Melbourne, didn't he head for the Eastern Wilds?"

The Old One picked up a photo. It was the one with the four young teens.

"Warragul was outside the Republic, and yes, it was a free colony, but where the lancers were being dropped off wasn't on the road to Warragul. It wasn't even on the way to the wilds. It was on the road to San Remo and Phillip Island. Like the Mornington Peninsula, those areas were part of the Republic. Those boys weren't escaping Melbourne's tyranny. They were being herded south to its furthermost region where they could be contained."

The Old One passed the photo to the girl.

"But if you're curious about cuspers who escaped from the Republic, they soon discovered that most civilised colonies didn't want males over the age of twelve. The lucky found their way to one of the lancer enclaves while the unlucky discovered there were worse places to be.

INVERLOCH

FRIDAY 10 DECEMBER 2049 - 6:00 A.M.

So far nothing had gone to plan and the more Benny thought about it, the more he realised he liked it that way.

Plans, especially other people's plans for him, sucked. Like that plan to go to Warragul. That had never felt right. Yes, he needed to get out of Melbourne. And the smugglers who got him out were nice enough, although he wasn't so sure about that red-haired girl who called herself Cherry. He didn't say anything to Steve but he was secretly glad when those pirates abducted her. Partly, it was because she was so condescending when the smugglers handed him and Steve over to her at Venus Bay, but it was also because he never liked the idea of one woman pawning him off onto another. In his early days as a stud, that's how women treated him until he learned how to manipulate them as much as they manipulated him. Then studding became a game. Nothing more. That was until he met Monika. But Monika was no longer part of his story.

Then there was Steve. Steve wanted to stick to the plan and head for Warragul despite what happened at the rendezvous point. That plan got scuttled when they met the boys from Warragul. They'd been run out of town and said that the place wasn't safe for males any more. Their plan was to head for the lancer colony at San Remo and they convinced Benny and Steve to join them. Now that plan might have worked if they hadn't stopped to check for supplies in this sleepy little town of Inverloch. To his credit, Steve took the initiative last night when they found themselves surrounded. He tried to explain that they were refugees from Warragul and that they only wanted to get some supplies and move on but their captors weren't interested in either their explanations or their plans. Instead, they hustled them into this warehouse and then disappeared. Fortunately, the place came supplied with food and water. Unfortunately, it also came with locks on the door and bars on the windows.

Having given up on plans, Benny wasn't sure what to expect when he woke this morning but that added an element of surprise to his day that Benny found he liked. It was like when he decided to ditch being a grunt and signed up as a stud. For a grunt, every day was pretty much the same. They showed up for work when they were told, did what they were told and clocked off when they were told. They all knew their days were numbered but instead of making the most of it, they lived as if they'd already climbed into their graves. Benny wanted more. He wanted to live as much as he could for as long as he could.

He glanced over at Steve who didn't know what it felt like to live with a number over your head. He was sitting under the only window in the place and despite the dirt caked on the window and the heavy bars across the outside, was using what light there was to read that flyer he'd found yesterday. Benny thought that the way he was studying it, you'd think it was a treasure map or held the secret to staying alive. Staying alive, now that's something worth reading about but not some piece of trash. Not that there was anything wrong with reading. Benny's best friend Josh read all the time, and Benny enjoyed listening to Josh retell the stories he read, but as for himself, life was too short. He preferred pictures to words. He particularly liked those pictures in Monika's vintage magazines. His favourite featured a beautiful women draped across the front of a sleek red car. They were long gone, those combustion engine cars. All of them except that big black limo he'd seen Evelyn Perkins arrive in. That was the day he overheard the women's conversation. At the time, he thought it was great that Monika was likely to be the next Premier but more importantly, he thought that he would've given anything to have a ride in that car. Now, the magazines, the limo and Monika were all gone.

He was starting to understand how women must've felt after the Desolation was finished and the world they knew no longer existed. Monika was one of those women. She'd been born into the world pictured in those magazines and knew what had been lost. But then so had Steve. He wasn't as old as Monika but he was old enough to remember what the world had been like. It was while they were travelling the countryside looking for the road to Warragul that they got to know each other. Benny told Steve about how he'd wound up in the smuggler's boat. They'd been sitting in the half-dark, but Benny was pretty sure he'd seen a strange look cross Steve's face when he said that Premier Anderson had been murdered on French Island. It only lasted for a second and Benny figured he might not have noticed if Steve hadn't been quick to change the subject. Accommodating rich, powerful women, had taught Benny to pay as much attention to what was not said as to what was, so he knew Steve was hiding something. But that was another thing he learned while studding. It was an unwritten rule but one they all stuck to. You never pried into another stud's past unless they wanted to talk about it. And Steve didn't want to talk about his days as a stud. Nor did he want to talk about how he came to be at Hastings Pier but that was obvious. The smugglers had to get him out because he was a survivor.

Despite the mysteries, Benny liked Steve. It was like having an older brother. There were boys Benny's age who could remember having an older brother but no one remembered having a father. Benny's generation was the last to be conceived by the pre-pandemic males and the first to grow up fatherless. Like Monika's magazines, Steve's memories, particularly those of his father, gave Benny a glimpse into that other world. The one his mother refused to talk about.

Once when he was searching for something he could use as a cape for one of his musketeer adventures, he stumbled across a picture of a man standing next to a happier version of his mother. Excited, he showed it to her, hoping it would make her smile and for a moment, it almost happened. She looked at the photo, her hard face softening, but it didn't last. There was bitterness in her voice as she said, "There's no point going backwards." Then she tore up the photo and tossed it in the rubbish.

And it wasn't only his mother who didn't want to talk about that pre-time. His friend Josh found books that talked about men; adventurers, warriors and scientists. Their stories were interesting, but none of them mentioned fathers and sons. Like those cars in the magazines, they were an anachronism. Benny remembered that word because he liked the way it sounded. Males over 20, sons with fathers, cars with combustion engines; they not only belonged to a time that not only no longer existed but one that had been deliberately and methodically erased.

Shaking his head, Benny returned to the question of planning and the only plan that made sense to him now, was how they were going to get out of here. He pressed his ear against the heavy metal door and listened for sounds of activity but outside was quiet. It was like playing hide and go seek only he wasn't sure who or if anyone was going to come looking for him. Thinking of his childhood reminded him that there was a time when he'd had, not so much plans as dreams. Along with his friends, Josh, Zane and Karen, he'd imagined a life of adventure: pirating, swashbuckling, finding hidden treasure, but whatever plans any of them had had been crushed the year they turned 10. That's when they brought in the Selection. It was a test boys had to take, and it was used to categorise and pigeonhole them into what was deemed acceptable male work. At least he'd been quicker than most to suss out the new system. By law, he had to wait until he was sixteen to become a stud but Benny found that there were ways around everything. He'd met ex-studs, who'd become lancers. They introduced him to a world outside the system.

"Join with us and you have the option to say no," they said. "Join the bath house and they sell you to anyone who's willing to pay."

But Benny figured there were more advantages to working within the system so once he was old enough, he signed up with a local bath house. And he never regretted it. Pleasing women was a whole lot better than hauling rubble from construction sites. Sure, the women who frequented the bathhouses expected sex, but he gave them more than that. He discovered that what they liked better than sex, even good sex, was someone who listened to them. Someone who made them feel valued and someone who made them feel happy again. Personally, he preferred younger women, but it was the older ones, the ones who'd lived through the Desolation, who seemed most appreciative of male company, and he quickly learned how to spot the wealthiest ones. They were his ticket up and out. And the more he charmed, flattered them, and amused them, the more they asked for him by name. It wasn't long before he moved from the bathhouse to private positions in well-to-do houses. Yes, they passed him among themselves like a cherished plaything, but he lived better than he ever thought possible. He was using them as much as they were using him. That is until he became Monika's toy boy.

Like the other women he serviced, she was wealthy and well-connected. In fact, as Infrastructure Minister, she was the most powerful woman in politics next to the Premier. That alone was enough of an aphrodisiac but when she dropped her superior attitude and let herself go, he thought of her as more of a person than a client. Perhaps that was how he messed up or maybe it was because of the 'cusp'. Either way, he'd broken one of the cardinal rules, the one that stipulated only females could initiate sex.

It had all seemed innocent enough at the time. They had both enjoyed their early morning session, but then she went for her shower, and he followed her. Even now, he thought they had both enjoyed the impromptu climax but when he saw that look on her face, he knew he'd gone too far. Perhaps, he overreacted by running away, but he'd heard tales about others who crossed that line, and he wasn't about to stick around.

Hiding at his friend Zane's, he mentioned that conversation he'd overheard and Zane got all excited.

"Are you saying that Evelyn Perkins instructed the others to lie about when and where the Premier was murdered?"

Benny had nodded, not understanding his friend's enthusiasm.

"It's all over the news. They're saying the Premier was murdered on her yacht on Sunday morning."

"So?"

"So, I have contacts who'll be willing to trade your story for free passage out of the Republic."

Benny was glad Zane had come up with a plan but he wasn't so keen on getting involved with the Subversives. He'd heard his clients talking about them. They said they were dangerous terrorists who wanted to disrupt this new age of prosperity. But there was nothing dangerous about Zane. He was as kind and gentle as anyone. And if the Subversives were so dangerous, why would Zane have recruited Karen? He loved her. But they were secretive. So secretive that even Josh didn't know that Zane and Karen had joined. But all that was ancient history now. Zane was probably enjoying Benny's bike, the one Monika had given him, and Karen and Josh were undoubtedly continuing their illicit relationship, and here he was, stuck in a warehouse in Inverloch, wondering what his captors planned to do with him.

Movement on the other side of the warehouse caught his attention. The boys from Warragul were waking up, stretching and yawning loudly. Like Benny, they had no idea what to expect in San Remo, so they talked about the life they left behind. Two of the boys, Craig and Malcolm, had been smuggled out of the Republic when they were babies while Jai was found as a toddler on the steps of the Arts Centre. His mother was assumed to be a wilding. All of them had been raised in Heart House and when they went uni, they decided to room together in a place they called the dorm. When Benny said that they must be really smart to have passed the Selection, they laughed. The oldest one, Craig, said that Warragul didn't have a selection test. Anyone who wanted to attend classes could do so. Benny didn't understand why anyone would choose to be a student. To hear Josh talk, it was a degrading experience and he wanted to quit but his mother made him continue.

"Don't the female students ridicule you?"

Malcolm, the red-headed freckle-faced one said that boys were sometimes treated as inferiors but generally they were accepted. If Craig had said that, Benny would have dismissed it as bullshit because

Craig was in his last year, and late-stage cuspers often exaggerated things, if for no other reason than to make their lives sound better. But it was Malcolm who said that females accepted them and strange as it sounded, Benny was inclined to believe him, if for no other reason than Malcolm was as transparent as a window pane. Benny would've bet that the kid couldn't tell a lie if his life depended on it.

Still, Benny had to ask.

"If the female students accepted you, why did they run you out of town."

"It wasn't the female students," said Jai, the blue-eyed, latte-skinned boy with the short brown matted hair. "it was a group of traders riled up by the woman who runs the markets."

He went on to explain that there'd been an incident and one of the traders was found dead. Her truck, with her body in the back, was found on the road to Melbourne but not far from San Remo.

"Before that, life was pretty good in Warragul," said Jai.

"Yeah, you could go to uni or learn a trade," added Malcolm.

"Or join the CFA," said Jai.

"What's a CFA?"

"Community Fire Authority."

"Like being a firefighter with hoses and trucks?"

"Pretty much," said Craig. "But the important thing is that Warragul doesn't have forced labour camps, and there's no stud farms or bathhouses."

Benny and Steve had exchanged looks when Craig mentioned the lack of stud services.

"So none of the women want sex with men?"

"There's no law against it," replied Jai. "Ask Craig. He's got a girlfriend back in Warragul."

"It's nothing special," said Craig. "Lots of girls try out sex with us to see what it's like, and then for others, it's just a way to get pregnant. Either way, females don't get too involved cause they know it won't last."

At first, Benny thought they were pulling his leg. In the Republic, the law was very clear. Heterosexual relationships, except for therapeutic cases, or entertainment, were illegal. It was, as the law stipulated, a perversion that only pre-pandemic women succumbed to. And what female would choose, like Craig said, to take a partner who was destined to die young? Tand yet, Benny knew that some females got involved despite knowing that it couldn't last. There were couples like Karen and Josh, who became lovers despite the laws and despite knowing what the future held.

All this talk of freedom and friendships with girls had made Benny wonder if he would have made different choices if he'd had the same opportunities. He thought of Karen and how grown up she'd looked the last time he saw her. He even made fun of her when she picked him up in Footscray by pretending to flirt with her. But when he reached over and touched her hair, she got angry. He'd apologised saying that it was just his way of saying goodbye but he couldn't help wondering if he hadn't decided to be a stud would she have chosen him over Josh? Putting his hand in his pocket, he confirmed that he still had the strand of hair that had come away in his fingers.

Frustrated at the thought of his last conversation with her, Benny banged his head softly against the door. Karen and Josh were a couple and they were both his friends. Besides, he wasn't likely to ever see either of them again.

On the other side of the room, the twins, TJ and Vaz were also waking and, of course, arguing. One said that if they'd taken the bypass as he suggested, they'd be in San Remo now. The other responded, saying that they'd come to Inverloch because they needed supplies to get to San Remo.

Now that's lack of planning, thought Benny.

They'd been in the warehouse when Benny and his companions were shoved in last night. Even after spending a night in close quarters with the two, Benny couldn't tell them apart. They were both tall and thin with short brown curly hair, amazingly long hands and fingers, and striking eyes. In fact, it was only their eyes that differed between them but even that difference was unique. One brother's left eye was green while the right was blue. The other brother had the same mismatched eye colour but in the reverse. Benny couldn't remember which was which and he suspected them of deliberately swapping names to keep everyone confused.

On top of that, they had a way of talking as if they were a single individual. Like last night. Before the group from Warragul could introduce themselves, the twins had started talking.

"Where you guys from?" The one with the right blue eye asked.

When they heard Warragul, they looked at each other knowingly. Then the other one said, "We're from a wilding colony farther to the east."

His brother continued, "We'd still be there if it wasn't for those new laws."

"Yeah, our community signed some agreement with Melbourne."

"Sold us down the river, that's what they did."

"So we left," they said in unison.

Steve asked what kind of agreement and Vaz, or was it TJ, said that the agreement offered the community protection in exchange for testing and fingerprinting all the boys.

Benny said the same thing was happening in Melbourne but when Steve asked why, everyone looked at each other and shook their heads.

"Never even heard of it," said Malcolm.

Then Jai asked, "Why'd you choose to move to Inverloch?"

"We didn't," said one twin. "We planned to stay at the lancer colony in Sandy Point."

The other brother took over. "But when we got there everyone was talking about going to the lancer meeting in San Remo."

"So if you were all heading to San Remo," asked Steve, "where are the others?"

"With all the rumours about the missing trader, the lancers at Sandy Bay got scared about going anywhere," said one twin.

"No," said the other. "They didn't come because they're too old."

"Yeah, they're all cuspers and likely to be dead within the year."

"Definitely dead within the year."

"But we're only 16."

"We have our whole lives ahead of us."

Thinking about what the twins had to say about cuspers made Benny think about how each of them measured time differently. For

Craig who was already 19, time was measured in heartbeats. For Malcolm and Jai, who were Benny's age, time was measured in the months they had before they turned 19, while Steve had the luxury or burden, depending on how you looked at it, of not knowing how to measure his days.

So deep in thought about mortality was Benny, that he almost missed the sound of footsteps.

"Someone's coming," he said, scooting away from the door. The twins stopped arguing, the boys from Warragul turned to face the door and Steve set the flyer on the ground. The room became silent as they all waited in anticipation. There was the sound of a key sliding into place, then the click of the lock. The knob turned slowly and the creaking of the door hinge echoed in the silent warehouse. A blast of heat and light entered the room. Shading his eyes, Benny stared at the figure in front of him, then scrambled to get to his feet. He'd seen that short stocky build before Steve recognised it too.

"Bulldog?"

CHAPTER 5
THE OLD ONE'S CABIN

SEPTEMBER 2069

"Bulldog? Wasn't he one of the lancers who met Steve and Benny when the smugglers dropped them off at Venus Bay?"

"Exactly," replied the Old One. "Are you surprised to see him back in the story?"

"Well, it does feel a bit contrived," replied the girl. There was the hint of a smile which the Old One dismissed with the wave of a hand.

"Everyone in this story has a reason to be there."

There was a gruffness in the voice but no malice.

"Besides, the world was a much smaller place in 2049 than it is today."

"With half the population dying by the time they finished their teens, that's not surprising," said the girl.

The tension created by the Old One's assertion that Evelyn Perkins was the villain in this story was subsiding and the girl found herself feeling more comfortable as the story shifted back onto the fate of the teens. How and why Dr Harris left Melbourne was interesting, but historically, she was famous for her discovery, not for her escape. And

Evelyn Perkins, even if she had been responsible for the deaths of all those boys, in the end, she was the one who brokered the peace and brought an end to the Great Upheaval. Those were the facts and they were incontrovertible. But, on this, her last night in the cabin, what the girl wanted to know was, what had happened to the teens. Fact or fiction, it was their story she identified with. Good-natured Zane, who only wanted to do something useful with his life, had gotten caught up in politics and paid for it with his life. Benny, who only wanted to enjoy the short life he was granted, wound up exiled, and Karen and Josh, who wanted nothing more than to be together, were now separated. Their lives, much like her own, seemed to be under everyone's control but theirs.

"Are you listening?"

The girl realised she'd drifted off.

"Of course I was. You were saying that the world was a smaller place and I said that's because half the population was dying before they finished their teens."

"It wasn't only because boys had shortened lives. The birth rate was also lower."

"But I thought the fertilisation clinics made artificial insemination readily available?"

"Artificial insemination, yes. Pre-implantation fertilisation, no. That was still in its infancy and gender testing before implantation wasn't introduced until late 2049.

"I don't understand. How did that affect the birth rate?"

"Think about it. In random fertilisation of eggs, what percentage would be male and what percentage female."

"I believe the figure before the pandemic was 50/50."

"The pandemic altered how long males could live but it didn't alter the percentage of eggs that developed into one gender or another. Now consider that before early gender testing techniques, the gender of the foetus isn't detectable until the eighteenth week—"

The girl's face brightened.

"I get it!" Then immediately, a frown replaced her smile as she realised what that implied.

"You're saying the birth rate was lower because half the foetuses implanted were subsequently terminated because they were male."

"Not quite half. Some women refused to destroy the life that was developing inside them but a significant number took that route. They then had to start the process all over again and that was also hard so many women decided not to have children at all."

The Old One sifted through the photos and pulled out the picture of the young Catherine Williams.

"Gender wasn't only an issue for the woman carrying the baby. It was something that could either strengthen a relationship or destroy it altogether."

"I can understand why choosing to keep or not keep a baby might cause a couple to break up but how could it bring them closer together?"

"Overcoming adversity strengthens not only individuals. Those couples who decided to raise boys faced a number of hurdles. It wasn't only because boys died young that women decided to discard baby boys. There was the stigma imposed by society. By the closing months of '49, males were forced to leave school by the age of thirteen unless they were selected as sperm donors so the majority of boys were uneducated and considered ignorant. Then there were financial considerations. Because boys could only do menial jobs, the compensation they received barely gave them enough money to feed and clothe themselves. Crimes reported on the news were more likely to be attributed to boys. Current affairs programs regularly featured boys who acted out because life seemed unfair. These stories only reinforced the negative stereotypes, and by default, their families were stigmatised."

"Are you referring to Dr Harris?"

"Not Bonnie. She never cared what others thought and besides, Josh was in that first post-pandemic generation. Discrimination against males didn't become rampant until he was in his teens. No, I was thinking of Catherine and her wife. Even though they were a high-profile couple, I think they could have managed to stay together if a third party hadn't come between them."

"Are you referring to Evelyn?"

"I'm referring to Catherine's ambition."

CATHERINE

FRIDAY 10 DECEMBER 2049 - 6:00 A.M.

"Thom? Thom, sorry I'm late but you're not going to believe who came by my office."

Catherine opened the bedroom door and flicked on the light. She'd only been away for 24 hours but it felt like an eternity. Her ordeal had started yesterday when her mother burst into this same room demanding they take a walk. Catherine had said that as the new Infrastructure Minister, she needed to get to her office but her mother insisted. That so-called talk was about some crackpot conspiracy theory that Evelyn Perkins was sabotaging research on the disease. If her mother had been some stay-at-home carer, that would have been one thing but her mother was Dr Geraldine Williams, the administrative head of Gentech. That made her more than a pain in the ass. She was now officially a political liability. Well, that was a problem she would have to deal with later.

Her most pressing issue yesterday had been the emergency in the Old CBD. Arriving at her office late and already distracted, she'd learned that the fire raging out of control in the old high rises had spread to two more buildings. The day got progressively worse as the fire began to sweep through more and more buildings until it threatened to jump into the surrounding middle-class neighbourhoods. And it wasn't only the fires that made the inhabitants of those neighbourhoods nervous. It was the lancers. The mere thought of them roaming the streets made her and every other respectable woman cringe. At least boys who took the Selection test and accepted their assigned jobs provided some service to society but the lancers only caused problems. Homeless and unskilled they survived on charity, theft and occasional day labour. They were a perennial problem and the fires allowed the authorities to do something about it. Fortunately, that problem was under the jurisdiction of the police and military.

The fires were her problem and they had quickly overwhelmed the resources she had at her disposal. That's when Monika Thomas stepped in. It wasn't what the former minister did but the way she did it that upset Catherine. Without consulting her, Monika had organised Steele Industries to supply equipment and resources to create a firebreak, and it was the firebreak that brought the fires under control. That manoeuvre had publicly undermined Catherine as the newly appointed Infrastructure Minister but then, to add insult to injury, Catherine was fairly sure that Monika's new fiancé, Stephanie Steele, was responsible for setting the fires in the first place. There'd been a history of fires in areas where Stephanie had planned developments. The frequency and locations were far too convenient to be coincidence, so Catherine had asked Monika for an inquiry, which Monika promised to do after the election. This fire, unlike the others, had gotten out of hand. But instead of being caught out as an arsonist, Stephanie was now being hailed as the city's heroine. Catherine had screamed in frustration when she heard the news and that made Monika look even more in control. The only thing worse would have been if Monika got on TV and told everyone that she'd taken charge of a situation that Catherine was obviously unqualified to handle.

It had been an exhausting and demoralising day but then something miraculous had happened. As Catherine was preparing to go home, Evelyn Perkins paid her a visit. Not only did the grand old lady of politics congratulate her on doing such a splendid job but she sat and asked Catherine about her future plans. Which was why Catherine had rushed home to share this news with her wife Thomasina. The problem was that their bed was not only empty. It looked like it hadn't even been slept in.

Knocking on the bathroom door, she called out again. There was no answer and a cold chill ran down her spine. She yanked the door open but that room too was empty.

"Thomasina!" She walked back down the hallway and opened the door to the new nursery. The early morning light filtering through the yellow curtains had painted the white crib in its same colours. Even though their pregnancy had just entered its third trimester, Thom had the room already set up. She'd chosen yellow not only because it was cheerful but because, as she said, it was gender-neutral. Catherine winced at the thought and closed the door. Evelyn Perkins had made it patently clear that gender screening was going to be mandatory. The NOP candidate couldn't very well introduce further restrictions on males while raising one of her own. That conversation with Thomasina, like the one with her mother, could wait. First the good news. Then the bad.

Passing through the formal sitting room, illuminated only by the hall light, she was vaguely aware that everything was where it should be but that only served to make the silence more ominous. The light coming from the kitchen, however, was a good sign, so she headed in that direction, expecting to see Thomasina sitting in the breakfast nook or perhaps on the outdoor patio. Of course. That would explain why she hadn't heard Catherine's calls. She rushed into the room only to be met with that same sensation. The refrigerator hummed silently, the light on the coffee maker glowed in readiness and the microwave dutifully displayed the time. Everything was as it should be, except Thomasina was missing.

Catherine walked over to the large sliding glass doors that opened onto the yard. There too, the early morning light bathed everything in a warm glow but the warmth she needed was missing. Shivering, she turned back towards the kitchen, and that's when she saw it.

Sitting on the small round table in the breakfast nook was a single sheet of paper. There had been several messages during the night from Thomasina asking Catherine to call back. In all the chaos and frustration, Catherine had ignored them. But now, the empty house, the unslept bed, the note on the table; all these elements made those calls sound more desperate. With shaking hands, she picked the note up. At first, all she noticed were the delicate curves of Thomasina's script. Running her fingers over the neat, elegantly formed letters, she appreciated their artistic quality. They were the essence of Thomasina. Then moving into the light of the kitchen, she read the note out loud.

Cat,

I tried calling you several times last night but they said you were too busy to talk.

Catherine flinched, remembering how she'd discarded those messages thinking they were a nuisance.

I know you're busy because I watched the news briefs but I needed to ask you where they were taking the lancers.

What? Why was Thomasina asking about lancers? Something cold and chilling pushed Catherine to read on.

Nick

As soon as Catherine saw the word, blood rushed to her head. Gripping the paper, she quickly scanned the rest.

Nick didn't come home last night, and Mum and I are worried sick. No one will tell us anything so I'm going to look for him.

XXX

She stared in disbelief.

She'd come home excited to tell Thomasina about her meeting with Evelyn Perkins but instead of an adoring wife greeting her at the door, she'd come home to an empty house and a piece emergency. But it wasn't a frantic note to say that she was ill or in danger nor was it a sweet note to say that she'd gone to stay with friends or family because of the emergency. No. She'd gone out after dark to look for her brother Nick. What was she thinking? Catherine rubbed her temples with her free hand.

Nick! At 18 he was entering that age when he should be sent away. Everyone knew that cusp-aged boys were unpredictable. With only two years left to live they were as likely to become wild and uncontrollable as they were to fall into severe depression. In Nick's case, he'd announced that he was going to join a stud farm. Thomasina had begged Catherine to dissuade him. Dissuade him? How could anyone talk reasonably with an 18-year-old boy? But she'd done what she could. She offered to get him a better job as a public gardener.

Her temples were throbbing.

Knowing Nick, he probably hadn't listened. Well, she thought, if he has gone off to some bath house or stud farm, he's in for a rude shock. Evelyn Perkins is planning to shut them down.

Catherine's fingers curled around Thom's note. There was something satisfying in the way it crumpled.

This was exactly why women chose to get rid of male babies. They were nothing but trouble and heartache. Apparently, Thomasina was going to have to discover that the hard way.

Releasing her fingers, the note unfurled revealing once again the graceful curls and squiggles. Catherine pictured Thomasina writing the note and raised the paper to her lips. Perhaps she should have returned Thom's calls, but there had been so many other things to deal with: the fires, the ongoing animosity between herself and her mother, and the pressure from Monika Thomas. And then Evelyn's visit. Catherine was sure she'd passed some kind of test that the old lady had set her because Evelyn ended the conversation by asking Catherine to sit next to her at this morning's memorial service. Undoubtedly, Monika would sit on the other side but Catherine now saw herself as Monika's equal as well as her rival. It was a victorious moment but now it was spoiled and by what? A crumpled piece of paper.

The throbbing intensified and her eyes watered.

What good was a victory without the celebration? The black ink swirled on the white paper. Why today, of all days, did Thomasina decide to disappear? Why had the woman she loved deserted her for a worthless boy?

The pain in her head was so intense that she closed her eyes only to see flashes of light like lightning against the night sky.

A hot shower. That's what she needed. That and a nap and then she'd be able to deal with everything. She crumpled the note into a ball and tossed it against the wall.

Retracing her steps through the house, Catherine turned on the lights and then the TV. She needed to fill the emptiness. The voices of the presenters on the sunrise show followed her into the bedroom as she stripped off her clothes.

"The fires in the Old CBD are now under control but residents in the evacuation zone are not being allowed back in as emergency crews continue with the clean up."

They followed her into the bathroom.

"In other news, Premier Dorothy Anderson's memorial service will be broadcast later this morning. The service at St Patrick's Cathedral will be attended by friends, family and government officials. The general public, however, will not be permitted inside due to security concerns. Acting Premier Monika Thomas ...."

They faded away as Catherine turned on the shower. While the water pummelled down on her, she grabbed the shampoo and massaged it into her hair until the pressure in her head receded. It's going to be alright, she told herself. Tension was giving way to exhaustion and her eyes momentarily closed. She was in a wooded area walking with her father. Not a lush green one, a burned-out one. It was the one she'd visited with her father after the bushfires. Feeling herself slip, her body jerked and she was awake and still in the shower. A drop of shampoo ran into her eye but like her earlier frustrations, its sting was quickly washed away.

The sting of her mother's words, however, weren't so easily banished. She squeezed conditioner on her head and using her fingers combed it through her hair. While her father was alive, he'd been her ally. He'd smoothed out the tangles. And Evelyn, like her father, listened to and encouraged her. If he were still alive, he would be congratulating her on her achievement, not undermining it with conspiracy theories. Fortunately, it was Evelyn and not her mother that she would be spending today with.

Turning around, she let the water wash away the conditioner. It slid down her back, ran down her legs and disappeared down the drain. Washed away. That's how Evelyn's chat this morning made Catherine feel about Monika. Not only had the retired leader intimated that Catherine's career was on the rise but she'd indicated that Monika's position wasn't that secure.

Everything was turning in her favour, so where was Thomasina? She should be here, helping Catherine get ready for the memorial service. After all, they were meant to exemplify the modern couple. Using the loofah to scrub her back, she remembered the way Thom looked at her the other night when Evelyn asked if they were having a girl to carry on the family name. On the way home from that party, they'd argued for the first time. Thomasina said she was upset that Catherine hadn't told Evelyn that they didn't know their child's gender. How could she explain to Thom when that explanation would only have made things worse? Instead of reasoning with Thomasina, she'd shut her down by saying that politics was none of her business and that when they were in public all Thom had to do was smile for the cameras. Was that too much to ask? Replaying her words in her head she scrubbed harder. Not only were her remarks calloused and insensitive but she also hadn't confided to Thom what Monika had told her. How would Thom have reacted if she knew that Evelyn was not only requiring gender testing but testing for Element X as well? No one knew what Element X was but any fertilised egg, or fetus for that matter, carrying the defect, was to be destroyed

She turned off the water and stepping out of the shower reached for the warm towel that always sat waiting for her on the vanity. She stared stupidly at the empty spot before she realised that without Thom, there was no towel. In fact, she had no idea where Thom stored the towels. Thom was the carer, the one who organised the house and made everything warm and inviting. Without her, Catherine wasn't sure where anything was kept anymore. Opening the linen cabinet, she found the towels neatly folded and stacked, but like the house, without Thom, they had no warmth.

She opened the top drawer of the vanity looking for her hair dryer but like Thomasina, it was nowhere to be found. She yanked open the other drawers, messing up their contents even though what she wanted was obviously not there. Wadding up the towel, she dropped it on the bathroom floor and stormed into the bedroom opening drawers and checking table tops until she found the missing appliance sitting in front of her makeup mirror. It was where she'd left it and the thought crossed her mind that Thomasina must have forgotten to put it away.

Nothing is going to spoil this day.

The excitement that had carried her home, followed by the anger on finding her home deserted, was evaporating, like the dampness in her hair, leaving behind only her exhaustion. If she climbed into bed now, she could grab a quick nap before the memorial service, and by then, Thomasina would be home, and everything would be the way it should be.

As her head touched the pillow, the TV announcer in the other room said something about locating the lancers who were believed to have murdered Premier Anderson, but Catherine's eyes were already closed.

MONIKA

FRIDAY 10 DECEMBER 2049 - 6:00 A.M.

"We're almost finished, Ms Thomas. I just need to adjust the mike. There. That's perfect. Now the announcer –"

"Thank you but I know how this works," said Monika. Then feeling she sounded a bit harsh, she added, "It's been a long night so forgive me for being so abrupt."

Putting on her well-rehearsed smile, beaming white teeth offset by her signature red lipstick, Monika reinforced her apology by asking, "Do you think someone could bring me a cup of coffee? Plain black, and if it's instant, better add sugar."

On the sound stage, the morning show hosts were relaxing and chatting among themselves as the station switched to the news segment. Sitting off to the side, Monika who'd been up most of the night, appreciated this brief moment of privacy. It reminded her of her first time in this studio. Back then she'd been left alone because she was a nobody, an insignificant government representative sent to speak on behalf of the one who really mattered, Evelyn Perkins. There was a wartime frenzy back then, as Australia responded to that last wave of invasion. The enemy had breached the closed borders and now stalked the country, invisible, insidious and inescapable. And Monika was the young, 20-something politician who'd risen to prominence for no other reason than everyone else had abdicated. Her father had collapsed and died on the floor of parliament. Innumerable friends and colleagues had disappeared. Harried, drained, demoralised she'd been pushed out of the way that day as camera crews, newscasters and production staff rushed to take their assigned places. She recalled looking at the stage lights and thinking there was no light at the end of that tunnel. Only fear. Fear and death.

She glimpsed someone standing off to the side and was surprised to see Tom. He was encouraging her with his smile but his eyes betrayed his thoughts. Death was stalking him just as it was dogging the steps of every man. Urgency. That was the message she had to deliver. Men, the important ones, the privileged ones, were being summoned for their own protection. Scientists were to report to their labs where they could be sequestered and continue their search for a cure. The government, the male element, were being sent to bunkers and important military personnel were being transported to special camps. It was a bold move but what else could they do? Evelyn Perkins, the acting Prime Minister, had proposed the plan, and Monika was here to deliver it.

A young woman held out a disposable cup containing coffee. Monika thanked her and turned back to look at Tom but the person at the edge of the set wasn't Tom anymore. It was a young woman with short brown hair and round-shaped glasses. She returned Monika's look with a smile and 2032 faded away. It had been a frightening time, but in early 2032, there had still been hope. This was 2049, almost 2050 and all hope had been lost, at least when it came to men. The young ladies manning these cameras and fussing over her had never known that time. It had been a different era, a different world, a different Monica.

"Over here Ms Thomas," said the producer.

Monika, set aside her coffee and walked away from those ghosts of the past. She took the seat opposite the interviewer as the producer counted down with her fingers.

3. 2. 1. Cue the the interviewer and--

"This morning we have the Acting Premier with us, the Honourable Monika Thomas. Ms Thomas, we appreciate your time this morning. We know you're very tired given the disastrous events of the last couple of days."

"Thank you, Emila, for having me. Yes, it's been a difficult time but thanks to the hard work of the many, the fires are now under control."

"Tell me, Ms Thomas. How did you arrive at the decision to use bulldozers to create a fire break? That was the turning point, wasn't it?"

Monika had rehearsed this answer with Steph the night before. They wanted to highlight that Monika had only stepped in as a last resort. Faint praise was what they were aiming for.

"The fire commissioner told me that the fire was beyond their ability to contain and the new Infrastructure Commissioner, Catherine Williams, had provided them with all the resources that were at her disposal but obviously, it wasn't enough. Well, when what you have isn't working then you have to look further afield, don't you? It was something I learned from my years working beside Evelyn Perkins throughout the Transition. So I asked the fire commissioner how they stopped out-of-control bushfires, and she said they created fire breaks to starve the fires into submission. And how do we create firebreaks, I asked. She explained that they would need to demolish the buildings around the fires. While it meant destroying parts of the Old CBD that weren't on fire, it was what had to be done to save the surrounding suburbs."

"So you decided to sacrifice the few to save the many. But how did you manage to rally so many bulldozers and workers? Surely that sort of response requires planning and negotiation with business leaders. How did you get such a fast response?"

"I have always been a big proponent of government and business working hand in hand to deliver the best outcomes for the citizens of the Greate Republic of Melbourne so I called on the head of our largest construction company, Stephanie Steele. She was the one person I knew who had the necessary resources. Without hesitation, she offered her equipment and personnel. All at no cost to the government, I might add. It is a classic example of government and business pulling together to provide a solution."

"Well, it sounds like we all owe a debt of gratitude to Ms Steele. Tell me, the personnel that assisted last night, what do we know about them? I understand there were some injuries."

"They were a mix of trained workers and conscripts."

"Conscripted workers? You mean young boys."

"Boys trained in scavenging and clearing work. They were hardly young by male labour standards and they weren't untrained as some have suggested. I also think it's important to remember that last night was an extraordinary event and dangerous work sometimes results in injuries. Fortunately, none of our skilled workers suffered anything more serious than smoke inhalation."

"And what about the inhabitants of the Old CBD?"

"Those women who've lost homes as a result of the fires will be reassigned to homes currently being reclaimed in the outer suburbs."

"And the lancers?"

Monika paused. Was this interviewer one of those bleeding heart sympathisers? She considered her response and decided to go with largess. Davina could take the heat for any backlash regarding boys who were ill-treated.

"I understand they have been relocated to lancer enclaves outside the city limits where they can be properly looked after. Having said that, I have been told that in the process, they identified the young men believed to be responsible for Premier Dorothy Anderson's murder."

"Well, that's certainly good news. I'm sure the residents of Melbourne will sleep easier on both counts."

The Producer signalled them to wrap up.

"Ms Thomas, I'd like to thank you for taking time out of your busy schedule to talk with us. I know you have a busy morning with Premier Anderson's memorial service so we won't keep you."

"My pleasure," said Monika smiling into the camera.

As soon as they switched to the hosts behind the main desk, Monika rose. Without acknowledging the interviewer further, she ripped off the mike and handed it to the girl off-stage who had retrieved the untouched cup of coffee. Staffers shuffled the girl and the offered cup aside as they escorted Monika out of the studio, passing along updates to her even as she climbed into her waiting vehicle. They were all issues that could wait. For now, she needed to go home, get a couple hours sleep and then head to the cathedral with Stephanie.

Despite that unscripted question about the lancers, the interview had gone well and she hoped that Catherine was watching and had got the message. Her opponent might be Evelyn's new plaything but she still had a lot to learn when it came to politics. As for Evelyn, Monika knew that once the service was over and Dorothy was put to rest, it was time to push ahead with the election. That meant that Evelyn was going to have to stop playing games and announce her support. This election, the first in two decades, was meant to be an affirmation of government policies so why was Evelyn fomenting dissent? For example, that demonstration the other day. It was supposedly organised by some unknown group calling itself Catalyst for Change but it had actually been organised by Evelyn's head of security, Davina Warren. While it had netted some important dissident leaders, it had also stirred up dissension in the wider community, particularly in the business sector. If it was part of the overall strategy, then why hadn't Evelyn warned her beforehand? And if it was something else, then what was it Evelyn wanted to achieve? And then there was Evelyn's increasing pressure to limit the number of male births. It wasn't only the male rights activists who were expressing concern over that issue. Steph had been quick to point out that it was one thing to establish restrictions on male's activities, but Evelyn's plan looked more like the wholesale elimination of males. Aside from the ethical aspects, Steph pointed out that industry leaders relied on cheap male labour. Monika had been Evelyn's protégé for years and had followed her mentor's instructions to the letter but now, for the first time, she was beginning to question her leader's judgement.

As Monika's self-drive turned the corner, Parliament House came into view. Passing through the park, the car slowed to pass a bus that had stopped to pick up passengers and something else Steph said came back to her.

"The overthrow of Evelyn is already underway. What you need to decide is whether you want to get hit by the same bus or be the one driving it."

The jury is still out on that, thought Monika, but one thing was certain, now that she had the office of Premier, she wasn't about to let it go.

CHAPTER 6
THE OLD ONE'S CABIN

SEPTEMBER 2069

The Old One finished speaking and stared at the tea leaves in the bottom of the cup as if they held some salient piece of advice. Mesmerised, the girl watched as the leaves shifted shape with the ebb and flow of the liquid in which they floated. Expecting the Old One to make some oracular announcement about how they were controlled by the forces around them, she was disappointed by the silence that ensued and so she decided to make her own, "If Evelyn Perkins was such a —"

The cup toppled, splashing its contents onto the table, stopping the girl in mid-sentence. As the tea flowed across the table, it spread to the girl's textbook, staining the edges. She grabbed a tea towel and forgetting to finish her statement, concentrated on mopping up the spill but it didn't matter. The Old One finished it for her. "Misandrist."

"What?"

"Man-hater. She was a man-hater. Always had been."

The cavalier way the Old One accused Evelyn Perkins of gender bias surprised the girl and she stopped wiping at the spill.

"I thought you were apolitical."

"The politics of pre-pandemic Australia never interested me but looking at Evelyn's life, I can understand why she resented the power men had in those days. She was brighter than most and worked harder, while they privately laughed at her, secure in their sense of entitlement. I could understand her resentment but she let that resentment ferment until it turned to hatred. It was well disguised, mind you, but it was there."

Reaching again into the stack of photos, the scarred hand pushed aside a picture of two smiling women and pulled out a framed picture of Evelyn placing the Order of Australia over the head of a man. He was much taller than Evelyn and the photo captured him bowing down so she could place the sash over his head.

It was a photo that the girl had seen before but now she studied it. Evelyn Perkins was wearing her customary smile, but now the girl asked herself if the smile was for the cameras, or if it was for the power she had over this man. Pictures might be worth a thousand words but they could also be contradictory.

The Old One picked up on the girl's uncertainty.

"I know you want evidence. We all want evidence that proves that what we thought all along was right but sometimes that confirmation isn't forthcoming. Take Patricia, for example, even when she'd been the one uncovering the evidence, she wasn't sure she wanted to accept it. And what about the case against Jocelyn? How was Sofia to accept that her dearest friend was guilty, even in the face of her friend's confession? Evidence or not, sometimes we just don't want to hear the truth."

Then, setting the cup back in its place, the Old One said, "Now, are you going to make me another cup of tea, or am I going to sit here with a dry throat all night while I fill you in on Sofia's dilemma?"

SOFIA

FRIDAY 10 DECEMBER 2049 - 6:00 A.M.

The monitor with its constant beeps, flashing numbers and multi-coloured lines that spiked and rolled across the screen had accomplished its purpose so the nurse disconnected it. Having killed the liveliness, it displayed only moments before; she now pushed it aside. Next, she removed the drip. Its wheels squeaked, or perhaps it was her shoes, as she pulled it away from the bed. Sofia, standing off to the side, watched as the nurse completed each task with silent precision. Neither spoke nor did they acknowledge each other in any way. As the nurse opened the door, voices drifted in from the hallway. The people standing there; police officers, councillors and reporters, were talking amongst themselves, ignoring the two women in the room. Then the door closed with a barely audible click, and the room was silent except for the gentle breathing of the patient who'd slept through these last-minute rituals.

Pulling the only chair in the room closer to the bed, Sofia sat down. She was loath to wake her friend. Instead, she studied the dark purple and yellowish-green hues of the bruises on her face and arms. The features on that strong face had resumed their familiar contours now that the swelling had receded and as the monitor testified, her blood pressure was good, her heart beat strong, and her temperature normal. All her vital signs attested to the fact that the woman was fit to give testimony which was why May, as Commissioner of Police, proposed that the trial proceed without delay. It was imperative, May said, that they get this trial out of the way quickly because Jocelyn was not an ordinary citizen. She was Council Chair and given the unrest caused by recent events, a council without its leader was bad for everyone.

Sofia argued that if Jocelyn were ill then the council would have selected someone to fill in, in her absence. May, however, replied that this was not a question of absence. It was a question of leadership. How could Jocelyn chair the council when she was accused of premeditated murder? A crime that if proven, resulted in banishment. And how could they remove her from the council while her guilt or innocence was still in question? No, delaying the trial would be bad for the council and that would be bad for the community.

Sofia protested. Couldn't the council vote to have Jocelyn removed due to health concerns? That way they could hold their special elections and get on with business. But the council members saw through Sofia's argument. They knew she was trying to buy more time because of Jocelyn's pregnancy. Six weeks or a month and the baby was likely to survive, with or without its mother. It was a reasonable request and some agreed that it might be best to let Jocelyn have the baby first. That child was, after all, innocent of any crime. Other councillors argued that Jocelyn should have considered the fate of her child before she despatched its father. It was Jocelyn who was to blame for the lives of her husband, her child and herself and not those who convicted her.

The arguments flowed back and forth, for and against until May motioned that they take a vote. Nay to move to trial. Yay, to delay it. Going around the table, asking each councillor for a yay or nay, Sofia watched the secretary note each response in the minutes. As expected, the council was split along their usual lines. The protective services, May, on behalf of the police, and Alicia, as Commissioner of the CFA, voted nay on delaying the trial. Jacinta, as Housing Commissioner and Ginger, as Health Commissioner, along with the Head of Education, Terry, voted yay. Two more votes but Sofia knew how Earnestine, the

Treasurer, was going to vote. She was May's cousin and never strayed from her family's position on anything. Her vote was a predictable nay. The council was tied, with one vote left to cast. If only that vote were mine, thought Sofia. But as mediator, hers was an appointed position, not an elected one. She could pass judgement but otherwise was not allowed a say in council decisions. The last vote, the determining vote, was left to Claudia, the Secretary.

"Well, what's it gonna be, Claudia?" said May.

For what seemed like an eternity, Claudia stared at the pad of paper in front of her. She and Jocelyn had grown up together. Played on the same netball team. But she also thought Jocelyn was wrong to get involved with Reg. He was only 16 when the rumours of their affair started to circulate. She was 34. Old enough to be his mother but Jocelyn was admired and well-liked. Her supporters said that it was understandable that a woman in her mid-30s would want to reproduce. That was only natural. If Warragul had fertilisation clinics, like they had in Melbourne, she would have had other options. But she was a colonial. And in the colonies, what recourse did any woman have except intercourse with a teenage male?

Her detractors acknowledged that they didn't object to a woman having sex with younger males but doing it openly, now that was another thing. They were quick to suggest that there was more to the relationship than getting pregnant. It was when Reg moved in with Jocelyn, however, that the rumours went into overdrive.

Letters appeared in the local paper saying that maybe the Free Colony of Warragul needed to institute some laws of propriety like the ones in the Republic. It was not unusual for Jocelyn to hear the word pedophile whispered as she walked past a group of older women. Younger women were generally more sympathetic. They said they could understand the need for sex but not the need to live with someone of the opposite sex. Jocelyn told Sofia that some of her closest friends had even shown up at her house, as a kind of intervention. It was one thing, they said, to treat boys with respect but quite a different thing to treat them as equals. In other words, it wasn't the age difference so much as the difference in social standing. As Sofia waited for

Claudia's response, she wondered if the secretary had been part of that group.

Noticing Jocelyn twitch in her sleep, Sofia reached out to straighten the covers. Theirs was a relationship that went beyond mere friendship. United in a shared love of community, they had worked together for years to shape the values of the colony and central to those values was maintaining Warragul as a free colony; one that gave boys more opportunities than the Republic. While Jocelyn wasn't involved in Sofia's smuggling activities, she nonetheless provided council support to integrate the Republic's refugees into Warragul's community. That's why Sofia hadn't judged Jocelyn's choice of lover but that didn't mean that she didn't have concerns. Boys in their cusp years were unpredictable and in the case of Reg, Sofia's concerns were justified. But why did this have to happen now?

Sofia's mother always said that disasters came in threes. Not that Sofia believed in superstitions, but in this case, her mother was right. First, there'd been the news that Premier Anderson had been killed, along with the rumour that she'd been murdered by lancers. For those women who were biased against cusp-aged males, this news had rekindled fears regarding lancers, but for Sofia, it had even further ramifications.

She had long hoped for Warragul's citizens to gain access to the Republic's health services. Then by chance, a couple of years ago, Sofia and Jocelyn came into contact with Premier Anderson. Their initial talks about border issues segued into the broader issues of trade and then onto that of human rights. That's when the Premier cautiously broached the subject of bringing Warragul back into the Republic. She said that recreating the former state of Victoria had long been a goal of Evelyn Perkins, and now, as leader of the NOP, she thought it was time to turn that dream into reality.

"Imagine," said Anderson, "Warragul would have access to improved health facilities, higher education, libraries, museums, shopping."

To sweeten the deal, she confided that there was going to be an election held in 2050. If the NOP won that election, under her leadership, then she would have the necessary backing to eliminate the anti-heterosexual laws and greatly reduce restrictions on males.

"Won't that place you in opposition to powerful members within your own party?" asked Sofia.

"There are strong interests opposed to my agenda but there are quite a few in favour. More than you might realise but it's colonies, like Warragul, that will make the difference. If Warragul were to become part of the Republic and back me in the leadership, we could control the NOP and thereby control the Republic."

Premier Anderson was playing a dangerous game within her own party but so were Sofia and Jocelyn. There were many in Warragul who feared the Republic and others who hated it for deserting them during the pandemic. Paving the way for Warragul to reintegrate was risky, but then again, the benefits were equally worth it. They agreed to continue the conversation with both sides committed to secrecy. Then came a special request. Premier Anderson asked Sofia to locate a facility in the wilds but not too far from Melbourne, that could be turned into a laboratory. She never specified what this facility might be used for but she did say it was part of the larger plan and that Warragul would benefit in the longer term. She asked Sofia to nominate someone who could be trusted to transport goods to this secret facility. The person Sofia picked was the trader Jackson.

But now all that hard work had come to naught. Premier Anderson was dead, and shortly after that, Lauren, the trader, was murdered. When her truck was found dumped not far from the lancer community at San Remo, the women of Warragul, already on alert about dangerous lancers, started talking about banning all cusp-aged males. One of the strongest anti-male advocates, Ursula, had even rallied some of the traders and chased the male uni students out of town. It was only when Sofia and her friends intercepted them that she was able to keep the younger boys at Heart House safe.

What everyone, other than a select few, didn't know was that Lauren was doing a special smuggling job. Everyone knew Lauren was involved in smuggling boys out of Melbourne's labour camps, but this time she was delivering two individuals who needed to be kept out of sight and protected. While Sofia couldn't prove it, she had reason to believe that at least one of the individuals was a survivor.

Then, on top of the other disasters, Reg had attacked Jocelyn. While it was uncharacteristic behaviour for the boy, it was exactly what Jocelyn's friends had warned her about. The attack, coupled with the murder of the Premier and Lauren, added fuel to a fire that was already underway.

"Are you still here?"

Jocelyn's voice, groggy with sleep, pushed aside Sofia's other thoughts.

"I went home and had a good night's sleep," responded Sofia. "How about you?"

Jocelyn patted her bump. "I slept as best I could with this one squirming around."

It was an attempt at humour but it also highlighted the most contentious aspect of Jocelyn's trial. Banishment was hard enough for a fit and healthy woman but it was a death sentence for a woman about to give birth. But now, none of that mattered any more than the voices that hummed in the background. At yesterday's special council meeting, Claudia had cast her vote and now it was up to Sofia to tell Jocelyn that she was to stand trial immediately.

The hospital room door, shut and guarded by Kerry, the bailiff, dampened the noise of those waiting in the hallway but the open window failed to filter out the voices passing by outside. It felt like everyone in the town and the surrounding area had come for the trial. Last night, Sofia had watched as the first spectators arrived to stake out their spots in front of the Warragul Arts Centre. Florence and her mob had been among them. Sitting in a circle, arms linked, they were silent supporters of the woman who was part of their tribe. Fireflies, those little bugs whose abdomens lit up to attract males, joined in the vigil like tiny floating votive lights. Watching the women and the fireflies, Sofia was struck by all the changes that had occurred in her lifetime. The Desolation and its aftermath had changed the social structure, not only of Australia but of the entire world. Those changes had been so quick and so extreme that they overshadowed that other major shift, the climate. The summers were drier and hotter now, while the winters were colder and wetter. Storms were more severe and droughts lasted longer. These changes were advantageous for some species, allowing them to thrive farther south than before but for those that couldn't adapt fast enough, the only outcome was extermination. Along with the climate, it seemed that the community, too, had become more extreme. What had once been a happy community of like-minded people was fragmenting and Sofia wasn't sure which group would survive and which would perish.

When Sofia and Florence brought the first group of rescue boys from Melbourne, the community welcomed them. Those first boys had grown up in Heart House and some of them had gone on to university while others worked at the co-op or took jobs around town. It seemed like a situation that suited all parties, but in the last couple of years, there had been an undercurrent of unrest. Ursula was the most vocal opponent but she wasn't alone. Just as the climate had changed nature, the Desolation had changed human's social structure which often made Sofia consider the question of adapting. During the Desolation, Florence and the women in her family had coped better than Sofia. Was that because their family ties between women were stronger or was it because the arrival of Europeans had already inflicted so many changes to their way of life that adapting was ingrained in them? The Indigenous people of Australia had survived in this land of extremes long before Sofia's European ancestors arrived. Like the invasive species moving south with the shifting climate, those of her ancestors that came from the old world had not only brought with them new crops and animals, but also deadly diseases and foreign laws. Despite that, the indigenous people had adapted and survived but what about Australia's newest arrivals? Did they have what it took to survive?

Jocelyn, like Sofia, was of mixed heritage, but unlike Sofia, who was more European, Jocelyn was more indigenous. Their differences, subtle as their similarities, were only a question of degrees, but that didn't make them any less significant. Sofia knew that the Florence faction would always choose family over law while Sofia's allegiance lay with the law. The European in her believed that without laws, society collapsed and by extension, where there were laws, there were punishments. Whereas Florence believed that Jocelyn's murder, premeditated or not, was justified, Sofia, knowing the law, only had to prove that Jocelyn's murder of Reg was not premeditated. The law, just or not, stated that only premeditated murder was punishable by branding and banishment. Where Florence argued that the law didn't make sense in Jocelyn's case, Sofia focused her energies on finding a loophole.

"Joc, I need you to tell me, in your own words, exactly what happened."

Sofia held Jocelyn's hand while she spoke. They'd been granted this short time alone because no one knew the protocol for a murder trial. Was the accused allowed visitors before the trial? Was the mediator restricted from pre-trial questioning? Who knew? There'd only been that one murder trial prior to today and that had been different because it had involved a male killing a female. The law suited that situation but didn't seem appropriate now that a woman was accused of killing a male. For once, Sofia wished Warragul's system of justice was more like the Republic's. There, if a woman murdered a male, she might be chastised, or if the boy's family were particularly aggrieved, the woman might have to pay compensation, but no woman could be punished for murdering a male just as no woman could be accused of raping one either.

Sofia, sitting in her straight-backed chair, said, "There's a lot of rumours circulating but most of the community believes you murdered Reg in self-defence. It doesn't matter what you said to May at the time. You were a pregnant woman under stress. One who'd just been beaten. We can claim you were under duress when you confessed. We can say that now that you've had time to recover, you want to clarify the sequence in which things happened. We don't need to change your story so much as—"

"Sofia, stop. I can't take an oath to tell the truth and then lie."

"It's not a lie. It's clarification. He beat you. You defended yourself."

"It's true that he beat me but it's also true that I loved him."

"That doesn't make any sense."

"What is the punishment for beating a woman?"

"If you're a male it's the same as murder," replied Sofia. "The culprit is marked as a woman beater and banished to the wilds."

"When you saw what Reg did to me the first time, were you going to let him get away with it?"

Sofia took a deep breath before she spoke, "It was up to you to accuse him."

"But I didn't."

"Which is why no actions were taken against Reg." But even as she said the words Sofia's voice faltered because she knew that wasn't totally true.

"And when you saw what he did the second time, what were you planning to do?"

"Once a boy becomes abusive he's a danger to the community."

"So you would have had him brought to trial with or without my pressing charges?"

"The laws exist to protect the ones we love."

Jocelyn sat forward in her bed and placed her good hand on top of Sofia's.

"Remember last Sunday when we were talking about that strange prehistoric shark that the lancers brought in ages ago?"

Sofia recalled the conversation but couldn't understand what that had to do with Reg's murder.

"I remember, you said it started to smell so they took it into the bush and buried it unceremoniously. What does–"

"That's what would have happened to Reg," said Jocelyn. "I know what you were planning after he hit me. I could see it in your eyes. That's why I asked you not to interfere."

"Jocelyn, I don't know what you're talking about."

"I know what the women of this town do when a cusp-aged male becomes a problem."

"We banish them," said Sofia.

"And send them on the road to Inverloch," interjected Jocelyn, "with the mark of their transgressions."

Sofia looked up but didn't speak. How could she? To deny it would be a lie while to agree would be to admit her own guilt.

Jocelyn continued. "I know what happens. I came across one of their solutions."

Sofia wasn't sure she wanted to hear the rest of Jocelyn's account.

Some things, things that were left to chance or fate, should be forgotten. Ignored. But Jocelyn pressed on.

"Remember, oh, about 10 years ago, around the same time as the sea creature, there was that fifteen or sixteen year-old boy who attacked a young girl at Heart House."

"Are you referring to Caleb?"

"That's the one."

"Jocelyn, he was marked and banished which is what would have happened to Reg."

"Once I knew that you were planning to have him charged, I knew what I had to do."

"Jocelyn, you're not making sense."

"I know what wilding women do to young men who are branded as women beaters." Dropping her voice to a whisper, Jocelyn said, "I saw what happened to Caleb."

"Oh, Jocelyn. We can't control the actions of those outside our community. If fate drove him into the hands of –"

"You and the women of Warragul set Caleb on the road to Inverloch. You could have put him on the road East, where he might have reached a lancer colony, but you didn't. You set him on the road to Inverloch because you knew what they would do."

Jocelyn's brown eyes stared deep into Sofia's, not with anger but with sorrow, a deep penetrative sorrow.

"I found what was left of Caleb," continued Jocelyn. "I was passing by Inverloch on one of the backroads when I encountered a terrible smell. I figured that's where they'd dumped the sea creature so I thought I'd keep walking but then I saw something."

"Jocelyn that road leads to a lot of places. He could have bypassed Inverloch and gone on to San Remo."

"But he didn't and you know why, don't you?"

"Jocelyn, you're talking nonsense. He may have wandered into Inverloch but he wasn't intentionally sent there if that's what you think."

"Worse. I think the women of Inverloch were told where that boy was going to be dropped off and they were waiting for him. Sofia, you have no idea what they did to that boy."

Sofia didn't want to know any more. She'd been the one to pronounce judgment, and she knew that May's officers had taken him to a road that led West, but she hadn't known that those same officers were going to make sure he was properly punished. On the other hand, she hadn't asked for specifics and that was because she didn't want to know. It was enough that May said that her officers would make sure he never returned. That boy Caleb was a threat and everyone knew it was only a matter of time before he committed a truly violent act. Sofia hadn't asked how they knew he wasn't coming back. She'd done her duty and left it up to them to do theirs.

"We are not responsible for the women of Inverloch," she reiterated.

"But you are responsible for sending a boy, for that's what he was, into the hands of those women. He was marked and handed over. We left the punishment to them but we delivered him into their hands and in the end, the choices we make always come home to roost."

Sofia wanted to deny Jocelyn's allegation but a little voice deep inside stopped her. It had been easy at the time to condemn and leave the rest to chance.

Jocelyn was crying openly. "I couldn't let that happen to Reg. He hurt me but I couldn't do that to him."

"So why didn't you send him away?"

"I did. After that first time. I told him to leave but he came back."

"So you took it upon yourself to punish him."

"He would have been 20 in June. I would have loved for him to hold his child, even if only for a few months but something got into him."

"Jocelyn, every boy has a different way of dealing with the cusp. That's why sometimes it's best to let them go."

"He wasn't bad Sofia. It's just that he found it so unfair. He didn't want to die."

Another lively, chatting group passed by the window on their way to the Arts Centre. These late arrivals were nothing more than curious bystanders who only came because public trials were rare. They had no vested interest in the outcome of the trial so they spoke about the weather, their plans for the rest of the day and whether they were going to stay in town for the night's festivities. For them, the trial was entertainment, much like tonight's play. But for those who'd arrived last night and early this morning, they had a vested interest in the outcome. They were the ones who sat in opposition to each other. They were the ones that highlighted how far this once close knit community, had become divided.

As their voices faded away, Jocelyn reached over to the side table and picked up a little brass broach.

"After the first time," she stopped to swallow down her emotions and then said, "When he came back, he gave me this. He said he made it to say he was sorry."

She placed it in Sofia's hand.

"They're going to take everything I own away from me but I don't want them to take this."

Before Sofia could respond, there was a knock and Kerrie, the bailiff, opened the door. "May says it's time."

CHAPTER 7
THE OLD ONE'S CABIN

SEPTEMBER 2069

The afternoon sun had moved below the trees, taking with it both light and warmth. As the Old One finished speaking the girl shivered then automatically wrapping her arms tight around herself, said, "How could Jocelyn have done what she did in the name of love?"

The Old One replied, "Times were different and maybe it's a good sign that you don't understand. Sometimes understanding becomes a kind of accepting. It's a fine line that's easily crossed."

Having come back to the topic of Jocelyn, the girl thought that now was a good time to ask her own question. The one that no one ever wanted to discuss but as she opened her mouth, the kettle screamed and the Old One said, "You'd better attend to the tea."

The girl stood and again started to speak but the kettle's screams became more insistent so instead she headed for the kitchen while the Old One turned the wheelchair towards the table and picked up the faded photo of the young man with the dark hair. While Jocelyn was being prepared for her encounter with colonial justice, he and his group were also being prepped.

INVERLOCH

FRIDAY 10 DECEMBER 2049 - 8:00 A.M.

"Well, if it ain't Shepherd," said the stocky lad standing in the doorway. Scanning the room, he spotted Benny and laughed, "And Blue. I thought you two were headin' for Warragul. What're you doin' down here in Inverloch? You take a wrong turn somewhere?"

The voice was mocking but not unfriendly. Scratching the growth on his chin, Steve stepped forward and pointed in the direction of the uni students.

"These refugees from Warragul convinced us that the Colony was no longer male friendly."

"So, I've heard," replied Bulldog.

Without moving from his position blocking the exit, he turned his attention to the other occupants of the warehouse. The twins standing side by side garnered barely a glance. He took more time, however, to appraise the three lads from Warragul. Steve knew how that felt. He remembered the way Jack and Bulldog had sized up him and Benny when the smugglers dropped them off at Venus Bay. It seemed that lancers took the measure of a person before welcoming them. But it wasn't the lancers who renamed him. It was the girl Cherry. She, too, sized him up and then pronounced that his lancer name was German Shepherd. Bennie, she renamed as Blue Heeler. At the time he'd wondered if all women in this part of the world saw men as dogs or if that was the girl's particular world view. Even if she hadn't been kidnapped by those women in the trader's truck, he probably wouldn't have asked. Something about that girl stilled questions.

Finishing his assessment, Bulldog clapped his hands and said, "OK, listen up. I'm going to let you guys out of here but before I do, I need to tell you the rules."

"Rules?" squeaked one of the twins. "When did lancers start having rules?"

"Yeah," agreed his brother.

Snickering and jostling each other, they looked towards the others for support, but instead, the Warragul boys stayed focused on the lancer. His face changed, the way the landscape changed when a cloud blocked the sun. Then with a movement so quick and fluid that even Steve didn't see it coming, Bulldog kicked the door shut. Hearing it slam, the twins turned back to face Bulldog who was heading straight towards them with a look that wiped the smiles from their faces.

He stopped directly in front of them. Speaking calmly and firmly, he said, "We may be lancers but we're not uncivilised or uncouth."

He let that sink in before he turned around and strolled back over to Steve saying, "Now, Shepherd, you and your flock need to listen up 'cause 'round here, you violate the rules, you get punished." He stood eye to eye with Steve for a moment, then swung back towards the boys. "Don't matter if you're one of us or not." Scanning the faces in the room, he settled back on the twins. "That's rule number one." He held up his fist. One finger emerged on its own.

The twins, at first shocked into silence, decided to complain. Together, they said, "That's not how it is with lancers. We're not—"

Jai told them to grow up and listen. Both twins turned on him, but Craig stepped in between, so they backed down. Bulldog, standing still, feet planted firmly in place, waited till he had their attention once more, then asked Steve.

"So what's your plan? You guys stayin' here or movin' on?"

Looking past Bulldog, he searched Benny's face before he spoke.

"At the moment there is no plan."

"Maybe you should stay till you get one."

Steve considered the offer as he scanned the faces of the others. What he realised, as he looked from one to the next, was that they trusted him to talk on their behalf. All, except the twins. But then, they weren't part of his group.

"I guess we need to hear the rest of these rules before we decide."

"Right-e-o." Bulldog crossed his arms. Letting his eyes shift from one boy to the next, he proceeded.

"This here's a lancer wilding community. That means there's women and children sharing their town with us. They got their own area so rule number two is that you don't enter their area without their approval."

Steve could see the question in the boy's eyes but they remained silent as Bulldog continued.

"Females are free to move around the town from dawn to dusk and you can talk to them but you must be civil and courteous. Everyone understand what that means? You speak to pass along information or to say please and thank you, but otherwise, you do not speak unless spoken to. You fancy a female, you wait for her to tell you that she's interested. That's rule number three."

"But how do we—", Malcolm looked confused. "I mean if we can't start a conversation—"

"Don't worry. If they want a yak, they'll let you know. Now, rule number four. If a girl does approach you to say she's interested, you can tell her how you feel about that but you do not touch her without permission. You wait and let her make the offer. Even then you do not go further than she wants you to."

As he talked, he walked along the line inspecting each individual to make sure they understood him.

"If she takes your hand, you can accept it but you want more than that, even a kiss on the cheek, you need the head woman's permission and that too is left up to the female. So rule number 5, and this one is very important, you need the head woman's permission to go beyond holding hands."

"As for sex," here he stopped directly in front of the twins, "it's only allowed within the confines of the women's area and that definitely requires the approval of the head woman. Rule 6, and you do not want to break this one, says that there is no spontaneous coupling, even if the female invites it."

Steve noted the serious looks on the faces of the boys from Warragul. The twins, however, smirked at each other as soon as Bulldog turned away from them. Turning abruptly as he opened the door, the smirks quickly disappeared but Steve got the impression that Bulldog was aware of them nonetheless.

"Never forget rule number 6. If a female invites you into her space, you first gotta have the head woman's permission. If she agrees, then you can stay the night but by breakfast bell, you leave. Is that understood?"

Outside, a bell clanged several times.

"That's the breakfast bell. Remember that sound. You hear that and you get the hell out of the female sector. That's rule 7 and trust me, you do not want to forget it. Do you understand?"

Steve signalled the boys to nod their agreement but his real focus was on Benny. The boys from Warragul were clueless and the twins even more so, but he and Benny had both served as studs. They both knew about the ramifications of breaking the rules. Punishments might differ between Inverloch and Melbourne but they were still rules made up by women to ensure that men didn't take the upper hand.

Standing with his hand on the door, Bulldog said brusquely, "Am I clear?"

When there was no response, he placed his hands on his hips and stuck out his chest. A muscle in his jaw tightened and he bellowed.

"I said, do you understand?"

This time, the boys responded by nodding emphatically, which seemed to satisfy the dog.

"Right. Now I'll take you to breakfast and then we'll assign you temporary quarters while you decide if you want to stay or not. But

Inverloch hospitality is not free. While you're here, you'll have assigned duties. Everyone contributes. Is that understood?"

The group exchanged confused looks and Bulldog reiterated, "Is that understood?"

"Yes," replied Steve who signalled that the others should respond as well.

Cautiously, they replied "Yes."

That didn't seem to satisfy Bulldog so he said, "I asked if you understood?"

This time they replied 'Yes', in unison.

"Right. Let's go then."

As Bulldog led the way out, and the boys followed, Benny came up next to Steve and said, "Does this seem odd to you?"

"Yeah, odd as in oddly familiar."

Benny nodded in agreement and said, "Well, one thing's certain."

"What's that?" asked Steve.

"I could use a good breakfast."

And with that, he walked out and caught up with the other boys.

The town that had been empty the night before, now bustled with activity. Women and children came from the direction of the houses Steve and his crew had passed last night. They wandered in various directions, some heading towards the western beach, others wandering down the main street. A few males emerged from the houses that had females but they hurried to the other side of the road where they joined up with the males who were coming up from the eastern beaches.

Bulldog came to a halt at the main intersection and waited for Steve and the others to gather round him.

"Women and children can either eat at home or in the communal kitchen at the church, over there."

He pointed towards a spire to their left.

"The main road here marks the limits of the women's section. You do not cross to the left without permission. The male area is to your right."

At this point, one of the twins whispered in his brother's ear and they both giggled.

"You have something you want to say," barked Bulldog.

"We want to know how we get permission."

Bulldog walked towards them, and Benny and the others parted so that he stood in front of them. They towered over him but the smiles slipped from their faces.

"I thought I was clear on that point but I'll repeat for the slow learners. You wait for the girl to step forward and ask the head woman for permission. The female does the asking."

He looked around. "Anyone else have a question?" When there was no response he turned and said, "We have breakfast at the bar. Follow me."

Bulldog led them up the male side of the Esplanade to a squat brick building. As they approached, a group of three teens exited with mugs in one hand and paper-wrapped sandwiches in the other. The greasy smell of bacon was overpowering as Bulldog held the door and the hungry boys pushed past him. On the polished wood bar sat platters stacked with parcels individually wrapped in brown paper.

"Egg and bacon sandwiches," exclaimed Benny. "Is this for real?"

The others jabbered excitedly but it was the twins who found it hardest to curb their enthusiasm. They jostled each other, trying to gain a better position until the lad in front of them turned and gave them a dirty look. Apologising, they settled into line like everyone else.

That line moved with the precision of a finely tuned machine. Each boy grabbed a sandwich and moved on. Empty platters were whisked away, only to be replaced by another. The replenishing was done by a couple of elderly women who scurried between kitchen and bar. There were no girls or young women in sight.

"How many people live here?" asked Steve.

"Well, the male population has been in decline but I think it's around 600. The female population is around 1,500 and that includes about 250 kids."

As they moved up in the queue, Steve noticed how one of the twins took a sandwich and backhanded it to his brother, who slipped it into his pocket. Then they both reached for another. If Bulldog or anyone else noticed, they didn't say anything. Given the size of the town, it was interesting that food didn't seem to be an issue. At the Big House on French Island, food also wasn't an issue but that was part of being a stud. Some of the new kids spoke about going hungry when they were growing up. They usually came from the inner suburbs of Melbourne. According to those boys, the government issued food stamps as a kind of wage. If a boy took his assigned job, the family got a food allocation for him. Otherwise, the family received food allocations for females only and they added, the food allocations were barely sufficient. Women with jobs received wages on top of their food allocation but even they struggled to raise boys who didn't work. For low-income families, it was almost impossible to raise boys because boys didn't get assigned jobs until they took the Selection test, and they had to be ten to take the test. That meant taking food from others in the family to feed the boys. The government solution to help struggling families was to offer to take over the care of young boys. Babies, toddlers, any under-age boy could be dropped off at one of the official boy care centres. The centres were basically labour camps. That put the boys to work as soon as they were able. It was common to see boys as young as six working on construction sites. It wasn't much of a life but it was better than being dumped in the wilds or left to fend for themselves in the Old CBD.

Following the others to the beverage table with its urns of hot water and its choice of coffee or tea, Steve noticed the stacks of bottled juice. He recognised them as the same bottles he'd been given on the boat trip from Hastings Pier to Venus Bay so he asked, "Are these women smugglers?"

Bulldog looked up from the tea he'd made for himself and noticed how Steve was staring at the juice.

"Most of the women here are wildings but there's a group from Melbourne that call themselves Subversives. They don't mingle much with the wilding women but they do bring supplies in as their way of contributing. Other than that, they mostly come and go on their own."

"And Cherry?" Steve thought of the red-haired girl with facial piercings who'd been in charge at Venus Bay. Somehow he couldn't imagine her abiding by the wilding rules. "Was she a Subversive or a wilding?"

Bulldog ignored the question. Instead, he asked, "Want coffee or tea?" When Steve shook his head Bulldog tossed him an orange juice and headed towards the door.

Outside, Bulldog pointed towards the green where there were a number of picnic tables and Steve followed him.

"So these rules. Who makes them up and who enforces them?"

"It's the women's rules and they do the punishing but the rules are as much for the safety of the males as the females."

"How so?"

"Well, let's say a girl goes walking on the beach with a lad and they get interested. He says she asked for it. She says he took something that wasn't on offer. The penalty for rape is not something you want to know about. This way, if a girl gets permission from the head woman, everyone knows what she's agreeing to. They're given a room for the night but each time has to be approved. No long-term stays."

"What about the children," asked Steve as a group of young pre-teens ran past."

"You asking when boys get separated from their kin?"

"Basically, yes."

"Boys are removed once a year. Everyone that turns 16 in that year is removed. We have an initiation ceremony to bring them into our group. We assess their skills and decide which work to assign them."

The Warragul boys were seated at a table and Bulldog sat down next to them. He finished his sandwich, balled up the paper and drained the last of his tea. Then he asked, "Any of you guys know how to fish?"

Benny looked up. "Steve does."

Bulldog chuckled. "Why am I not surprised? Well, after breakfast I'll take you lot down to the boats. We'll see who can catch, who can clean and who can mop up guts."

Later, as they headed towards the beach Steve asked about supplies.

Bulldog explained how the lancers mainly fished. Most of their catch was sent to Melbourne or the bigger colonies like Warragul where it was traded for chits, a kind of currency. The women, for the most part, managed the orchards and farms outside of town.

"During planting and harvesting, everyone works together but the women are in charge. They also look after the livestock but once a year, we have the roundup. Everyone has a hand in the slaughtering, but the butchering is left to the women."

As Bulldog said this, he gave Steve a knowing look before he added, "They're good with knives, which is something you lot need to keep in mind."

CHAPTER 8
THE OLD ONE'S CABIN

SEPTEMBER 2069

"It's getting dark, and I think I'd better light the fire," said the girl, placing the teapot on the table to let it brew.

The Old One set the photo aside to watch the girl scoop the ashes from the firebox and into the tin bucket. Methodically, the girl proceeded to lay a bed of dry logs stacking them so there was plenty of airflow. Meticulous and precise, the next layer was composed of lighter, disparate materials, assembled so that they could support their weight and form a bed to contain the tinder she placed on top.

The Old One, intent on the girl's actions, almost missed what the girl was saying.

"So Jocelyn's trial was on the same day as the Premier's memorial service."

"Exactly," murmured the Old One.

"But why didn't they wait until the service was over?"

"You could say that justice in the Colony was swift –"

Then the Old One paused, saying thoughtfully, "But maybe other forces were at play." Then, as if speaking to no one in particular said,

"Sofia too wondered why Police Commissioner May insisted on that particular day."

The girl looked up, but as nothing further was said, she returned to the fire. Striking a match, she carefully held the flame next to the dry leaves and grass. Once they caught, she blew on it until the kindling, too, began to smoulder. After that, it didn't take long for the logs to catch. The Old One had witnessed the same attention to detail in another. That woman had fire in her too and like this one, had learned how to control it.

As the girl closed the heater door, the Old One said, "There was never going to be a good day for that trial but having it on the same day as the Premier's memorial service certainly kept everyone in the Colony distracted from events outside Warragul."

The girl looked in the direction of the Old One to ask the question she'd been putting aside but seeing the distracted look in those old eyes, decided that now was not the time either.

"Like that fire you're building," said the Old One, "individual events and people were being stacked in just the right combination to be set ablaze. Whether it was coincidence or conscious design, I don't suppose we'll ever know but certain events seemed convenient for keeping people where they needed to be so that events could play out the way they did.

MONIKA

FRIDAY 10 DECEMBER 2049 - 8:00 A.M.

"You look like you could use a pick me up."

Stephanie held a glass with a bubbling reddish-orange liquid.

"Is that Berocca?"

"Normally, I'd suggest a Bloody Mary but today you'll be sitting next to Evelyn and we both know how she feels about drinking on the job."

"But where did you get your hands on a Berocca?"

"Money has a way of locating things that everyone else has lost sight of."

Monika took the glass. She hadn't heard that effervescent sound since, well, since the Desolation. Overseas trade came to a dramatic halt during the pandemic and Monika remembered all too well how something as simple as needles and as essential as antibiotics became hard to get. Berocca wasn't as life-saving as antibiotics, but it had been her standard 'post-nightout' cure.

"And hangover cures aren't the only surprise I have for you this morning."

Stephanie sat in the chair next to the bed Monika had thrown herself into after her early morning interview.

"A little bird told me that," she paused, "Are you going to drink that or stare it into you?"

"Let me enjoy the fizz a bit longer," replied Monika. "But tell me what titbit you learned while I was snoozing."

"It appears that our friend Davina was quite busy last night."

"If you're referring to the lancer roundup, I already know about that."

"But did you know that the roundup went beyond the Old CBD?"

Monika nodded her head with that slight tilt that conveyed the message, 'Continue, but I already know what you're about to say'.

Steph waited until Monika had a mouthful and then said, "They picked up some cuspers from one of my work sites."

Monika swallowed so quickly, she nearly choked. "Why would they do that? Were they looking for someone in particular?"

"I believe that's exactly what they were up to."

Steph leaned back in her chair. A smug smile plastered across her face.

"Well, are you going to tell me?"

"Sure you don't want to finish your Berocca first?"

Seeing the look in Monika's eye, Steph continued, "Well, if you insist. They picked up everyone at the construction sight in Collingwood, where we are upgrading the substation. They held them overnight, and Davina selected three for her special brand of interrogation."

Monika felt the blood rush from her head. Carefully, she placed the glass on the bedside table, consciously steadying her hand.

"Are you saying some of your workers are linked to the Subversives?"

Steph placed a reassuring hand on Monika's.

"Relax dear. Everyone has one or two Subversives lurking among their workers. There are probably some on your own staff. No, the one who needs to be concerned is your little nemesis, Catherine."

"Why should she be worried?"

"Because her brother-in-law was one of the three lancers Davina held for questioning."

"You're not saying that he's one of the lancers accused of murdering Dorothy?"

"Juicy bit of gossip," said Steph getting back on her feet. Then she added, "If it's true, that is."

Monika felt the colour returning to her face. It hadn't been Steph's labourers she worried about. It was Benny. Davina had left his bike on her veranda. A clear message that hed'd been found and dealt with. Linking Catherine to the Premier's murder seemed like evening the score. But what if that was exactly what Evelyn was doing? Benny had been her liability so was this brother-in-law, Catherine's?

CATHERINE

It was the quiet, not the lack of it, that woke Catherine. Abruptly, she opened her eyes. Feeling confused about where she was, the fog lifted and then she remembered with a jolt that she was meant to be at the memorial service. Grabbing her phone she looked at the time. 9:30. With a sigh of relief she lay her head back on the pillow and stared at the ceiling. She'd only slept a couple of hours but it was more than enough to recharge her batteries. Then something else hit her. The TV was silent. The sound of voices from the other room that had lulled her to sleep were gone.

Sitting up in bed, she scanned the room. Her hair dryer no longer dangled precariously on the edge of her makeup table. The area in front of her mirror was tidy. Everything was in its place. She glanced toward the bathroom. Her wet towel no longer lay crumpled accusingly in the middle of the floor and the clothes she'd stripped off and discarded like trail markers from her bedroom door to the bathroom had disappeared. The room was as tidy as her make-up table.

"Thomasina?"

Silence.

She desperately wanted Thomasina if for no other reason than to push her away. Her wife hadn't been here when she needed her but that didn't stop her from needing her now. Conflicting emotions jostled for her attention. Love. Hate. Longing. Fear. At the familiar sound of padded feet on the polished wood floors, a dopamine hit swamped Catherine and she thought she might cry.

There was Thomasina standing in the doorway smiling.

"You're awake. Did you see my note?"

At the mention of the note, Catherine's euphoria wavered. She hesitated. Like that night, when Catherine and her father had surveyed the remains of that burned-out town, she now felt both relieved and angry. Back then, she'd been angry at herself for being afraid but at the same time, she was relieved to see the lights of the relief centre. She wasn't sure who she was angry with this time but she knew that she was relieved. Note or no note, it was a relief to have Thomasina home again. On the other hand, remembering the note revived her anger.

Catherine replied, "The one about Nick?"

She hoped that she sounded objective, matter of fact, but all the while, the rage she felt earlier was returning.

"That's the one sleepyhead."

If Thom noticed the restraint in Catherine's voice, she didn't show it.

"Need some coffee to clear those cobwebs?"

Catherine's inner voice was screaming but outwardly she said, "That would be greatly appreciated and then we need to get moving." Shoving back the covers, she swung her feet out of bed. Deliberately averting her eyes from Thomasina's, she rapidly added, "We have to be at St Patrick's by 10:45 and with the road closures, there will be detours, so we'll need extra time."

A cool hand touched her cheek. In that moment, the hurt and anger dissipated. A single touch was all it took to exorcise her inner demons.

"Coffee first, then we can sort out the rest of the day," said Thomasina.

Far too soon, the hand was gone and the room was empty and sterile again. What was this day going to cost her?

Standing up, Catherine took a deep breath and opened the curtains. She'd inherited this house from her father after he disserted her for his self-imposed exile. At least, that's how she saw his retreat to the government-supplied bunker. Officially, it was her mother's but she'd abandoned the house for her lab long before the pandemic. Not that her parents separated. Oh, the famous Dr Williams had slept here but she never seemed to feel at home. When Catherine was young, it was her father, not her mother, that raised her. Then during the Desolation, when men were dying or being sequestered, her mother returned. During the worst of the pandemic, she deigned to haunt the house, passing from room to room, never talking, never offering comfort. Then, once the pandemic had devoured its prey, Dr Williams returned to her true love, Gentech. In what seemed like a totally selfish act, Catherine's mother abandoned her living daughter and for what? To rebuild Gentech? When everyone who was important was dead, what was the point in searching for a cure? Wasn't it more important to look after the living? If her mother had simply disappeared, or better, if she'd died like so many other women who lost their husbands during the pandemic, then maybe Catherine could have forgiven her. Instead, her mother kept dropping in and out of her life, coming and going as she pleased without any consideration for her only daughter's feelings. And in all that time, the one thing they never spoke of was the loss they both suffered.

Looking out across the valley that separated their leafy green suburb from the Old CBD, Catherine thought how beautiful it was. It had been ages since she took time to take in this view but as a child, this had been her favourite place. This window. This view. Before the Desolation, this neighbourhood had been highly sought after because of its outlook and the way the lights of the city illuminated the dark like a man-made Milky Way fallen to earth. This had been her parent's bedroom back then and her father would seat her on his lap, in front of this window, while he told her a bedtime story. Pointing to those city lights he would say that this was her castle on the hill and that this valley was her dominion. One day, he'd say, she would be the queen of all she surveyed, including that far-off city of stars. How many times had she fallen asleep in his arms listening to his deep, resonant voice? Then the pandemic hit and the lights went out. The lesser lights, those that occupied the heavens, reclaimed their rightful place. There had been a kind of poetic justice last night when the smoke obliterated those lights as well.

Last night, she'd watched the conflagration from a different vantage point. It was from the window of her office that she watched the fires wipe out the last vestiges of those derelict man-made structures. In that scene of destruction, Catherine saw, for the first time, Stephanie Steele's vision for the future. Even though she didn't like the woman, she could see that Stephanie was right about the Old CBD. It had to go to make way for the new. As the flames consumed building after building, Catherine had thought of her father. He'd been a builder, not of structures, but of society and that made him part of the power elite who'd fashioned those monuments to mankind. And now, they, like the men who'd built them, were gone.

Smoke, dark and menacing, clung to the higher floors of the buildings. A reminder that while the fires were over there was still a lot of clean up to be done. Undoubtedly, Monika's fiancé Stephanie, would get the contract, along with the kudos for knocking down the condemned buildings to form a firebreak. Yesterday, the inequity of that had galled her but this morning after her meeting with Evelyn, she felt buoyed. Monika, Stephanie, and yes, even her mother belonged to a generation that lived in a male-dominated past. She could see that, even if they couldn't. Evelyn, on the other hand, was a woman ahead of her time which was why the grand old lady had recognised Catherine's brilliance. For the first time since her father's death, she felt that someone recognised the greatness in her. In the past, it had been Monika who'd been the heir apparent, but after this morning, Catherine knew it was no longer a one-horse race. The kings' castles had collapsed, but they would be rebuilt only this time; the world belonged to queens, and she, Catherine, was raised to be a queen.

"Coffee's ready."

Should she confide in Thomasina or wait to see the look on her face when they were seated next to Evelyn at the memorial service? That was something she could decide over coffee but first there was the tricky subject of the ultrasound and the genetic test.

As Catherine sat down at the little kitchen table, Thomasina looked up. Her smile was welcoming but Catherine could see the fatigue in her eyes.

"I missed you when I got back this morning," said Catherine, surreptitiously glancing in the direction where she'd tossed the note. There was a pang of guilt when she realised it was no longer there.

"I'm sorry. I tried calling but you were so busy with the fires and I thought it was something I could handle myself."

Catherine wrapped her fingers around her mug.

"And did you?"

"Not really."

Catherine's fingers tightened. Here it comes, she thought.

"When Nick didn't come home by curfew my mother called to see if he'd come here instead. There was so much confusion with the evacuation zones and the road closures..." Her voice trailed off as Catherine took a sip of coffee.

When Catherine didn't respond, Thomasina continued.

"So I went to his work site."

Catherine swallowed and looked up with alarm. "You did what? In the middle of all that chaos, you went to a work site? What were you thinking? And how did you get there?"

"First of all, I was thinking my brother might be in trouble." This response came out with an unusual harshness but then Thomasina softened her tone. "I walked. It wasn't that far away and it wasn't dangerous."

"Not dangerous? You're six months pregnant and the streets were crawling with lancers and you think that's not dangerous?"

"Women walk, even pregnant women and the streets were hardly crawling with anyone."

Thomasina stood up taking her mug into the kitchen.

Catherine turned to watch her walk away.

"So, did you find him?"

Even with her back turned, Catherine could feel her wife's anguish.

"No. He hasn't turned up this morning either." She turned to face Catherine. "I went back to the site this morning and no one's there."

Catherine heaved a sigh of relief and turned back to her coffee.

"Everyone's got the day off because of the memorial service. In a day or two things will be back to normal."

"But what if he was picked up by the police."

"If his fingerprints are on file and he's registered, he'll be sent home with a fine for violating curfew. Now come and sit with me while I finish my coffee. I have some news of my own. Amazing news really."

Thomasina sat back down.

"I don't think you understand. My mother says cusp-aged males were being herded into trucks. There are rumours that they're being taken to the wilds."

"Thom, first you were worried about Nick signing up for the stud house, now you're worried about him being transported to the wilds. Why is everything about Nick these days."

Catherine pushed her mug away.

"I don't mean to sound insensitive but he's cusp-aged. He's as good as dead so what's the big deal?"

"The big deal is that cusp-aged or not, he's my brother and I need to know where he is."

"So what exactly, do you think I can do?"

"Make a few phone calls?"

Thomasina's voice was weak, pleading.

"Fine. But now I need you to do something for me."

"Anything."

The relief in Thomasina's voice was apparent so Catherine decided that this was her best chance to give Thom the news.

"This morning Evelyn stopped by my office."

"Evelyn Perkins! The Evelyn Perkins."

"The same."

Catherine allowed a small smile to emerge.

"She wanted to thank me for the way I handled the fires but more than that, she asked for my opinion on certain affairs of state."

She watched the effect of this disclosure on Thom's face. It was gratifying to see the enormity of Evelyn's visit sinking in.

"That's incredible. She asked for your opinion. It's the opportunity you've been waiting for. It's what we've both been waiting for. Did you tell her about giving all women, carers and guardians a stipend? Did you talk about daycare and –"

"Slow down. It was a short meeting but we touched on a couple of those things and she's asked me to come up with some, shall we say, strategies."

The glow of recognition in Thomasina's eyes was almost as exciting as receiving Evelyn's praise.

"I think I'm being fast-tracked. Now, would you like to hear the best part?"

"There's more?"

"Evelyn wants us to sit with her at the memorial service."

"In the same pew?"

"Not only in the same pew but right next to her."

"Oh Cat, that's amazing."

"Thom, I'm starting to think she might back me in the race for the Premiership."

"But I thought Monika Thomas was the designated—"

"I think Evelyn knows that Monika has aligned herself with the developers and everyone knows they're opposed to limiting male births. And after yesterday's fire, I think Evelyn sees how dangerously out of line they're becoming."

"But surely you don't believe in full gender testing. I mean we've talked about this."

"Thom, it's the way of the future. If we want to eliminate male exploitation, the only real solution is to eradicate all but the most essential males. I mean, look at all the trouble Nick is causing you and your mother and for what? In a few months, a year at max, he'll be dead and what purpose did he serve?"

"Purpose! What purpose? He's my brother. I love him regardless of whether he lives to be 20 or 200. How dare you, of all people, speak of purpose. Nick has worked all his life and what did he receive for it?"

"Thom, you're taking this personally. Calm down, you're not doing yourself or our baby any good by getting upset."

"I won't calm down. You've had everything handed to you. You had a well-connected family, so you never served on the death squads. And you've been allowed to pursue your career with government support while artists, like myself, were told we were unproductive. And with all that entitlement, what have you actually accomplished?"

"Thomasina, I don't think you know what you're saying." Catherine tried to sound objective and conciliatory as she continued. "I understand that you're upset over your brother and I also accept that your hormones are impacting your judgement—"

"My judgement? So it's my judgment we're calling into question. What about yours? Today, the problem is Nick, but what if our child is a boy? Are you just going to wipe your hands of him as well?"

Catherine leaned back in her chair and staring into Thomasina's eyes said, "And that's something else we need to talk about.

CHAPTER 9
THE OLD ONE'S CABIN

SEPTEMBER 2069

"Wait a minute," said the girl pausing the recorder. "I've asked before about Thomasina. There's no mention of her or of Catherine having children."

"Child." corrected the Old One.

"OK, child. As far as I know, Catherine Williams has no offspring."

"An interesting point."

"There's something you're not telling me? Did she have a boy?"

"Interesting observation. If she'd had a boy it would certainly have been an embarrassment to her and to the NOP. They were, after all, the party opposed to males."

"So was her child key to her position during the debates?"

"Offspring always hold the key."

DR HARRIS

FRIDAY 10 DECEMBER 2049 - 8:00 A.M.

"Josh has the key," Bonnie told herself.

She could see Patricia removing the chain from around her neck and placing it on Josh's but it was more than the key to her family's old apartment. It was a promise. It was their promise that they would come back for him. That key was the reporter's lucky charm, her talisman and it was meant to protect him while they went in search of a way out of Melbourne. The key was meant to keep him safe just like the building they were hiding in was meant to be his sanctuary. As an unregistered male on a wanted list, leaving the building risked being arrested on the spot. The danger was supposed to be on the outside not inside.

"He has the key," she murmured. It wasn't a statement. It was a mantra. It was hope.

She found herself in the Women's Peace Garden sitting next to her friend and boss, Geraldine. Gerry was giving her something. Like the key, this something was meant to protect her. A fog was rolling in, gobbling away at the Peace Garden until all that was left was Geraldine's voice repeating her message. Something about X. Element X. The key to the cure was inside. Inside what?

The fog turned black, a deep, dark choking cloud that smelled like—

Smoke!

Suddenly she was awake. Wide awake. Sitting up, she looked around, confused. Light seeped in through a caged area to her left, but the rest of the space was packed with boxes, and above her hung a rack of garments. To her right, a closed door offered the only visible exit. It took some concentration on her part but finally it sunk in. She was in some kind of van and it smelled of smoke but not the burning building kind. It reeked of cigarettes.

Flashes of last night emerged. She and Carla had rushed to the Old CBD. Then the bulldozers had arrived and the last thing Bonnie remembered was getting jabbed in the arm with something sharp. But what were they doing in the middle of all that confusion?

Josh held the key. Of course. That's what her muddled mind was telling her. She'd been trying to get to him but his building, along with the others in that area, was ablaze and she remembered screaming, "My son's in there."

Disoriented, and still feeling enervated, she crawled to the door of the van and tried to open it. The handle was jammed. She yanked harder but it wouldn't budge. Summoning what strength she could, she banged on the door and yelled but her voice was hoarse and feeble. She crawled to the window that spanned the width of the door and wiped at the dirt. All she could see were trucks and beyond that road and beyond that trees. Nothing looked even remotely familiar. It was a totally foreign landscape. If she was in a Melbourne suburb, it was unlike any she recognised. She pushed her face against the window in an attempt to see what lay further to her right or left. The city she knew was nowhere to be seen as if it had been obliterated while she slept. Panic gripped her. Frantically, she banged again on the door and jerked at the handle. It remained immovable. She readjusted her position and kicked at the door with her feet.

"No need to break down the door. I'm coming."

A woman's face appeared in the window, and Bonnie stopped as the woman pushed a cigarette between her lips and held up a key.

"Stop all this fuss," she said while the cigareet dangled precariously on her lower lip, "and I'll let you out."

Bonnie paused. Her body tensed in expectation. She heard the key go into the lock. Heard it jiggle. The woman swore and banged the door with her hand while Bonnie, once again, swallowed down her panic. The woman inhaled, removed the cigarette and blew out smoke. Like a cat trapped in a closed room, Bonnie backed away from the door and assumed a defensive position.

"Who are you? Where am I?"

On the other side, the woman absorbed in the complexities of the van door, replied, "No need to panic. We're only a bit over an hour out of Warragul."

The key made a satisfying clunk and the woman added, "You'll be home and hosed—"

But Bonnie wasn't interested in the woman or what she had to say. As soon as the latch released with a satisfying clunk and the door swung open, Bonnie scrambled out. Her legs, however, weren't as prepared as she was, and they caved under her so that the woman grabbed her and set her back on the edge of the van. Bonnie clawed the woman's hand away, nearly dislodging the cigarette now stuck between two fingers and the woman backed up. While Bonnie rubbed life back into her legs, the woman raised the cigarette to her lips, inhaled deeply, then lifted her head and blew three smoke rings into the air. She studied Bonnie who retaliated by staring straight back at her. They were boxers who'd returned to their corners and from the safety of that vantage point, caught their breath while assessing their opponent.

The look the woman gave Bonnie was a poor imitation of one that Geraldine used to great effect. It was meant to intimidate but Bonnie sensed that this woman was putting on an act. She lacked Geraldine's conviction as if she was playing a part she hadn't rehearsed well enough. Geraldine never had to put on an act because she had the goods to back it up. All this woman had was the fact that she knew where they were and Bonnie didn't.

Cautiously getting back on her feet, Bonnie tested her theory by taking a few steps towards her jailor. Quickly, the woman backed up, her skirts rustling like dry leaves on a windy day.

"Where am I?"

Dropping the cigarette, the woman squished it underfoot and said, "At a truck stop on the way to Warragul."

"What am I doing here?"

Sticking out the tip of her tongue, the woman used a finger to dislodge a bit of tobacco. Wiping it on her skirt, she said, "We needed to recharge. You're lucky I came out for a smoke, otherwise I wouldn't have known you were awake. Best go inside and have brekkie cause we still got a ways to Warragul."

"Warragul? What am I doing in Warragul?" This last question Bonnie posed to herself.

"I never asked your business," fussed the woman. "Your little friend said I was to take you to Sofia Vargas in Warragul and that I'd be paid handsomely for getting you there. Now, if you're hungry, follow me." The woman checked the charging pump. "Should be ready to go in another 20 minutes."

The name Sofia Vargas rang a bell, but Bonnie wasn't sure why. Slowly, deliberately she moved away from the van, taking in more of her surroundings. Charging stations lined the pavement in front of her, and looking up, she read the sign overhead: Leongatha Truck Station.

The van door shut with a bang behind her and the lady with the jangling jewellery brushed past, heading towards the restaurant. Bonnie glanced around for signs of anything that made sense. Across the road, a green sign, leaning badly to one side, read Melbourne 136 kilometres.

"You coming?"

As she followed the stranger, something came back to her.

"Genesis," she whispered.

"What's that?"

She stopped. "I've got to go back. I told them, I can't go without Josh."

It was coming back to her now. Energized by the recollection, she said, "I have to go back. This is a mistake."

"Nonsense," replied the woman. "I took a big risk getting you out of Melbourne and I didn't ask any questions but I tell you one thing, you try to take off before I get reimbursed, and I'll knock you on the head myself and drag you to your destination. So come on and be a good girl, and don't give me any trouble, or I'll shove you back in the van."

Bonnie didn't think the woman would really attack her, but not having a better plan, she followed the woman. As she walked, yesterday came back into focus. Geraldine had told Bonnie about Element X. It was a new marker that the government was screening for along with other genetic defects. Fertilized eggs with this marker were to be labelled inviable. Then she remembered why she told Carla that she needed to get back to Josh. His chance at life was already encoded in his DNA and she was the one that had passed that code onto him. The key to changing boys' lives lay inside their mothers. That's why the government was searching for Element X. They weren't searching for what had changed, they were eliminating that which hadn't.

She leaned against the pole that supported the giant overhead sign.

"You OK?"

The woman took her by the arm and pulled her in the direction of the diner.

"Your friend said you were likely to be disoriented and might need some restraint at first."

By friend, the woman must mean Carla. The same Carla who asked, "What if you don't find a cure before it's too late for Josh? Will you give up?"

That question took on greater meaning now that she knew what she was up against.

Then she remembered Geraldine saying, "You can stay here and watch Josh die or you can go to Warragul in the hope of finding a way to save him."

Everyone around her was saying it was too late to save Josh but not too late to save other boys. What they failed to understand was that the only reason she'd spent the last twenty years looking for a cure, was to save her son. Without him, there was no reason to get to Warragul.

There was no reason to continue her research. She was finished. It was over.

Bonnie stared at the sign across the road. 136 kilometres. Hope might be fading but it wasn't dead. Not yet. Taking a renewed interest in her keeper, she asked, "Who are you?"

"I'm Bertha, owner and director of Bertha's Traveling Shakespeare Company."

She pointed to a couple of vans parked on the other side of the lot.

"That's the rest of my troop. They're inside having breakfast which I would also like to do. Now, you feel up to eating?"

The brightly painted vans were decorated to look like gypsy wagons but that was an illusion. They were ordinary delivery vans not unlike the one she'd found herself in. This woman and her troop were in the business of disguises and Bonnie realised that was exactly what she needed.

"How much longer did you say before we get to Warragul?"

"It's not far but first, let's get some coffee and food. Don't you worry, I'll deliver you to Sofia, as soon as I can."

The bangles on the woman's wrist chimed as her hand tugged on Bonnie's elbow. Her long skirts swished and the reflective plastic circles sewn on them, captured the sunlight, casting rainbows in the direction they were heading. Bonnie had always believed in following rainbows just as she believed in miracles. Something would send a sign her way. All she needed to do now was keep her eyes and ears open.

Inside, the diner was noisy with the sound of chatter and clanging dishes. If anyone thought it strange for this brightly dressed woman to be dragging a dishevelled and slightly disoriented middle-aged woman behind her, no one showed it. They looked up as Bertha guided Bonnie through the door but aside from a momentary lull and a curious glance, they returned to the company of their companions with hardly a break in the conversation.

Bonnie's ears, however, pricked up as they skirted around a couple of traders heading for the door.

"Roads south are clogged. Every male in Melbourne-"

She wanted to stop and ask questions but Bertha pulled her along, stopping only as they reached a booth where a couple of other women dressed in similar long skirts and flowing blouses sat.

"Make room, you two."

The women looked up, then slid over, taking their plates and mugs along with them.

"Ladies this is our new wardrobe mistress Bron."

Bertha then introduced the two others.

"Becca here is Ophelia and Mags plays Hamletta's guardian. The others are at a booth over there."

She pointed towards a booth on the other side of the room, then shoved Bonnie into theirs.

"Hamletta?"

"It's our new, revised Hamlet," said Bertha. "We're previewing it in Warragul where we've already sold out Sunday's performance."

As Bertha answered Bonnie's question, she sat down herself. Raising her hand, she yelled out to the waitress, "Gina, can we get a couple of big breakfasts and two mugs over here."

After giving Bonnie a quick glance, Mags returned to the conversation she was having with Becca.

"One of the traders told me the town is on edge. Seems a trader was found dead in her truck."

Bonnie was only half listening. She was more concerned with what she'd heard the trader's heading for the door had said.

Every male in Melbourne—

Was what? They said the road south was clogged. Did that mean that lancers from the Old CBD were heading south? And where was this road heading south?

CHAPTER 10
JOSH

FRIDAY 10 DECEMBER 2049 - 8:00 A.M.

"Do you have any idea where we're headed?"

"It's called the Colony."

Josh was loath to admit to his companion that he didn't actually know where to find the Colony. All he knew was that Karen had said that it was east of Melbourne, somewhere along a road labelled M1. He also knew that East was the direction the trader named Jackson was heading with Karen and Dr Cutter. Armed with that knowledge, a few supplies and more than a bit of his mother's faith in the future, he'd convinced himself that he was doing the right thing. His companion hadn't needed any convincing. Once they'd gotten out of the city, he was happy to let Josh take charge.

It had been different last night. In the maze of streets that made up the Old CBD, it was the kid who'd known exactly what to do and where to go. He'd led the way, ducking down laneways, crossing under overpasses and guiding them through shadowy parklands. Without the kid to guide him, Josh would've perished in the fires or been picked up like the other boys seeking to escape the flames.

Shifting the backpack to a more comfortable position, Josh thought about how different his life had been from that of his companion. The kid had obviously spent years living on the streets with no one looking after him. He'd survived by using his wits. Josh, on the other hand, had been lucky all his life and yesterday proved it. His mother told him to stay put in the apartment on the twentieth floor but the reporter, Patricia suggested he raid the other apartments in the building for supplies. Was she just trying to keep him occupied while they were gone or was she being practical? Either way, it worked out to be lucky.

At first, he thought going from floor to floor, slowly working his way down to the lobby, was a waste of time. Most of those apartments had already been broken into and ransacked. The only supplies he found were in apartments that still had the remains of their former occupants which was probably why they'd been left alone. It was in that last apartment he broke into that he noticed how thick the smoke had gotten which was why he rushed down to the lobby. Flames were shooting out from the shopfront across the street. There were no fire trucks. No alarms. Not at this point. He touched the glass door and felt the heat. A group of four or five cusp-aged boys ran past, yelling at each other to run faster. He pushed the door open, still hesitant about whether to take his chances on the street or back in the building. What he saw was that the whole block of buildings was ablaze. A kid appeared, running at full tilt and bumped into him.

"C'mon."

The kid had stumbled but as he picked himself up, he had called out to Josh. Josh hesitated and the kid yelled at him again.

"We gotta go."

The key dangling from a chain around his neck burned his skin. Still, he hesitated. His mother told him to wait. Patricia said the building was safe but seeing the flames climbing the walls of the other buildings on the block, Josh realised it was only a matter of time before his hiding place became an inferno. The kid was waiting, willing Josh to make a decision but as soon as Josh moved to follow, the kid raced ahead.

They ran several blocks and Josh stopped to catch his breath. He reached into his pocket to get his phone and then remembered that they'd left their phones at the morgue to confuse the secret police. The kid appeared next to him, pulling on his arm and yelling, "We can't stop. C'mon."

They ran a few more blocks. Ahead Josh could see the fire trucks and the flashing lights of police cars. He could also see, groups of boys being herded towards army trucks.

"This way."

The kid was waving at him from a boarded-up wall, then disappeared. Josh thought his eyes were playing tricks. One minute the boy was there. The next he was gone. One of the boards moved and a hand reached out.

"C'mon."

Josh followed the hand and found himself in a demotion site. Deftly, the kid navigated his way around the rubble and Josh followed in his own clumsy way.

Today, the roles were reversed.

They'd been walking on the highway for at least an hour since they left the border and Josh realised that the kid's filthy rags emitted less of the smoke and urine odour now that they were in the open air. Or maybe it was simply that the boy was downwind of him. Either way, the air felt different as they left the city and its suburbs behind.

"What we need is a sign."

"A sign?" replied Josh.

"Yeah, a sign like Noah sending out the dove or Moses seeing a burning bush."

"Where did you read about that stuff."

"I didn't. I mean I can't read but there was these women that used to come to the old market. They brought us food and clothes. If we listened to their stories, they fed us."

Now that the boy had broken the silence, he seemed eager to talk.

"Well, I don't know about doves or bushes but a while back there was a sign that said Warragul was 43 kilometres."

"Is that far?"

"Well, at the rate we're walking and allowing for necessary breaks, I think we should get there sometime tomorrow."

Josh noticed how his companion's pace slowed at the thought of the distance they had yet to cover. It had been a long night, of dodging and weaving, heading in any direction that took them away from the flames and bypassed the street patrols. Several times they'd had to stop and double back as they saw groups of boys being rounded up and herded towards waiting trucks. At one point they'd hidden behind a dumpster with another stowaway and watched as each captured boy was facially scanned, then shoved into a waiting vehicle. As each truck filled, it headed down a main road leading away from the city and another took its place. Josh had felt his blood run cold as he realised they were looking for someone and wondered if that someone was likely to be himself.

Slipping past a ring of uniformed guards, they'd risked hopping a late-night bus that moved, empty and forlorn, down the deserted street. Taking turns sleeping on the back seat, they rode until the mechanical voice announced the last stop. Josh read the sign to his companion. Dandenong Train Station. The name meant nothing to either of them but exhausted and out of options, they found a spot under the overpass and slept.

It was still dark when the train alongside them, came to life. The vibrations of its motors woke Josh and he nudged the kid awake as the lights came on in the carriages. Someone walked down the ramp above them, speaking on their phone and climbed into one of the front carriages.

"Where's it going?" whispered the boy.

Josh had wondered the same thing but once he realised the train was heading east, he made up his mind.

"That's a very good question," he replied. "but I think there's only one way to find out. Are you game?"

The kid stretched, looked around. Overhead a car sped by. It wasn't the quiet whoosh of a self-drive. It rumbled with that distinctive sound made by firing pistons. Only government vehicles ran on petrol. When the sound disappeared into the distance, the kid said, "Anything is better than getting picked up by the brownies."

"Brownies?" Josh had never heard that term.

"Yeah, the ones in the brown uniforms. The police are bad but brownies are the worst. They get you, you don't come back."

"How do you know?"

"There's this building near the old markets where I used to sleep. I'd see them take boys inside. They went in but they never came back out. Except one time. There was this one boy who leapt from the balcony. Crashed through the window and all. Jeez those brownies cursed and swore. Probably cause he dented their car. Anyway, they found him on top of it, so they threw him on the ground and left him for the ambos."

"Was he still alive?"

"Naw. Smashed his head on the way down. Now, we gonna hitch a ride on the back of the train or risk going inside."

It hadn't occurred to Josh to cling to the back of a moving train and he wondered how this kid, who couldn't be more than thirteen, knew how to do all this stuff.

"It looks pretty deserted. I think we'll risk riding in style."

So as the train announcement advised passengers that it was departing, they rushed through the closing door of the last carriage.

Hallam, Berwick, Beaconsfield, Officer. Standing next to the doors they stared as the station names flew past. Platforms on the opposite side, the ones heading into the city, had passengers waiting but it wasn't until a stop named Cardinia that someone invaded their space. By then they'd relaxed so the sound of the door opening, followed by the appearance of someone entering, shocked them as much as it did the intruder. The door closed behind her and seeing the boys, she eyed the Emergency button. They saw it too but no one moved as the train blew a whistle and pulled away from the station. She seemed to get over her initial shock much faster than they did because she spoke first, breaking the tension.

"Are you running away?"

"No," said Josh. "We're just-"

"We're going for a ride to the border." The woman completed the sentence for him but her look revealed her understanding. She glanced at the kid but addressed herself to Josh.

"Look, you're not the first to come this way. Packenham is known as the gateway to the eastern wilds but I should warn you, the borders aren't open these days. All the roads are blocked. Females with passes can get through but there's no hope for males. Maybe it has something to do with the Premier's murder."

Continuing to ignore the kid, she said to Josh, "You don't look like a dangerous lancer so I'll give you a bit of advice."

She then explained how and where to jump the tracks, telling him to follow the railway line east out of town. As she talked Josh felt the weight of the key hanging on its chain around his neck and wondered if its protection extended past the borders of the Republic because it seemed like they were going to need all the help they could get.

"The patrols stay on the main roads but I suggest you remain as inconspicuous as possible till you reach the freeway." As she said this, Josh noticed how she looked in the direction of his companion. Helpful as she was, that look irritated him but he simply asked, "By freeway, do you mean the M1?"

"Some people still call it that."

"What do others call it."

"They call it Freedom Way."

CHAPTER 11
KAREN

FRIDAY 10 DECEMBER 2049 - 10:00 AM

"That's the Fine Art's Centre," said Rega knowingly. "Council meetings are held inside but this crowd's too big. That's why they're holding the trial outside."

But even the outside didn't seem large enough to Karen. The only time she'd seen crowds like this was the day of the Catalyst for Change protest in Melbourne. At that gathering there'd been signs demanding rights for males, along with light and dark blue striped flags that symbolised the movement. Here there were no protesters, no signs, nor were there any males. There were, however, plenty of spectators. They gathered in tight-knit groups that crowded the paved areas and flowed over onto the grass. The girls from the co-op, undaunted, dispersed, slipping through the cracks between the groups. Karen was just as keen to find a good vantage point but tethered to Rega, she was limited in her movements. They were jostled aside as new arrivals joined their friends' groups. The farther back they were pushed, the more Karen craned her neck in order to see the pavilion.

Feeling a tug on her shirt sleeve, she looked over to see Rega standing on a park bench. Her companion was motioning for Karen to join her. Someone in the back yelled, 'Get down', but Rega gave them the finger, then leaned down and said, "The view is better from up here."

More voices objected as Karen climbed up but they quickly died away as the doors to the Arts Centre opened. Pointing to a woman coming out, Rega said, "That's Kerry. She's the bailiff."

Karen nodded. She had no idea what a bailiff was but given her instructions, she wasn't about to ask.

Rega, at 16, was a couple of years younger than Karen, but she had the advantage of having grown up in town. Karen figured that's why Georgina had pulled the girl aside as the others piled into the truck.

"I'm putting you in charge of Tanya," she'd said. Karen hadn't recognised the name, at first because everyone referred to her as the new girl, even when they were talking directly to her.

"But George, I'm—"

"It's not up for discussion," the co-op owner had said. "She's a wilding unaccustomed to the Colony so you stick by her the whole time. Understand?"

Not only had Karen been given a new name, she'd been given a new identity. That of a wilding. Like lancers, wildings' reputation had preceded them and it wasn't complimentary. Back in Melbourne, being called a colonial was bad, but to be called a wilding was truly insulting. And now that she'd been classed as a wilding, Karen discovered that colonials held a similar disparaging view. Not only did the Warragul girls shun her but on top of that, they treated her as if she were a simpleton. They explained everything slowly and in great detail. It was condescending and offensive, but then again, it was a good thing because when it came to life at the co-op, she was clueless.

Rega was nudging her and saying, "Now pay attention. There's eight councillors." Pointing in the direction of the pavilion, she said, "Oh, here they come now."

Six women filed out and sat in the chairs that had been set in a straight line that ran the width of the pavilion so that the crowds were in the periphery of their vision, instead of being central to it. Moments later a seventh woman emerged wearing a uniform. Her appearance produced both boos and cheers but she ignored both as she walked to the opposite side of the pavilion. There, she turned and faced the other councillors.

Rega stood on tiptoe to speak in Karen's ear. "That's May. She's the Police Commissioner."

There were two seats still empty. Both were straight-backed wooden ones which sat in the middle of the pavilion. One faced the crowd, while the other had its back to it. Karen figured one must be for the remaining councillor, and the other for the accused.

The cheering and jeering had subsided into the buzz of normal conversations when Karen felt a change. It wasn't so much in the level of the noises around her as in the intensity. Rega pointed toward the door as a short woman with cropped greying hair stepped into view. Despite her diminutive stature and lack of a distinguishing uniform, Karen picked up on the vibe that accompanied her. Solemnly, the woman followed the bailiff to the chair facing the audience. As she stood before the chair, looking out over the crowd rather than at it, a groundswell of silence pressed through the crowd until there was only a sea of calm. Then the woman sat.

"That's Sofia Vargas " whispered Rega. "She's the council mediator."

Karen scanned the scene, the police Commissioner, the mediator, the councillors and the empty chair. Like those around her, there was a feeling of anticipation, as if something was about to happen. She desperately wanted to ask the girl next to her but the trader Jackson had warned her to keep a low profile and not to ask too many questions. It was asking questions, after all, that had gotten her and others into trouble.

Back at the co-op when Karen had first asked if she could attend the trial, Dr Cutter, who everyone now called by her first name of Helen, had vehemently opposed the idea.

"All of Melbourne will be looking for her."

"This isn't Melbourne," Karen had replied. "And besides, if I'm supposed to make Warragul my home, wouldn't it be out of character for me to miss this event?"

"The girl's right," agreed the co-op owner, Georgina. "Everyone'll be going. If she stays away, it'll raise questions."

"But what if someone recognises her?" Helen had argued.

"As far as anyone knows, she's a wilding girl. If anyone's likely to be recognised, it's you," said Georgina, "You're the one that used to live here."

"That was before the Desolation and even if someone from the past recognises me, they won't know that I worked as Melbourne's coroner."

"I agree with George," said a voice coming up behind them.

Karen didn't have to turn around to see who had taken her side. It was the trader, Jackson.

"The girl needs to learn how things work here in the Colony but," she looked at Karen with those steel grey eyes, "I suggest you keep your mouth shut and don't ask too many questions."

Following Jackson's edict, Karen observed but in her mind she was comparing this public trial with the town hall meeting in Melbourne.

Sofia, staring straight ahead, deliberately ignoring the audience, was the antithesis of Catherine Williams, who'd engaged with her audience that night. What was supposed to be a serious discussion of election issues had been turned into a publicity event for the NOP. That was until Karen asked that uncomfortable question about why the government shut down Dr Harris's lab. That question had caused a flurry of excitement and if that reporter Patricia Bishop hadn't whisked her away, she might have been arrested on the spot. As it was, she had put Dr Harris at risk and been forced to leave Melbourne and Josh behind.

Off to the left, a wave of excitement caught her attention and that of those around her. A vehicle was approaching. Moving slowly, lights flashing, it occasionally let out a siren blast to make sure bystanders got out of the way. Like a broom sweeping aside dust balls, it advanced through the crowd till it arrived at the base of the stairs. There a uniformed officer stepped out and opened the back door. As the figure of a woman wearing only a hospital gown emerged the ripple of whispers that had followed the car became something more ominous. It was the angry buzz of a hive that had been disturbed and Karen wondered what had caused the upset.

"That must be Sofia's idea," said Rega.

Karen gave Rega a questioning look so the girl explained, "If Jocelyn is found guilty, all her goods will be confiscated. Do you understand what I'm telling you?"

The girl's eyes glowed with admiration but Karen's face must have conveyed her confusion because the girl explained further. "If she's found guilty they take everything she owns, then and there." Seeing that Karen still didn't understand, Rega spelled it out. "She's not wearing her own clothes. She's wearing the hospital's so they won't be taken away. She won't have to walk through town naked. Now, do you understand?"

The realisation hit Karen and she looked back at the woman ascending the steps, then over at the seated woman who sat unmoving despite being at the centre of these events.

As Jocelyn took the last remaining chair, someone from the back yelled out, "Boy lover."

Karen looked over her shoulder and saw a spindly woman. She was surrounded by women who wore jeans and blue cotton singlets like Jackson so Karen figured they were traders as well.

"That's Ursula." Rega spat the woman's name out, "She's the one that should be on trial. She threatened to burn down the boy's dorm but then Alicia stopped her. I wish she hadn't."

Karen couldn't stop herself. "You wanted her to burn down—"

Rega didn't wait for Karen to finish. "There's no laws protecting boys, but there are laws protecting property. If Ursula'd lit that fire, she'd have been prosecuted. As it turned out, they only put Ursula under house arrest for disturbing the peace. For the boys, however, it was too late."

Rega stifled her anger with a shrug of the shoulders, turning her attention back to the proceedings. "It's just as well. I was getting too attached to one of the older boys and that's never a good thing. Still, I think Ursula had no right to do what she did."

Back on stage, the Police Commissioner held her hand up, silencing any further talk.

The mediator, Sofia, filled the silence with her commanding voice.

"Jocelyn, you have been brought before your community to answer the grievous charge of premeditated murder. As Colony Mediator, I am your sole judge and jury. Do you understand?"

Karen watched the woman with her back to the audience, nod her head. She wished she could see the woman's face because she wanted to know what kind of person could murder someone. She thought of her friend Zane. He'd been murdered for nothing worse than a case of mistaken identity. If he hadn't been riding the bike that Monika had given Benny, he would still be alive today. And Benny? What had become of him? Had the smugglers gotten him out of Melbourne? She thought about the night she'd dropped him off outside the deserted stadium and the way he'd looked at her. She'd been afraid that he might lean over and kiss her and that scared her because she'd have been tempted to kiss him back. It was a moment and it had passed. Instead of crossing that line, he'd climbed out of the car and her self-drive continued on its way. Two childhood friends gone and now Josh hiding in Melbourne while she was tucked away in Warragul. She might not be a murderer but there was a judge and jury inside that was holding its own trial.

Sofia was asking, "I want you to tell me about your relationship with Reg."

Karen strained to hear the response and she wasn't alone. Everyone was listening intently. Even the birds had ceased their warbles.

"Reg was my partner and the father of our child."

"And how old was Reg?"

"Nineteen."

"So he was in his final cusp year. Did you know he was violent?"

The word violent caught Karen off guard. Her mind moved from the image of her friend Zane to that of the lancers who'd frightened her at Flinder's Street Station. She had wondered after that event, if there were two types of cusp males or if boys at nineteen went through some kind of change? Josh and Benny would both be entering their cusp in a few months so the answer to this woman's question had the potential to answer her own.

"Until this week, he was a caring and devoted partner."

"So you had no reason to believe he would physically attack you?"

"He was looking forward to the birth of our child."

"But despite that, he hit you didn't he?"

"He wasn't himself."

"I'll repeat the question, he hit you didn't he?"

"Yes."

"And after he hit you, what did you do?"

"I sent him away."

"Did you tell him to go to the male dorm or leave town?"

"I told him to find a lancer community." There was a pause, then the woman on trial added, "Preferably to the East."

"And did he do as you asked?"

"No."

The crowd murmured but the Police Commissioner signalled for silence.

"He came back and this time he beat you again, didn't he?"

When Jocelyn didn't answer, Sofia repeated the question. "He beat you and this time it was more than a punch wasn't it?"

Karen could feel the tension as everyone waited for Jocelyn's response but it was the question inside herself that really longed for the woman's answer. Did normally gentle males turn violent? Was violence inevitable?

The woman in the hospital gown said nothing so Sofia continued.

"He returned and this time he beat you so badly that you required hospitalisation. Isn't it true that this time he terrified you and threatened the life of your unborn child?"

Every muscle in Karen's body tightened.

"He wasn't an animal. Something got into him—"

"Isn't it true that he was so violent that you had to wait until he fell asleep before you could do what you had to do to protect yourself and your child?"

"What's she doing?" mumbled Rega.

Karen wasn't sure if the girl was referring to Sofia or the woman on trial but something was amiss because the air was once again electric.

"I killed him." The response was a confession that sounded like a plea to stop and Karen felt something in her own heart break.

"You killed him in self-defence," insisted Sofia. "You couldn't protect yourself while he was awake so you did it while he slept."

"I couldn't let him live." Jocelyn was openly sobbing.

"You'd been badly beaten and were in a state of shock. You feared for your life and grabbed the only weapon you had at your disposal. The knife."

Under her breath, Rega shook her head saying, "Sofia's pushing the boundaries."

"He was sleeping," said Jocelyn.

"You were in shock. Sleeping or not he was a threat. Your actions were delayed because you feared he would wake at any moment. Your life was in danger."

Other voices around Karen were whispering now, but she was only interested in Jocelyn's response.

"I knew he wouldn't wake."

"How could you know that?" Sofia's voice was incredulous.

Jocelyn straightened up. Holding her head high, she spoke loudly and clearly.

"Because I put a sedative in his food."

Voices erupted around Karen and next to her Rega said, "Oh my god." Even the councillors in their chairs talked openly among themselves.

Sofia stood, raising her voice.

"Jocelyn, I need you to understand that Reg's death, as you have described it, is premeditated murder. You understand that the sentence for that crime is banishment. Are you sure you have provided us with a thorough and correct version of what happened?"

The voice was stern but Karen felt the anguish in it. The crowd, however, was in an uproar. Groups of spectators were turning to their neighbours, some yelling at each other while others started shoving the ones next to them. The Police Commissioner frantically signalled for silence but when that didn't work, she signalled officers to move into position between the crowd and the actors on the stage. With another signal, the officer in the car sounded the siren. As that noise quelled the crowd, Karen heard Rega say, "She's done for now."

The Police Commissioner moved over to Jocelyn and taking her arm forced her to stand.

Sofia was speaking softer so it was hard for Karen to catch all the words but it sounded like a plea.

"Are you sure you haven't left –"

The Commissioner cut her off. "Sofia, Jocelyn has confessed. The verdict is obvious."

Sofia ignored the statement.

"I need to know why. You could have come to me or May."

"That's enough," said May.

Rega also expressed her disbelief. "I don't understand either. Why would you risk banishment for a boy? He was going to die in a few months anyway and now she'll be stripped of her title and everything she owns."

"Title?" said Karen

"Jocelyn is, or was, Council Chair."

Karen looked at the stage and realised that the woman accused of murder wasn't just an ordinary citizen, she was a senior politician.

On stage, the Police Commissioner was demanding a response.

"Sofia, we need your verdict."

Voices in the crowd picked up on her order and started chanting.

"Verdict. Verdict."

Sofia held up her hand and the voices petered out.

"Jocelyn the law is clear." The silence was intense as if everyone were holding their breath. Then Sofia spoke, "Premeditated murder violates the peace of the Colony. You are found guilty of violating that peace. You are, therefore, to be marked for your crime and banished."

Among the spectators, cries for and against the verdict rose up.

One voice yelled, "Murderer."

Another yelled, "Boy lover."

Others were openly weeping but Sofia and Jocelyn faced each other, ignoring the mayhem that was breaking out around them.

Karen, however, was more interested in Sofia. Reading the woman's lips, she wondered the same thing.

"Why?"

CHAPTER 12
THE OLD ONE'S CABIN

SEPTEMBER 2069

The Old One filled both tea cups. It was a simple act of moving hot liquid from one place to another, an act performed hundreds of times and like all the other daily tasks that people performed for each other, it might have gone unnoticed except that tonight, watching the brown liquid shift from pot to cup, the girl felt as if she were the empty vessel being filled. While she identified with the teens from a previous generation the Jocelyn in these stories was sounding more and more familiar.

The Jocelyn she remembered was associated, not with Warragul, but with a big red brick building. That Jocelyn had been one of the women the girl called mother but then Tanya arrived and moved her to Warragul. She might have forgotten that Jocelyn if the woman hadn't shown up years later. It was market day and the girl was helping Florence set up the fish stall. The fishmonger was fussing over the unseasonable heat and yelling to one of the girls to fetch more ice when suddenly she dropped the box of clams she was holding and dashed out of the stall. It was strange to see the large black woman move so fast but then the girl saw Florence wrap her arms around a stranger who'd emerged from the crowd. The girl sensed something familiar about that person but had stood there, unsure, until Florence reintroduced them.

"This is Sara," Florence had said and then a look of recognition followed by hugging, kissing and remarking how she'd grown. That had been such a happy day and perhaps the girl, even then, thought Jocelyn had come to take her home. But Jocelyn didn't speak of the past and when she moved into the abandoned cottage at the end of the square, she didn't invite the girl to move in with her although she often invited her to visit. It was as though the past never existed and now the girl was beginning to understand why.

"Jocelyn, in town, and the Jocelyn on trial is she the same – I mean, how could she—"

"Spit it out, girl."

It was a gentle rebuke but the question refused to take shape so the Old One said, "Are you asking why Warragul allowed her to return or why she allowed herself to return?"

"Both, I suppose."

"Some say home is a physical place. Others say it's something you carry within you. Jocelyn was someone who carried a sense of home inside herself but even so, this town was always going to call to her. Despite what happened here, Jocelyn loved this town. But to answer your other question, I think she came back because the town needed her as much as she needed them. Her return helps them heal."

The girl took the cup of tea the Old One passed her way and figured now was the moment she'd been waiting for.

"When I was little, I used to ask questions."

"So I've been told," said the Old One.

"You have no idea how many times I asked Tanya who my real mother was."

The words poured out before the girl could stop them.

"You said Jocelyn was pregnant when she was banished. Is that why everyone avoided answering my questions about what happened to my real mother?"

The Old One sipped the hot tea and set the cup down.

"If you're asking if Jocelyn was your mother, then the answer is no.

And if you're asking why people avoided answering your questions, it's because they didn't know. As for Jocelyn letting Tanya bring you to Warragul, well, the decision wasn't up to her. We decided that it was safer if you were raised like all the other casualties of the Great Upheaval."

The girl wanted to know what the Old One meant by the word 'we' but the Old One didn't give her a chance.

"Before the war, Heart House housed boys smuggled out of Melbourne. It was a place to keep them safe and offer them some love and care but by the time the Truce was signed, all the young ones were gone. Heart House no longer had a purpose. Then someone, I suspect it was Juanita, got the idea to take in girls who'd been orphaned by the war. Jocelyn had looked after you but you weren't her child and it was her child that we felt she needed to spend time with."

"So why didn't Jocelyn tell me about my real mother?"

"Jocelyn didn't tell you because she never knew your mother."

The Old One sighed and placed the teacup on the table. For the first time in days, there was an awkward silence, and then the Old One said, "It was an uncertain time. We'd all settled into our day-to-day war existence, and then suddenly, this opportunity for a Truce arrived. We were unprepared. Not that we didn't want peace. It's just that it came faster than some people were ready to accept and it came with a price tag."

In the wood stove, the large log on top collapsed into the heap of grey ash. There the flames whittled away at what was left.

"Jocelyn was happy to take you in and love you but she also understood why we had to take you away."

That word 'we' again. Who were these people making decisions about her life and why? Before she could formulate her next question, the Old One said, "We only have tonight so I suggest we finish drinking this tea and get back to our recording. Now I suppose you want to know what Patricia Bishop was up to while Jocelyn was being run out of Warragul."

PATRICIA

FRIDAY 10 DECEMBER 2049 - 10:00 A.M.

"You and what army," said Penny.

Checkmate.

Patricia's instincts were screaming out that the answer to the question of the cure resided on French Island but Penny was right. If there were imprisoned men and they were unable to escape, and if the Subversives were opposed to invading, how could two unarmed women get access? Twirling the strap of her canvas bag, Patricia considered an even more difficult question. How was she going to convince Penny that it was worth trying? Especially since Penny, leaning nonchalantly against the wall, was making it clear that French Island wasn't the only place that housed prisoners. Like the men sequestered during the pandemic, Patricia was being held in this deserted western suburb under the pretence of keeping her safe.

A phone buzzed and Patricia instinctively opened her bag before she remembered that she'd left her phone in the DIY store to distract the police who were tracking her in order to find Dr Harris. Penny reaching into the pocket of her cargo pants, pulled her phone out and casually checked its screen.

First, her face darkened, then she straightened up, body taunt and muscles prepared for action. Patricia watched with interest as Penny listened to whatever her caller was saying, but it wasn't until Penny tossed the phone aside and bit her lip that Patricia perked up. Something was wrong. Penny headed towards her and Patricia jumped to her feet. Swallowing, she gripped her bag and prepared to defend herself.

"We need to get out of here."

Penny grabbed her arm before she could react and shoved her towards the back door.

"Where are we—"

"No time."

Penny kicked it open and pushed Patricia towards the stairs.

"What's—"

Penny covered the tiny yard in three steps and started pulling at a section of fence. The planks gave way giving access to the next yard. She slid through, sinuous as a snake and Patricia rushed to follow. As she squeezed through, Penny deftly put the planks back in place.

"Keep up."

It was an ultimatum, not a directive. Without so much as a glance back, Penny was running through the yard to another fence whose loose planks led onto a street. Behind her, Patricia heard the sound of sirens, so heart-pounding she raced after Penny. Wheels screeched around a corner and Patricia pressed her bag close to her side and ran faster. She was putting distance between herself and the safe house but she could still hear the sound of car doors slamming. Then pounding and the crash of wood splintering. Patricia lost ground as she looked over her shoulder, then had to push herself harder as she saw Penny disappear around the side of a house. With each deserted yard, she lagged farther and farther behind until at last she found herself standing in the tall grass with no sign of Penny.

Frantically she looked around for a sign, some fence plank slightly out of place, a gap between buildings, any sign of an exit, but there was nothing but empty space.

An arm reached out and pulled her down. Penny put a finger to her lips and then she was off again. Crawling through the grass they reached the back of a partially constructed house. Bracing herself against its foundation, Patricia tried to still her heavy breathing. Next to her, Penny's breathing, slow and steady, seemed relaxed, but the expression on her face said otherwise. She was listening. Following Penny's example Patricia also strained her ears. Obviously, they were running from someone, but now the question was, were they running to somewhere or simply running? Patricia took in their new surroundings. They had zigzagged from house to house, darted across suburban streets that ended in cul-de-sacs and ended up in this construction site. This was where the suburb, like their escape, had run out of steam. Electrical wire strung up the now collapsing framework was still attached like an umbilical cord to its roll. A hammer lay abandoned next to exposed joists, a saw sat rusting on a stand next to a piece of wood that waited for the cut that would never be made. Poignant reminders of the speed at which the pandemic had progressed. These artefacts were left behind by the men who collapsed on the spot or dashed for the safety of their homes only to discover that the enemy they were trying to escape was already in them.

The Transition that followed the Desolation had tried to reclaim these last vestiges of human expansion. Even after the male half of the population had collapsed, momentum drove the surviving women forward until they realised there was no point. No point in completing these aborted suburbs. No point in building anything new. No point in reclaiming that which was irrevocably lost. Patricia and Penny were hiding in one of these last vestiges of the pre-pandemic world. It marked the spot where surviving females surrendered and started their slow retreat into the sanctuary of the inner city suburbs.

Penny tapped Patricia's shoulder and pointed at a row of portaloos. Half squatting, half crawling she headed in their direction. Patricia mimicked her crouching run as best she could and headed after her. Opening the door to one of the portable toilets, Penny climbed in and turned the lock. Patricia had her doubts but reaching for the handle on the first door she came to, she tried to open it. The handle turned but the door was stuck so she stood up and pulled harder. It refused to budge but in the distance she could hear wheels racing around a corner. Thwarted by its obstinacy, she yanked at the door, bracing her feet against the edge until, at last, it flew open. The overpowering stench it emitted must have been trapped inside for years, and she reeled backwards, pulling her shirt up to cover her nose. On the seat sat a skeleton, the ragged clothing of a construction worker still clinging to its bones. She slammed the door shut and backed away, stumbling to the next one. The sound of wheels on pavement was getting louder. Their adversaries, whoever they were, were closing in. She turned the handle on the last toilet and Its door swung open. It smelled of ammonia and rotten eggs but at least it was empty. Stifling her gag reflex she climbed in and flicked the occupied switch.

Inside, it was hot and claustrophobic but despite the enclosure, flies swarmed around her. Fear and sweat seemed to have lured them through a hole kicked in the side wall. Patricia envisioned a panicked worker trying to kick his way out and felt the same urge welling up inside. The buzzing, the smell, the enclosed walls; only increased the panic she was trying to contain. Then she heard a noise that subjugated all her other fears.

A car door slammed and footsteps crunched on the gravel. Patricia held her breath, hoping her heartbeat wouldn't give her away.

A voice cried out, "You check the stalls. I'll check inside."

"Inside what? It's only a frame?"

"Just do as I say."

Patricia's heart jumped. Like a jackrabbit caught in a trap, it banged wildly against her chest.

"Why's it always me?"

The desultory voice was accompanied by the sound of feet on gravel. Steps approached and Patricia's body switched from flight to fight as it prepared to jump whoever opened the door. She heard the sound of someone trying a door but, finding it locked, moved on to the next. Another twisting door handle, then the squeak of a door falling open, followed by an expletive. Steps moved quickly, then slowly approached Patricia's hiding place. They stopped directly in front of her. The handle on the door jiggled as flies licked at the sweat rolling down Patricia's face. A swift hard kick shook the door and Patricia started. Another expletive and the handle jingled violently as Patricia braced herself.

"Find anything," shouted the voice from a distance.

"Bones. How about you?"

"Nothing."

Patricia waited long after the sounds had receded. Head resting against the wall, she didn't even react when she heard Penny's voice say, "It's OK. You can come out now."

Instead, she brushed the flies away and wiped the sweat with the edge of her shirt.

"We need to keep moving." Penny's voice was firm but it had lost that insistent edge.

With shaking hands, Patricia fumbled at the latch until the door freed up and swung open. Fresh air and light invaded the space but Patricia's body was spent. She stumbled out. Collapsing against the door as she shut it, she asked, "Now can you tell me what's going on?"

Penny, at her unflappable best, replied by grabbing Patricia by the shoulders and, looking her in the eye, said, "That was Joan. She got a tip-off that they found out about this place."

"The tipoff," Patricia was still trying to calm herself, "was that before or after she left us?"

Penny bit her lip and Patricia was desperate to know what was going on in her friend's head, but equally afraid to disrupt her friend's thoughts. That her friend realised she'd made a mistake was obvious but it was also obvious that she wasn't about to divulge what that mistake was. Instead, Penny was figuring out her opponent's next moves, so she could formulate her own counter move.

"They're making arrests," said Penny.

"But I thought Subversives don't know anyone other than their immediate link."

"Joan said they picked up Rose. Either someone from last night's meeting talked or –"

"Your forced silence came too late," finished Patricia.

"It doesn't matter now who's talking, we need to disappear. Our safe houses are compromised and they'll be checking our homes, questioning our families."

"What do you mean, questioning our families," said Patricia. "If they don't already think I'm one of you, they will as soon as that story appears with my name on it. I've got to warn my mother and there's all my notes and—"

"You can't go home," said Penny. "None of us can go home."

Patricia realised Penny wasn't thinking about her, she was thinking about her sister Carla. If their safe houses were compromised then Carla was also in danger. Surely, if Joan warned them, she would have warned Carla. But who would think to warn her mother? Patricia needed to get home and get home fast before it was too late.

"If they search my office," she said, "they'll find the note from the messenger boy's satchel. They'll put two and two together and –"

"Shit. If they see that note they'll head for the refinery. Why didn't you destroy it?"

"I was the innocent bystander in your cloak-and-dagger shenanigans, remember."

The words rolled off her tongue as glib as any habitual liar. That note was stuck in a book sitting on a shelf of books in a room filled with books, but Patricia felt justified given all the lies and half-truths Penny had used to manipulate her. It was a bluff but Patricia had nothing else and besides Penny seemed to be buying it.

"We're going to need transport," said Penny.

That proved to be easier than either of them had thought. In the next house over they found an abandoned ute, its charger still plugged into a bank of solar panels.

"Pre-fingerprint locks," said Penny opening the door. "Today's our lucky day."

"Except that we need the key card," said Patricia.

"It must be here somewhere," said Penny searching under the seats and checking the console. Patricia, however, was thinking about the body in the portaloo. One of them was going to have to go through the pockets of the deceased and she was already thinking of excuses for Penny to be that someone when Penny yelled out.

"Found 'it tucked behind the visor."

"That's a fob, not a card."

Penny climbed in the driver's side and pressed the fob. There was no click.

"Shit. The battery's dead."

"Try the key," said Patricia.

"What key? It's a fob there's no—"

Patricia snatched the fob out of Penny's hand, tugged on the end and as the parts came apart, revealed the key.

"There'll be an ignition slot in the console."

"Got it," said Penny as she put it in place. Pressing the start button, she waited for the ready indicator to light up. Penny pressed the start button again. She slapped the steering wheel.

"It's not working."

Dejected Patricia climbed out and walked towards the road. They were stuck in the middle of nowhere, without transport, and meanwhile, back in the city, her mother was unaware of the danger she was in. Dead on arrival, she thought remembering her days picking up bodies during the pandemic. Then it hit her. She rushed back to the ute where Penny was angrily pressing the start button.

"Hop out," she said, "These vehicles are pre-pandemic. Let me try." Taking Penny's place in the driver seat, she depressed the brake pedal and pressed start. The ready indicator glowed green.

"Hop in."

Once they found their way onto the old Western Highway, Patricia pressed down on the accelerator. Glancing in Penny's direction, she noted her friend's look of concern and said, "Don't worry, I know what I'm doing. I used to drive an ambulance, remember? Oh, and you might want to buckle up."

"This isn't an ambulance and driving like this is liable to get us pulled over."

"We're construction workers," said Patricia hitting the brakes and swerving down a side street. "This is how they drive."

Penny grabbed her seat belt and secured it in place.

"Where are you going?"

"I'm just going to swing by home," she said turning down another side street.

Penny fumed. "I told you it's too dangerous."

"Don't worry. It's under control."

They swerved through a roundabout and Penny reached for the dash.

"So what's your plan? Head for your house, walk in, get your stuff and waltz right back out?"

"Something like that."

Entering the more populated suburbs, Patricia drove more sedately even though the roads were devoid of traffic. Shops and businesses were closed which meant everyone would be home watching the memorial service for Premier Anderson, including her mother. As she turned down her street, she pulled over to the curb. As she expected, the self-drive she and her mother shared with Mrs Cardrew, was parked in their driveway. More importantly, there were no strange cars or vans parked on the street. In fact, the street was empty. There were no joggers or women with baby strollers walking past the house. No one and nothing. Everything looked as it should for a quiet suburban street.

Reconciled to Patricia's plan, Penny said, "I'll wait here and keep an eye on things. You have 10 minutes. If you're not back by then, I leave without you."

"Ten minutes and what? You drive away?"

Penny glared at her. "I remember how to drive a vehicle."

"Sure. Like you remembered how to start one."

"Just be quick."

"Don't worry. Nothing's going to go wrong."

As Patricia entered the house, her mother jumped up.

"Where have you been? I've tried calling you all night and again this morning."

"I don't have time to explain and it's best that you know as little as possible. I need to grab a few things and then I have to leave."

"It's those boy suicides, isn't it? What did I tell you about getting involved—"

Patricia headed for her office with her mother chasing after her.

"If someone comes looking for you, what should I tell them?"

"You don't know anything. Trust me, that's the best answer."

Her mother grabbed her.

"I won't ask what you're involved in but I need to know if Joan is involved."

Patricia looked at her steadily. Should she warn her mother about Joan?

"I can't tell you anything. Now, I need to grab a few things and go."

As she pulled away her mother said, "Where's your key? You never—"

Reflexively, Patricia reached up to her neck. The key, her lucky talisman was gone. In all the dramas since yesterday, she hadn't thought about it.

"I went to our old apartment and used it to let myself in. I must have left it behind."

"You were in that part of the Old CBD. How did you escape?"

Patricia stopped. "What do you mean?'

"That area was consumed by the fires. Wait, if you didn't know—"

"Do you know if our old place—"

"It's gone, Patricia."

Patricia pictured Josh standing on the balcony with no means of escape. Swallowing down the lump forming in her throat, she said, "I've got to go," and rushed into her office.

Her mother followed her.

"Whatever you're involved in, let me help."

"Honestly Mum, there's nothing you can do except pretend you know nothing."

She shoved her laptop into her canvas bag along with her notebooks then grabbing her grandfather's book off the shelf she kissed her mother.

"I love you," she said then rushed to the door.

Her mother caught up to her as she was halfway down the drive.

"At least let me buy you a little time."

"What do you mean?" said Patricia stopping next to the car.

Her mother looked around then noticing the car she said, "Unlock the car with your prints and I'll take it to the market."

"What? No, the markets are closed."

"Then I'll take it for a drive."

That's when Patricia realised what her mother was up to.

"You think if anyone is monitoring the house they'll think it's me in the car."

Her mother smiled hopefully and pointed at the door.

Patricia replied, "That's brilliant." Quickly she swiped her finger across the door lock, blew her mother a kiss and ran towards the end of the block where Penny waited.

"I've got what I need now. Let's get out of here," she said, throwing her bag into the back seat of the dual cab.

She paused to take one last look at her home. Her mother stood by the open car door and Patricia wondered when she'd ever be able to see her again. She waved as her mother got into their self-drive, then hopped in the driver's seat and did a quick u-turn to head back the way they came. They'd barely reached the intersection when the air reverberated with a massive explosion.

She slammed on the brakes and they both looked back. There in the drive sat Patricia's self-drive engulfed in flames. In a flash, Patricia was out of the ute and running. Neighbours were also coming out of their houses and by the time she reached her drive, they had gathered in a horrified group. Crazed, Patricia fought her way through them but the intensity of the blaze pushed her back. Placing one hand in front of her face she reached out with the other in an attempt to grab onto the door handle. The heat seared her flesh as arms pulled her away. A force stronger than herself moved her away as a second explosion rocked the ground under her feet forcing her backwards. There were voices all around her but they meant nothing as she stared in horror. In front of her, the little self-drive crumbled to the ground as fire ate away at its core.

But it wasn't only the car that the flames devoured. Patricia was melting away. The voices talking in her ear faded. Someone was wrapping something cold and wet around her hand but it was too late. Her hand felt numb and that numbness had spread through her body and was taking over her brain.

CHAPTER 13
PATRICIA

FRIDAY 10 DECEMBER 2049 - 10:00 A.M.

"We need to get away from here."

Penny's voice was urgent but Patricia was in a fog. Where was here?

Her mind was having trouble with the concept of here because she was no longer connected to her body. She was somewhere outside time and place and the commotion around her was something playing on a TV. Another blast sent more shock waves that elicited more screams. More panic. None of that impacted Patricia. She was riding her own sonic wave. Eardrums perforated by the blast stifled her hearing and muddled her thoughts but it was the vibrations inside her body that reverberated like a heavy clapper banging on the cast iron bell of her body. Waves rocked her. Tossed her about. Everything was in motion until at last, the energy played itself out and she felt herself sinking.

"No! No, you don't!" came a voice from far away.

A force shoved her hard against the wall and Patricia felt as if her bones had turned to glass. They shattered into a million pieces. Their sharp edges tore at her insides. Everything crumbled. Her world was crumbling. She was crumbling. The only thing holding her together was this force pinning her against the wall.

Slap!

Something hard slammed against her face. The sting of it burned like the heat from that first explosion. She absorbed the force of it. Let it wash over her but it came back and hit her again. That angered her and the heat of that anger had a curious effect. The pieces came together. Fused glass. Tempered glass. She pushed back at the force that held her.

"We've got to go now!" Penny held her firm. The urgency in her voice echoed that of wailing sirens. Their screams grew louder and louder. If they were firefighters then they were too late to put the fire out. If they were an ambulance then they were too late to save the woman trapped inside that little car. Too late. Too late. Everyone was too late. The damage was done. She fell against Penny's shoulder and cried out the jagged painful particles that had been her soul.

"There's nothing more we can do here," said Penny. Her voice now soothing.

"It's my fault," Patricia blubbered. "That was meant for me."

"Which is why we have to get out of here," Penny said, releasing her grip slightly. "We need to find someplace safe."

"I can't."

"You can and you will. Now let's go."

Penny wrapped her arm around Patricia's waist and pulled her along.

"My bag. I need my bag."

But even as she tried to free herself Penny gripped her tighter.

"I've got it. Now we need to move. Do you think you can drive?"

"Drive?"

The thought of getting into a vehicle sent more shock waves through Patricia and again she struggled to free herself but Penny was stronger.

"OK, then we walk out of here but however we do it, we've got to move now."

Anger replaced anguish. Someone had taken something precious from her and that someone had to pay. She pulled away from Penny.

"I'm going to find who did this and make them pay. I'll make them pay."

Her voice sounded as if coming from the bottom of a well.

Penny was holding tight even as Patricia swatted at her. The tears were flowing freely now.

"They're going to pay. Every last one of them."

"Then we need a plan."

Penny was standing in front of her, holding her by her shoulders. Intense eyes, dark, almost black, stared into hers. "Do you understand? To make them pay, we need a plan."

Patricia stared at Penny, lost in those black pools, then the words made sense. "A plan. Yes, we need a plan."

Penny nodded encouragingly.

"And the first step is to get out of here and get someplace safe."

"Safe. Yes, we need to be safe."

"Do you think you can drive?"

"Me? Why me? Why don't you drive?"

"Because, I.. I don't know how."

"What do you mean you don't know how? We all had driving lessons in school."

"Not me."

Patricia stared at her friend in disbelief. Trapped in a life and death situation and this woman, skilled in so many things, admits that she can't do the one thing they need to do to save themselves. A simple thing that they'd all learned 20 years ago. Everyone except Penny.

They were standing next to the ute with the passenger door open as a flashing light turned into the street.

"I'll talk you through it."

Penny shoved Patricia onto the passenger's seat, slammed the door and raced around to the driver's side.

"You'd better start talking." Hand on the wheel, Penny said, "Tell me what to do."

But Patricia was staring in the side mirror at the grey car with its flashing blue light. Deja vu. The car flew past just like it had on the day the messenger boy was hit.

"Those bastards."

"Later Patricia. Show me how to start this thing."

Patricia was fumbling with the door handle.

"The plan, Patricia," yelled Penny. "Remember the plan." She lowered her voice, "If they find you, they win and then there is no plan. Now, what did you do to start this thing."

"Press on the pedal and press start."

"Which pedal? There's no lights. We must be out of power."

Penny was banging the steering well and swearing but Patricia was caught up in the drama outside her house. The firefighters were tending to the fire, and the grey-suited officers were getting out of their car. She reached in her pocket and threw the keys in Penny's direction.

"The key. All this time you had the key?" Frantically she fumbled to get the key in the ignition.

Anger and thoughts of vengeance outweighed everything else. Opening her door, Patricia said, "Oh for god's sake. Change places."

Her head was pounding, her hands shaking but she got the ute started, put it in drive and pressed the accelerator. The vehicle lurched up onto the curb, as Patricia's hands felt a sharp pain and she momentarily let go of the wheel. Swearing, she gained control and pulled the ute back onto the road. It bounced down off the curb and as wheels and road connected the ute jolted sideways. Another searing pain as she gripped the steering wheel and pulled it back into line.

Penny struggling with her seat belt, yelled at Patricia, "You're not wearing a belt."

"Fuck the belt," said Patricia squealing around the corner. They careened twice over speed bumps, each time Penny's head banged on the roof followed by the ute banging as it bottomed out. Ahead the traffic light turned orange. The adrenalin in her system masking the pain in her hands, she pressed hard on the accelerator and sped through the intersection. It felt good to be in charge of a vehicle again.

"My god, slow down," yelled Penny, one hand hanging onto the door handle, the other braced against the roof as they careened on two wheels through a roundabout. The approaching self-drives, sensing the speed of the on-coming vehicle, slammed on their brakes, granting the ute the right of way it demanded.

"Do you even know where you're going?" shouted Penny as they hit a clear stretch of road.

It was a good question and one that Patricia realised needed answering. She eased her foot off the pedal. "I don't know," she replied. Then glancing over at Penny, she said, "You're the one with all the secret hideaways. Why are you asking me?"

"First of all because you're driving."

Patricia figured Penny had a point so she pulled onto a side street and stopped next to the curb. "OK, tell me where to go."

Penny bit her lip, which Patricia figured was not a good sign.

"Our safe houses aren't safe anymore," she responded. "You're the reporter, don't you have, I don't know, like secret meeting places."

"Don't be ridiculous. No one does secret rendezvous anymore."

As they sat in the quiet, each pondering what to do next, the sound of children laughing drifted over from the playground. It was an incongruous sound and at first Patricia wasn't sure if it was real or something playing in her head. How could that sound exist? Terrible things were happening and yet here children were laughing. Children's laughter. When was the last time she'd paid attention to that?

Penny also seemed to be listening. Was she wondering the same thing, or were her thoughts drifting back to her sister Carla and the boys at the refinery?

Breaking the silence, Patricia said, "In my bag there's a sheet of paper with a map scribbled on it."

Obediently Penny grabbed the bag and rummaged around.

"Is this it?"

Patricia's hand had started shaking uncontrollably, whether from shock or pain, she couldn't tell but she pointed as best she could at a line.

"That's Ballarat Road, and this other one is Rosamond Street." Tapping on a rectangle near the intersection of the two lines, she said, "We're going here."

"How do you know it's safe?"

"It's the hideout of the four musketeers and now that they're all gone—" The words stuck on the lump in her throat, but she swallowed them down. "It's the best I can come up with."

Painfully opening her door, Patricia said, "I think we can walk from here."

CHAPTER 14
MONIKA

FRIDAY 10 DECEMBER 2049 - 10:00 A.M.

"Walking would have been faster," said Stephanie putting her I.D. back in her wallet. "If we'd taken your car, we could have breezed through these checkpoints."

"I told you. We couldn't take my car because it's bugged."

"And what makes you so sure mine isn't?"

"Well, for starters, it's not a government issue," snapped Monika.

Immediately, she regretted being so ill-humoured. Was it lack of sleep, a distaste for funerals or her ongoing anxiety over who Evelyn planned to back? Whatever was troubling her, and it was likely to be all three, she'd been on edge since Steph mentioned that they'd arrested Dorothy's assassins. Why had Benny immediately come to mind? There was no way he was involved and besides, leaving his bike on the veranda was a clear signal that he'd been taken care of. No, it was Catherine who needed to worry about this latest development.

Absent-mindedly, Monika rolled and unrolled her copy of Dorothy's eulogy.

"Why so quiet?" asked Steph. "I thought the whole reason for taking my car was so we could talk."

"Sorry, I'm going through the eulogy in my head."

"Keeping it brief and full of faint praise I presume."

"Evelyn wants her disposed of as quickly as possible so we can move on with her agenda and the elections."

"Is that why there's no public viewing, no lying in state?"

"The official stance is that it's too dangerous."

"Even though they've arrested the so-called murderers?"

"If you're asking if all this is for show then you're correct."

Monika sighed. Staring into the side mirror, she observed the slow procession behind them and thought about Dorothy's legacy. Her eulogy started by saying that they'd known each other from their days in Canberra. There, they'd sat on opposite sides of the bench, but then the Desolation came along. It erased party lines and forged new alliances. And so they had become a team. She'd talk about was how the Desolation undermined the structure on which their society had been built on and how that affected each of them differently. If Dorothy had lived, would those differences have become part of the free and open debate that Evelyn promised? Even before Evelyn handed over the reins of government, she stated that without a cure, the world run by men had run its course. That men were as good as extinct. Dorothy insisted that the search for a cure continue but hedged her bets by saying that, with or without a cure, males deserved a place in society.

Despite this fundamental difference, Evelyn had named Dorothy her successor and Monika figured she understood why. Evelyn knew that the women who'd struggled through the dark days weren't ready to accept her vision of the future. Nor were the politicians, including Monika herself. Evelyn needed Dorothy to keep hope alive while she worked out a solution to the problem of conception. Something had changed their dynamic recently and their last argument had been particularly acrimonious. That's what led to Dorothy throwing that party on French Island. It was an act of rebellion. Monika couldn't help but wonder, if Dorothy hadn't died that night, would Evelyn have been able to close the lab at Gentech? The last one still searching for a cure.

As for her own thoughts on their dispute, Monika was less concerned with the outcome than her own political future. She'd stood on the sidelines, hoping to play one side against the other. With Evelyn, she positioned herself as a potential replacement if Dorothy didn't toe the line, and with Dorothy, she offered support for phasing out the anti-hetero laws if she won the election. It was no surprise then that Evelyn nominated Monika as Acting Premier. Nor was it inconsistent for Evelyn to introduce a wild card; Catherine Williams. Catherine, who was ten years younger than Monika and hadn't grown up thinking heterosexuality was normal, had a wife who was pregnant with a state-approved embryo. Together, they embodied the image Evelyn wanted for her new society. By bringing Catherine into the inner circle, Evelyn was telling Monika, in no uncertain terms, that she had to conform, publicly and privately. Otherwise, Catherine was there to replace her.

Looking at the papers on her lap, Monika, unaccustomed to self-reflection, found herself feeling self-conscious.

"Rose should be giving this eulogy, not me."

It was true that Rose was Dorothy's oldest friend and should be the one delivering these final words but Evelyn wouldn't hear of it.

"You are the Acting Premier, the official head of the NOP. Therefore, you are the one to give Dorothy her final send-off." Evelyn had then dismissed her but as Monika stood up to leave, her mentor had added, "Just make sure it's as bland as possible. Once she's in the ground I want the very memory of her deliberately and thoroughly erased."

It was clear that having served her purpose, Dorothy Anderson was to be discarded with as much thought as yesterday's trash. But was it only because Dorothy had been impolitic enough to get herself murdered at an illicit sex party? One that she'd organised at the notorious Big House on French Island to show her contempt for Evelyn's authority or was there more to it? To her inner circle, Evelyn said that today was as much about burying Dorothy's indiscretions as it was about burying her body. What Monika wondered now, is if Evelyn wanted to bury hope for a cure as well.

If that were the case, Monika had to consider the ramifications. Her engagement to Stephanie might fool the general public into thinking she was adhering to the new anti-heterosexual laws, but when it came to Evelyn Perkins and her vision of a matriarchal society, there was no room for half-measures. Evelyn expected complete and utter conformity. Like the paper in her hand, Monika was being twisted and squeezed into shape but both she and Evelyn knew that without a firm grip, Monika might veer off in the same direction as Dorothy.

As if reading her mind, Steph said, "Have you given further thought to my proposal?"

Glancing at Steph sitting behind the wheel, its functions controlled by the self-drive, Monika considered her fiancé's political plans. She was a businesswoman, so profits were her primary concern, and in conjunction with the retail and hospitality sectors, Steph's construction empire relied on the cheap labour supplied by boys. While Steph professed to be apolitical, she had no qualms about lobbying for her concerns. In that regard, Evelyn and Steph were similar. Steph might use the GPS to set her course while Evelyn gave instructions to her driver, but either way, they both controlled the destination without having to grab the wheel. And that was the crux of the problem. Whether Monika remained loyal to Evelyn or sided with Steph, she would not be the one in control. So the real question was, who was going to give her the greatest advantage in the coming election? And listening to the rhythm of Steph's nails tapping impatiently on the steering wheel, she couldn't help but wonder if Steph's consortium had made the same offer to Dorothy.

They came to a halt as they came to another checkpoint, but these weren't normal security guards. These ones were wearing the distinctive brown uniforms of Davina Warren's special forces.

"For trumped-up security, don't you think this is a little over the top?"

"It's being televised," Monika replied, but inside, her alarm bells were ringing. To quiet those thoughts, she added, "Evelyn thinks it takes the focus away from Dorothy's death and highlights the threat instead."

"It may do that but it also makes getting anywhere painfully slow."

As they progressed in the queue, Steph pulled down her visor to check her makeup in the mirror, and once again, silence sat like an uncomfortable third occupant. Up ahead, however, something was happening. It looked like the security guard was ordering someone out of their car. More guards arrived and the person was not only pulled but dragged away. Oblivious to the drama playing out, Steph chattered away.

"I suppose reviving the multi-party system of elections signals to the public that society has returned to normal but there's nothing normal about the way she treats males. I don't know about you but I find it ironic that she would use a system that disappeared, along with the men who created it, as a way to make sure they never come back."

The car that had been stopped, moved away on its own. Its inhabitant, escorted away, was no longer visible. Was this what the new democratic Republic looked like? If so, it was ironic that with freedom of expression came suppression. But there were other ironies and perhaps they worked in favour of this new democracy and Monika herself. Government House, which had been the residence reserved for the governor of Victoria, was now the Premier's official residence. The Desolation, with its ensuing dictatorship, had accomplished what democratic referendums had failed to achieve. Australia was no longer a ward of Britain and Victoria was no longer part of a federation of states. What had once been the home of an appointed individual, would now house an elected official.

The Republic had come a long way and Monika knew, as well as anyone, that if it hadn't been for Evelyn, Melbourne would have fallen apart as surely as the federation had. Retired or not, her word carried a lot of weight. During the Transition, it had ensured the survival of the new Republic of Melbourne and with the stability the Republic now offered the colonies, they might agree to be reincorporated. That which had been shattered could once again be made whole. It was quite possible that with Evelyn's backing, Government House could one day be the foundation for a whole new Republic of Australia, and Monika felt that that was her birthright. Her father had been the last prime minister of the old federation so it was only fitting that she be the first in the long road back. Could Steph's group of businesswomen offer her that?

Behind them, the sound of sirens caught their attention and that of the guards.

"What's going on now?" asked Steph as she flipped up the visor and adjusted the rearview mirror.

In the side mirror, Monika could see cars shifting to make room for a large black limo.

"She certainly knows how to make an entrance. I'll give her that," said Steph.

They both watched as the distinctive vehicle bypassed the queue of cars and pulled up in front of the cathedral. The unmistakable figure of Davina Warren stepped out of the front and opened the back door. Immediately reporters and cameras turned their attention, first to the famous black walking stick with the silver lion's head as it emerged and then to the woman who held it. Diminutive in size, there was no discounting the impact she had on everyone around her. Security rushed to clear the way but it didn't take much persuasion. Like Moses parting the waves, people automatically fell back, giving Evelyn space to enter the cathedral unimpeded.

"And you think I could go up against that?" muttered Monika.

Steph eyed her closely. "Not only do I think you can. I think you must."

Evelyn's entrance was completed, and cars again moved forward. With only a couple of cars in front, Monika freshened her lipstick and checked her hair. Looking beyond her mirror, she caught sight of a familiar figure exiting the car in front of them. She flipped the visor up to get a better look at the tall figure dressed in a conservative yet stylish pantsuit. As the cameras again came to life, the figure paused to wave at the crowds, her trade mark smile exuding confidence. Monika stared in amazement as Catherine's self-drive trundled away and her rival turned and walked into the cathedral.

She looked over at Steph and said, "She's expected to arrive after us. Am I missing something?"

The question was rhetorical but Steph replied anyway.

"Whether you are or aren't it appears your rival is."

CHAPTER 15
THE OLD ONE'S CABIN

SEPTEMBER 2069

"It's getting cold over here. Can you either move me closer to the fire or add more wood."

So engrossed in the story was the girl that at first she didn't realise the Old One was talking about the lack of heat in the cabin. While, she hadn't wanted to leave the topic of Jocelyn, at least not until she'd had a chance to find out who that mysterious 'we' consisted of, she immediately became engrossed in Patricia and Penny's escape. Before the Old One started telling these stories, the girl had never heard of Penny or her sister Carla. The same couldn't be said of Patricia Bishop. She was famous for her exclusive reporting of the Truce talks. And she was equally infamous for her book, Lost Boys which was banned shortly after its release. The girl had found a copy hidden among some papers on Tanya's bookshelf and knowing that her advisor would be away for a couple of days, had borrowed it and read it in one night. Unlike the Old One's version of events, Patricia had very little to say about Evelyn Perkins. Mostly, the book revolved around interviews with the boys who survived the attack on San Remo and Phillip Island. Those attacks, Patricia wrote were the result of increasing tensions between lancers and the women who lived in Gippsland. As for her mother, Patricia only mentioned her in the dedication, along with her father.

To my father for teaching me to speak the truth and my mother for giving me the opportunity to do that.

After hearing the Old One's account, that dedication took on a new meaning as did the supposed conversation between Monika Thomas and Stephanie Steele. But the Old One was right, the fire had died down and the room was getting colder.

She threw on her coat and moved the Old One's wheelchair closer to the heater, then headed outside for more firewood.

Left alone, the Old One watched the flames shoving and jostling against each other in the firebox while outside the sound of logs splintering sounded much like a cleaver landing hard on a wooden table.

INVERLOCH

FRIDAY 10 DECEMBER 2049 - 10:00 A.M.

"Now, I ain't one to teach me gran how to suck eggs so I reckon you don't need a lesson," said Bulldog casually tapping Steve on the chest with the back of his hand, "but these young blokes look pretty green to me."

As he spoke, he pointed at the boys gathered around the table. They were looking at the bits of fish guts and blood splattered on its surface and trying to avert their noses from the smell. Despite being on the pier and open to fresh ocean air, the stink was overwhelming. Bulldog, insensitive to the sights and smells, grabbed a plastic apron, slung it over his head and tied it around his back. With a flourish, he swung his meaty arm across the table, whisking the gore into the water where a flurry of splashes followed. Noticing the way the twins eyed the underwater commotion, he added, "Sharks. Bullheads." He then proceeded to set some knives in front of himself as if preparing to dine and added, "I don't recommend you swim near here."

Lifting the lid of a large cooler, he pulled out a fish that flopped in his hand as he slammed it on the table. Holding it firmly with one hand, he picked up the cleaver and with one swipe, severed its head. He exchanged cleaver for fileting knife and as the fish convulsed once more, ran a clean line down its belly, extracted the innards and tossed them into the water.

Benny looked on in fascination.

"Beats using a rock and your fingers," he said, glancing at Steve.

"Any job's easier with the right tools," said Bulldog tossing the fish fillets into a different cooler. "Who wants to have a go?"

The boys from Warragul didn't look that eager, nor did the twins, silent for once, so Benny said he'd give it a shot. Following Bulldog's example, he grabbed an apron and took the seasoned lancer's place. Gingerly, he stuck his hand into the container and, after a bit of splashing around, managed to get his fingers around a decent-sized fish. As he pulled it out, however, it gave him the slip, landing with a plop on the table. Reaching out to grab onto it, it coyly spurned his advances by slapping his wrist with a fin and moving just beyond his reach. Undaunted, Benny abandoned his position at the head of the table and followed after it. The others yelled encouragements as the fish led Benny on a merry chase down the length of the tabletop. Teetering on the edge, it finally fell victim to Benny's embrace. Basking in his audience's applause and smiling his victor's smile, he lifted it in triumph but then it wiggled free and escaped onto the pier. In a classic struggle of man against beast, Benny, on his knees, scuffled after it while others in its path made feeble attempts to nab it or at least kick it away from the edge of the pier. It was no longer Benny's lone pursuit as the others joined in the game. The frantic escapee eluded its captors until Malcolm dropping to his knees, managed to get a firm grip. Benny winded more from laughter than anything else, cheered along with the others as Malcolm held his catch high in the air.

Steve, who had joined in on the celebrations and was laughing along with the rest, stopped when he caught sight of a boat heading in their direction. As the others clustered around the table engrossed in Benny's attempts at killing the exhausted fish, Steve moved off to the side. Hands over his eyes to reduce the glare from the water, he studied the vessel. It was smaller than the boat that had brought him from Melbourne to Venus Bay so he figured it wasn't the smugglers. And it was moving too slow and too quiet to be a motorised launch like those used to patrol French Island. That didn't mean that it didn't pose a danger to himself and Benny. Over the last few days, he'd wondered why the woman who called herself Wendy would go through the trouble of smuggling him out of Melbourne and why she decided to hide him in Warragul. Whatever these women were up to, he'd decided that he wanted no part of it. Glancing over at Benny who had succeeded in chopping off the fish's head and was now working the fileting knife with jagged thrusts, Steve smiled. They'd only spent a short time together as they foraged their way around the countryside looking for the road to Warragul, but it had brought him a joy he hadn't experienced in years. That's how it was supposed to be with Matt. Matt, his cellmate from that prison on French Island, had convinced him that they could escape. The ex-soldier had filled Steve's head with visions of freedom. No rules. No barriers. Benny tossed the bloody guts into the water and Steve grimaced. Matt had killed that woman on the beach as efficiently and as callously as sharks attacking their prey. Was it fitting, then that sharks had taken Matt? The sight of blood in the water sickened him. Death hadn't bought Matt freedom. It had only brought his death.

Whack.

Steve jumped, thinking a bullet had whizzed past, but then he heard the cheers.

Bulldog had slapped Benny on the back congratulating him. Taking the apron, the lancer asked who wanted to be next. Steve, ignoring the shoving and good-natured jostling, headed out towards the end of the pier. He was more interested in the boat headed their way.

"That's most likely Jack comin' back from San Remo."

Bulldog had come up beside him.

"That one of your boats, then?" asked Steve keeping his eyes on the launch.

"Belongs to a relay based in Hastings. She runs reg'lar like 'tween here and Melbourne."

"Melbourne," muttered Steve. "Mind if I take a walk mate."

Bulldog considered the request and Steve thought he was about to say something but instead he shrugged his shoulders. "Yeah, mate. Just follow the path up into the scrub. You won't get lost cause the smell'll guide you back."

Tapping Benny on the back as he walked past, Steve said, "You and I need to take a walk."

Benny, saw the serious look on Steve's face and asked, "What's up?"

"Boat's coming in from Melbourne."

Without further discussion, Steve headed for the scrub and Benny followed.

When they were far enough from the beach to be out of earshot, Benny said. "Steve, you've been on edge since we got here. Is it something in particular or is it just a feeling?"

Steve dug his foot in the sand and stared out towards the open waters.

"There's something not right about this place but it could be that my imagination's running wild."

"I have to admit the rules are pretty strange but no worse than what you'd get on the stud farms."

"Maybe that's the problem. It feels like a stud farm. No matter where I turn I seem to wind up obeying rules set by someone else. But there's more to it. That flyer for instance."

"The one that wrapped itself around your leg last night?"

"Yeah. It says that there's a lancer council in San Remo and that every lancer colony should send as many delegates as they can spare."

"Maybe that's normal for lancers. You know, get together, have a party."

"Or it could be a trap."

"What makes you think that?"

"How many lancers do you think know how to print up flyers?"

"Well, the lads from Warragul went to uni. Maybe they learn stuff like that. You want me to ask them?"

"In Melbourne did you have access to computers and printers?"

"Steve, this isn't French Island, and it isn't Melbourne. We've only been here a few days so what do we know about lancers or wildings or any of this?"

"I s'pose you're right but just in case, I don't want some female from Melbourne knowing we're here."

"What woman from Melbourne?"

Steve pointed towards the boat which was closing in on the pier.

Benny watched as it slowed down and Bulldog grabbed the mooring line that was tossed his way.

"So that's what's bugging you. You worried about someone taking you back to French Island," said Benny looking back in Steve's direction.

Steve shrugged his shoulder, his eyes still on the boat. "I don't much like the idea of going back to prison in either place."

"You're right, there. I don't much fancy a trip back to Melbourne, either." Then he seemed to consider something else and added, "Except to see my friends. I'd like to see them one more time."

That phrase 'one more time' hit a nerve with Steve. Here he was worrying about going back to prison on French Island but this kid was already living with a death sentence. Benny's world wasn't just one devoid of grown men. It was one that offered boys no future. Matt hadn't known that his days were numbered but Benny did. Steve's mind flicked to the boys he'd known from his days in the Big House. No wonder they had lived each day as if there were no tomorrow. And earlier this morning, when he'd seen kids running around the grassy areas in the women's zone, it had dawned on him that the last time he'd seen kids playing was when he was at school. That had been a pleasant memory but now he realised that all those boys; the boys he'd grown up with, the studs at the Big House, Johnno and the other boys at the refinery, the kids running on the green and the lads cheering down at the pier, none of them would live to become adults. None of them would live to see themselves in their kids' faces. In another year, Benny too—he didn't want to finish the thought.

Instead, he looked back towards the pier where the boat was docking. A fit-looking woman in brown trousers and a beige t-shirt was climbing out of the boat as Bulldog tied it up. She strode off towards the village while a scrawny male hopped out. Steve and Benny watched as Bulldog said something to the smaller bloke, then pointed towards the path into the scrub. Even at this distance, both of them recognised the passenger and neither was surprised to see him striding in their direction.

"Shepherd and Blue," he said as he came up to them. "Bulldog said I'd find you up this way."

"Hi Jack," replied Steve but he didn't offer his hand and the two faced each from a respectful distance, cordial but wary. "I heard you were in San Remo. D'you find Cherry?"

"Too late, mate." There was a brusqueness in Jack's voice. It was not unlike his usual manner except that it had even more of an edge to it. "Met up with the officers that were looking into the murder of that trader who was s'pposed to take you to Warragul. They said rumour has it she was killed by lancers. Maybe the same ones that killed the Premier."

When Jack mentioned the murder of the Premier, Steve felt a queasiness in his stomach. He needed to move this conversation elsewhere.

"So you told them about the women that took Cherry?"

"Yeah, I did. They said they'd look into it but then they asked me how I knew about it. I said the dog and I had helped Cherry deliver a couple of males to the pickup point. They got real curious then. Asked what you looked like and what happened to you."

"What'd you tell 'em."

"What I knew. That you and the kid were headed for Warragul. They said that was funny cause you never showed but I said that you were injured or more likely, lost."

"All that's true," said Steve, but his mind was racing ahead, which was why he was surprised when Jack said, "You know Cherry was doin' someone a favour guidin' you from Venus Bay to Warragul."

"What do you mean?"

"I mean Cherry, she weren't one of them smugglers. This was a special job she took on. I don't s'pose you know anything 'bout that."

"Mate, I know less than you. I was the package being delivered, remember? But what do you mean she wasn't a smuggler?"

"Everyone knows those women in Warragul reg'larly take in young boys smuggled out of Melbourne. It's a free colony after all. For reg'lar runs, they bring them here to Inverloch and drive them in that lorry to Warragul."

Remembering the women and children on the green, Steve asked, "Why not leave them here?"

Jack shifted uneasily as he said, "Wildings look after their own but they don't look after those that can't look after themselves. Warragul's different that way." Then, switching the subject, he said, "Anyway, you two got taken to Venus Bay. It's off the usual route so the smugglers needed someone to guide you two to the pickup point."

"You said she took on this job as a favour. Do you know why?"

"She had her reasons but since we're sharing secrets, how 'bout you tell me yours."

Steve fell silent and Jack shrugged. "Those officers were mighty interested in you. So's that relay. She said they were searching this area for a bloke fits your description. Might be you murdered someone important and that's why you had to get as far from Melbourne as possible."

Benny, who'd been listening, piped up.

"That's not why Steve's got to stay out of sight. It's not what he did but what he is. Tell him, Steve."

Jack took a couple of steps closer so he was standing toe to toe with Steve. Despite the difference in height and build, Steve felt they were well matched for a fight.

"Tell me what, Steve," he said mimicking Benny.

"It's nothing."

Something dark and menacing was building up in Jack and Steve tightened his stomach, readying himself for whatever Jack decided to do next, but instead of getting physical, the wiry lad took a step back. The moment of confrontation ended as quickly as it had risen.

"Have it your way but if the head lady finds out that we're harbouring a murderer, a woman murderer, well, they got ways to deal with that."

"He's not a murderer," said Benny rushing between the two.

"Then what is he?" Jack shifted his hostility towards Benny.

"Stay out of this Benny," said Steve.

But the kid wasn't waiting for his approval. He blurted out, "Steve's in hiding because he's got what we all want."

"And what might that be?"

"Immunity."

"He's got what?"

"He's not gonna die."

CHAPTER 16
THE OLD ONE'S CABIN

SEPTEMBER 2069

The sound of wood toppling into the box next to the heater, woke the Old One.

"Was I gone so long that you fell asleep?" asked the girl.

Stretching the Old One shifted positions as the girl threw a couple of logs on the glowing embers. Whether it was due to the freshness of the night air, the stimulation of chopping wood, or perhaps the thought that this was her last night in the cabin, the girl was definitely in a cheerful mood.

Closing the heater door, she said, "I'm going to bring the recorder over and you can finish telling me about the memorial service. There's not much written about it, so this should be interesting."

"It wasn't meant to be memorable," said the Old One rubbing a leg that had also fallen asleep.

MONIKA

FRIDAY 10 DECEMBER 2049 - NOON

Monika felt in her gut that something was wrong. She couldn't pinpoint the problem but as she walked into the cathedral, the feeling intensified. She sensed that everyone was looking in her direction. Well, why wouldn't they? She was the Acting Premier and heir apparent in the coming elections. Her seat in the pew next to Evelyn confirmed that status. So what could be amiss?

Was it because Catherine had arrived without her wife? The spousal absence had caught her attention, but Steph's snide remark about a case of well-timed morning sickness hadn't elicited the chuckle it was intended to. Instead, Monika responded with,

"What do you mean?"

"Well, didn't you tell Catherine that Evelyn was going to require genetic testing for Element X?" replied Steph. "At this point in the pregnancy, that would be upsetting so you could hardly blame the young mother-to-be for not wanting to face Evelyn."

Steph had a knack for honing in on the heart of the matter, only this time, the mark she hit wasn't one of Catherine's foibles. It was Monika's impropriety. Attacking a political rival was one thing but dragging their family into the fray was bad form. That comment to Catherine had been made in a moment of anger fuelled by alcohol but what made it even worse was that it might be true. Evelyn was certainly pushing ahead her time table.

"I shouldn't have said what I did."

"Why not? Catherine is so self-righteous about the fact that her wife is carrying a government-approved egg. Let her wonder if something might be wrong with it. Besides, pregnancy isn't that big a deal."

"And what would you know about that?"

Monika wasn't sure why the remark about pregnancy irritated her, but it did. The thought that she might resent another woman being a carer or even becoming a guardian was quickly discarded. Neither she nor Steph wanted children. At least not at their age and maybe that was what galled her about Catherine and her wife. Being ten years younger, they were from a different generation. Women like herself, whose fertile years were lost in the Transition didn't have access to fertilisation facilities because they were still being redeveloped. As for the men of their generation, well, they were either scared to death of dying or already dead and buried. Both Monika and Catherine had struggled through the dark days, but being younger, Catherine had time to adapt. Hers was a generation that could have it all; children, security, and a bright future.

While they were still in their car, wondering about Catherine's solo appearance, Monika noticed a dark smudge at the base of her thumb. Absent-mindedly, she'd wiped at it, but when it didn't go away, she'd licked her finger and rubbed at it harder. Like the hurts of the past, it stubbornly refused to disappear. The closer they got to their destination, the more obsessive the rubbing became until Steph reached over and placed a hand on hers.

"That's a liver spot, darling. You'll get used to them. They come with age-like grey hairs and crow's feet."

Another Steph truism that seemed innocuous enough, while inflicting pain where it hurt the most. Before Monika could respond, the self-drive had pulled up to the entrance, where a security guard stepped forward and asked to see their I.D.s. Monika only had to lean over and say, "She's with me" for the guard to apologise.

"Ah, Ms Thomas. I didn't recognise the car. Wait and I'll come around and get your door."

Steph had already noted that the guards outside the cathedral didn't belong to the metropolitan police. While the regular police were managing the crowds outside the perimeter, it was Evelyn's personal police force that was deciding who was and who was not allowed in. Which made Monika wonder again about the woman the guards had surrounded only minutes earlier. She wished she'd been able to see who it was. It was normal to see Davina Warren, the head of Evelyn's brown uniformed guards, in attendance. She was always by Evelyn's side but seeing her officers taking control at a public event was unusual. Perhaps it was all part of Evelyn's plan. She'd insisted on heightening security not because she expected an attack but because she wanted the public to think there might be one. It reinforced that Dorothy's murder was an attack by lancers and by association, the Subversives. Furthermore, whoever the Progressives ran in the upcoming election, there would now be the suspicion that they were also linked to a group that sought to destabilise the government.

Steph had instructed the car to park itself and climbed out on her own but Monika dutifully waited for the guard to open her door. Her fiancé might be accustomed to making her way in the world but Monika's life consisted of having doors opened for her. Before the Desolation, it was her father's influence that paved the way, especially once he became Australia's Prime Minister. And when that door closed, there was Evelyn opening up new ones. It was Evelyn who brought Monika into the sanctuary of her fold when the world was falling apart just as it was Evelyn who held them all together. Monika, Dorothy, Rose, and Gloria; they were the nucleus of this fledgling government but it was Evelyn who bound them together.

Running the gauntlet of reporters, Monika had quickly mounted the steps, ignoring the questions thrown in her direction.

"When will you announce the election?"

"Will the fires impact the timing of the election?"

"Is it true that Premier Anderson's murderers have been caught?"

At the door to the cathedral, Steph had placed her arm around Monika's waist and whispered, "Give them a little something."

Coming to a halt, Monika realised that Steph was right. She'd turned and raised her hand to silence the reporters.

"This is a solemn day for all of us so I'm sure you'll understand if we decline any comments at this time."

Those few words had the desired effect but not before cameras snapped pictures of the couple who were credited with bringing the Conflagration under control.

Once inside the cathedral, Monika had been overwhelmed, not by the sight of the casket prominently displayed in front of the altar but by the smell of flowers. They lined the aisles and filled the alcoves so that the place smelled more like a florist's shop than a place of worship. Behind the flag-draped coffin, vases of lilies stood guard while a bouquet of white roses mixed with pink heath covered its lid. Both flag and heath were symbols of the old state of Victoria. And there, standing behind the casket was that other symbol of Victoria, Evelyn Perkins.

"No expense spared," muttered Stephanie.

Monika, ignoring the comment, shifted her attention from the coffin to the pews, particularly the front row where the dignitaries sat. Farthest from the central aisle sat Gloria Fenton, the party treasurer. Next to her was Catherine Williams. Monika's initial surprise at finding her rival in the front row was quickly swept aside. The woman now held Monika's former position, that of Minister of Infrastructure, so of course she would be front and centre. Switching back to Evelyn, Monika noticed how her mentor looked in her direction as she leaned forward and kissed the coffin lid. Then straightening, she gently placed her hand on it as if giving Dorothy a final blessing.

"She's quite the performer, isn't she?" whispered Steph.

Monika shushed her but Steph was right. Since last Sunday when Evelyn had announced that Dorothy had been murdered, Monika had had the feeling that Evelyn was putting on a performance, not only for the public but for her inner circle. That's why Monika felt compelled to find out what Evelyn was hiding. While she'd turned down Dorothy's invitation to the party, she knew that both Steph and Joan, the editor of the Daily Newsfeed, had attended. They'd both agreed that the boy Dorothy was in the boathouse could not have been her murderer, and they both stated that a small rowboat had left the scene of the crime. Then, in a quiet tete-a-tete, Joan had confided that one of her reporters, a Patricia Bishop, was getting close to unravelling the mystery of who was in that boat. Undoubtedly Evelyn was aware of the boat but what Monika wanted to know was whether Evelyn knew who was in it and if that was why Evelyn wasn't telling her inner circle, the whole story. Scanning the room, Monika looked for Joan. The editor-in-chief wasn't visible, and again, Monika thought of the woman being surrounded by brown uniformed guards.

Meanwhile, Evelyn had taken her place next to Catherine. Monika noted how the younger woman towered over the two elder stateswomen on either side of her making her appear even more prominent. But that wasn't the only thing. Shouldn't Catherine be sitting on the other side of Gloria?

Once again Monika squeezed the papers in her hand. They were the final words on Dorothy's life but what did they really have to say about the woman? They mentioned how Dorothy Anderson had been by Evelyn's side during the Transition, but they didn't mention how the young Independent politician had been the outspoken representative for the Brunswick electorate in the pre-pandemic days. Nor did they mention how Dorothy had a reputation for being both open-minded when it came to sex and judgemental when it came to calling out her male counterparts who used their power and influence to harass females who didn't play by their rules. Whereas Evelyn worked within the system, Dorothy had worked in opposition to it and that made her an easy target for the NOP leadership. Her adversaries had included Monika's father, who openly castigated Dorothy for her partying ways and frequent changes in partners. Well, that time like Dorothy, was dead. Still, the eulogy should have mentioned how the public loved Dorothy. Then, as now, she had championed the rights of the underprivileged, including that of sex workers. But then that might have raised the spectre of paedophilia. In a world where boys never reached maturity, where did one draw the line?

It was well known that Dorothy liked her males young and attractive. Still, she'd taken umbrage at Evelyn's remarks and struck back saying, "The bathhouses only employ boys over the age of 16 and they have all given their consent as adults."

"So you claim," Evelyn had countered, underscoring her point by banging her stick on the ground, "but there are plenty of boys under that age employed illegally. They either volunteer because it's a better alternative to slave labour on construction sites or worse, they're abducted and forced into the trade."

In that argument, Evelyn had honed in on the hypocrisy of Dorothy's stance on the male issue. The woman who publicly stood for male's rights was the same woman who took advantage of their inferior position in society. It also gave credence to Evelyn's position, that by exterminating males, she was putting an end to their exploitation. While she stopped short of calling for boys to be exterminated she had made the point that by prohibiting the birth of male babies, she was relieving them and their families of the anguish of lives that were always going to be held in contempt and servitude.

Gloria had stepped in to quell that argument, but Monika knew that Dorothy hadn't gotten over the slight because it wasn't long after that that she'd organised the party at the Big House on French Island. Ironically, that act of rebellion had cost Dorothy her life and possibly at the hands of those she had advocated for.

The usher wearing white gloves held out a program and Monika studied the off white paper which featured a recent picture of the middle aged Dorothy Anderson. Underneath the bold black letters of her name were the dates 2000-2049. The woman had served as Premier for only 2 of those years. Monika, four years younger, had expected to be next in line for that position but certainly not for another six. That was the term of office they'd agreed on when they drew up the new constitution for the Republic of Melbourne. Dorothy and Monika were supposed to be the bridge between the old guard consisting of Evelyn, Rose and Gloria and the progressive young ones epitomised by Catherine. Now, with the demise of Dorothy, Monika's turn had come early, but then so too had Catherine's.

As the usher turned to lead them up the aisle, Monika suddenly realised what was amiss.

"Wait. We can't be seated until Ms Walsh arrives," she said.

Rose Walsh, party Secretary and the other person designated to speak, was missing. The instructions for their arrival times had been very specific so that there would be no last-minute shuffling of seats in the pew. Monika as the first speaker was to sit to the outside of Rose. Then when Rose took her place at the lectern, Monika would take her place next to Evelyn. But like Joan, Rose was missing.

"There's been a last-minute change," said the girl. "I'm afraid Ms Walsh will not be attending today's ceremony."

Monika glanced towards Steph, who looked equally surprised and said, "Last minute change. That doesn't sound like Rose."

Monika's foreboding heightened as the usher guided Steph to her pew then led Monika to the front one. There, Evelyn looked up smiling as she patted the place next to her and that's when Monika saw how the balance of power had shifted. Evelyn's other hand rested on Catherine's knee but it was in her mentor's eyes that Monika finally understood what had been gnawing away at her. From the back of the church, the heavy doors closed with a resounding thud that matched Monika's heart. In that moment, Monika knew. Evelyn had written off her generation.

CHAPTER 17
THOMASINA

FRIDAY 10 DECEMBER 2049 - NOON

Thomasina heard the car pull up in the driveway. Putting down her pen, she wiped her eyes and took a deep calming breath. In the lounge room, the TV broadcast of the memorial service was introducing the dignitaries as they arrived but she'd already seen what she needed to see. Catherine was seated in the front row looking as sophisticated and elegant as ever. Seated beside her was Evelyn Perkins, the woman who was supposed to be the Saviour of the Republic. A week ago, Thomasina would have been thrilled at her wife's achievement but after this morning's argument, she knew the price they were expected to pay for that prominent position.

Ignoring the telecast, she sat with her journal on her lap. Part of her morning routine was to jot down her feelings each day as the child within her grew. It was a task she'd taken up as part of her pregnancy journey and it was meant to be a happy chronicle that they would one day share with their child. It had certainly started out that way. She flipped back to the first page. Dated June 1 2049, it read:

Went to the fertility clinic today to talk about our pregnancy options. We had sufficient credits to qualify for implantation and both of us had viable eggs in storage so it seemed like the right time. Catherine asked if fertilised eggs were segregated by any characteristics. The lab technician said that unless we specified preferences regarding eye or hair colour, the donor sperm was only restricted by the narrow criteria as specified by the state. The eggs used in the process would be randomly selected from those that had been harvested regularly from our wombs but we could choose whether to use ones from specific years or allow the lab to select the oldest or most recent. The technician explained that ten eggs at a time went through the fertilisation process. Those that successfully Fertilised were then screened for any of the known genetic defects. She added that if we were willing to wait a few months they might be able to provide gender screening prior to implantation. Our councillor jumped in and explained that the new procedures were still in development but if we decided to go ahead with the implant and the foetus turned out to be undesirable, then we were entitled to a new implantation at no extra charge. It sounded so simple and we were both so eager to start a family that we signed up on the spot. We were then faced with our first decision. We had to choose whose eggs to use. Catherine insisted on using mine. She said, "You're the one with all the talent" which was really sweet, adding that her contribution was going to be "paying the bills."

Rereading this line in her journal Thomasina realised that it was not sweet. It was condescending. Catherine, with her good-paying job, was asserting her superiority. Despite the expressed view that carers and guardians were equally valued, Thom knew that wasn't the case. That's why she'd only agreed to marry Catherine with the understanding that they were equals. And for a time, Thomasina thought they were. They both had jobs they enjoyed. Catherine worked for the local planning office and Thomasina worked as a teacher. Together they lobbied to get stipends for artists so that Thomasina could focus more on photography and less on teaching.

This decision for her to be the carer and Catherine, the guardian, changed the dynamic in their relationship. It seemed harmless at the time. Logical, really. Catherine, with her family connections and personal charisma, had moved from planning into politics, where she was advancing rapidly. At the same time, Thomasina was growing frustrated with the education system that insisted on hard sciences to the exclusion of art and literature. They jointly decided that Catherine would take on a public role but behind the scenes they would operate as a team. Together, they were going to make changes.

The problem, Thomasina now realised, was that working in the system was as likely to change the person as they were to change it. And at some point in this pregnancy or perhaps in response to her rising status in the NOP, Catherine no longer consulted Thom about political issues. Instead, she asked Thom for unconditional support.

A car pulled into the driveway and Thomasina heard a car door open then close. It occurred to her that Catherine might have asked Geraldine to drop in and check on her. Then a second door opened and closed. Realising it wasn't her mother-in-law, Thomasina was slightly disappointed. It was probably security guards. Since the Premier's murder, they'd been coming around. They rarely spoke to her. Just walked around outside, then disappeared. She returned to her journal.

June 15, 2049

Today we implanted the fertilised egg. Catherine said that as the carer, the choice of which egg to use was mine. There were five of them. They each sat in a test tube with a number in front of it.

Only one could be chosen so I asked, "What happens to the rest?" The technician said they would be destroyed. "But what if the one I pick doesn't implant?" I asked. "Then we start the process again from scratch," replied the technician.

I hated choosing one egg over the others but Catherine said she faced those sorts of decisions every day. She said that now perhaps I would understand how difficult it was to be in charge. She had a point, not about her job as a politician, but about life. Some decisions were a leap of faith so I made my selection and now it sits inside me. My only hope is that it will make itself at home until it's ready to leave my womb.

On the way home, I told Catherine that I felt bad about the unselected eggs. All those potential lives tossed away. It seemed cruel. She said you couldn't get too attached to things that were temporary. That's when the topic of gender came up. She reminded me that I shouldn't get too attached to this egg either. At least not until the gender testing stage. That's when I told her that I didn't want to go through with the gender test. Maybe I over-reacted because I was still upset about the other eggs being destroyed but at the thought that this egg too could be destroyed, I started crying and blubbering on about how I knew this particular egg was special regardless of its gender.

That was their first argument about gender but it hadn't been the last. As the pregnancy progressed, Thomasina pointed out to Catherine that as a highly visible couple, they were in a position of influence. They had the opportunity to improve the lives of so many by choosing to raise a child of the inferior sex. Catherine's response was that as a prominent couple, they needed to set an example by raising an intelligent, confident female. In the end, it was always Catherine who acquiesced. But today was different. Catherine not only insisted on gender testing, she stipulated that if it was a boy or had this new defect, this Element X, then the baby has to go. Thomasina had no idea what this new defect was but she was sure about one thing. She was not going to let gender deprive her of this child.

Rereading the last line in her journal:

Catherine says if it's a boy, we have to get rid of him but I'd rather leave than consider any option that means giving up my child.

She underscored the word 'my'.

Hearing a knock at the door, she set the open journal on the table and placed her pen on top. Surely the guards expected her and Catherine to be at the memorial service, so why were they knocking? Curious, she glanced out the window and saw a grey car with a blue light on the roof. It was not the usual security guards and Thomasina glanced at the TV to see if there was cause for concern but the service was proceeding as planned. Her next thought was for her brother, Nick. Had Catherine changed her mind and sent someone out to look for him? Of course. Finding Nick was Catherine's way of apologising. Rushing to the door, she opened it and saw two women in tailored grey suits staring back at her.

"Ms Williams?"

"I'm Thomasina Williams."

"Ms Williams, we need you to come with us."

"Is it Nick?"

"I'm sorry but we're not at liberty to say."

"I'll just get my things," she replied. As she grabbed her phone and purse, she glanced at the open journal and regretted that last remark. This morning's argument had been the result of fatigue and stress on both their parts. Catherine wouldn't really give up their child nor would she let Nick get carted off to the wilds. Even as she climbed into the backseat of the car she was convinced that she was on her way to see her brother. It was only when she heard the click of the door lock that she realised something was wrong.

GERALDINE

Geraldine poured herself another cup of coffee and carried it into her study. She checked her phone but there were no missed calls or messages and her inbox was also empty. The fact that Bonnie said she had a safe place to spend the night didn't make waiting any easier.

"I'll contact you," Bonnie'd said but there was no backup plan and Geraldine was blaming herself for that. She should have given Bonnie her spare phone. It was untraceable. But what if she lost it? Or worse, got picked up and had the thing on her.

Damn! Things were out of her control and she hated that. Bonnie said she had a safe place but refused to say where it was. All she said was that she was being looked after. But by whom? Probably those Subversives. They were a secretive lot and who else would use boys to carry messages? Bonnie might be a brilliant scientist but she was clueless when it came to politics. She was also clueless when it came to holidays and weekends. Had she forgotten that everything was closed for the memorial service? Did she send her go-betweens to the lab or did she remember to send them here? Hopefully not. Boys, any boys, all boys were being picked up. The last thing she or Bonnie needed was to be seen with a bunch of homeless boys.

Wrapping her hands around her mug, she swore. Optimism was never part of her makeup. That was Bonnie's territory. She took a sip of coffee and stared at the phone, willing it to light up. These were precarious times and Bonnie was not only a friend, she was a precious resource. Sure, there were other researchers but none of them were trained in gene therapy and none of them had worked alongside Dr Mark Connors. Bonnie had already discovered that an important study had been doctored but now they had proof. A colleague in San Francisco had learned that the disease was caused by a viral-influenced genetic mutation. This was a major breakthrough but they still had to identify not only the gene but what had mutated in it. Element X was a likely suspect. It was a genetic defect that the government had recently added to their fertilised egg screening program. If Bonnie had that information, she might be able to compare the good gene with the defective one then with her knowledge of CRISPR she might be able to repair the damage.

The problem from Geraldine's perspective, was the increasing number of 'ifs'. If Bonnie was safe. If Geraldine could get her the information. If Bonnie could get to the backup lab. If. If. If.

And all those 'ifs' hung on one big 'if'. If Bonnie would leave without Josh. Getting Bonnie out of the Republic was hard enough but Bonnie and Josh was impossible But all of these 'ifs' were moot if Bonnie didn't get back in touch.

Stressing wasn't accomplishing anything so Geraldine decided to review the research article that Bonnie had sent her. The results of that study had been altered but by whom and why? There didn't seem to be much point in searching the web for earlier copies because Bonnie said much of the research had been lost as internet links disappeared. Fortunately, she had copies archived on her personal computer. Unfortunately, they contained the adulterated copy. But that gave Geraldine an idea. Before she'd talked Bonnie into coming back to work, she'd been the one saving copies of research. It was possible that her files contained the original findings.

As she opened her archive folder, her black-market phone buzzed.

That's strange, she thought. Bonnie wouldn't have this number. In fact, there were only two people who had this number and –

She grabbed the phone and stared at the message.

Are you watching the service?

Puzzled, she pressed the Daily Newsfeed icon on her computer. What came up was not the Premier's memorial service but the words, Special Bulletin and an automated voice.

"Not only does Evelyn Perkins know the true identity of the Premier's killer, but she's hidden that information from her innermost circle, convincing them too that it was lancers. Her actions were meant to confuse investigators who actually wanted to know the truth. So what are you hiding Evelyn Perkins?"

Geraldine turned it off and switched on her TV but the same message was playing.

"—murdered on French Island, and the assassins were spotted leaving the island by several eyewitnesses. Shortly after the Premier's death, the lab researching for a cure to the disease that's killing our boys—"

Geraldine switched the TV off.

The message was carefully worded to highlight that the wrongdoing was limited to Evelyn Perkins, but Geraldine couldn't help but think of Catherine. She'd tried to warn her daughter about being too closely associated with Evelyn and now it appeared her concerns were justified. If the public suspected Evelyn Perkins of withholding a cure then they were likely to blame everyone in the NOP. But that wasn't the only danger. In fact, Evelyn's propagandists were probably already getting this smear campaign under control. No, the real worry was Evelyn Perkins. She would be wondering who leaked information about the Premier's death and, more importantly, why it was linked to the lab closure. As head of Gentech, and Bonnie's boss her name would be on that list and as Catherine's mother, Evelyn was likely to wonder if Catherine was involved. It wasn't only the public that Catherine had to fear. It was her own party.

Geraldine thought back to her demand that Catherine take a walk with her. In trying to warn Catherine had she implicated her instead? Had they been seen walking into the park together? Had Thomasina said something? Geraldine's mind was racing so fast that she barely noticed the sound of a car pulling into her drive. It wasn't until she heard car doors slamming that she decided to pay attention but by then it was almost too late. With shaking fingers, she typed a single word into her phone.

Genesis

Then as she heard the knock on the door, she threw the phone on the floor and stomped on it.

"Open up Dr Williams. We know you're in there."

Picking up the pieces, she lifted a pot plant out of its container and threw them under it. As she turned around, the door burst open. Two women in grey suits grabbed her arms, saying, "We need you to come with us."

JENNY

The unmarked grey car with the blue light, drove down the leafy green street. Without the use of sirens or lights, it was as inconspicuous as any other car, except that, on this day, there were no other cars. Everyone had the day off and was glued to their televisions watching the Premier's memorial service. As the car pulled up in front of the pleasant two-storey house, two ladies in grey suits stepped out. They glanced at the neatly trimmed rose bushes and the manicured lawn, then headed for the door.

"Nice neighbourhood," said the shorter one as she knocked on the door.

Her partner looked over her shoulder at the house they'd visited last time, the one with the pot of brightly coloured red and white petunias.

"Much nicer than mine," she replied. "Very up-market neighbourhood."

"This one's got one of those cushy government jobs," stated the short one as she knocked again, this time harder. When there was no answer, she banged on the door and yelled, "Ms Connors, we need you to come to the door."

"Instead of yelling, maybe we should just go in," suggested her partner. "We got reamed last time for being too cautious."

The one who'd been knocking tried the door handle.

"It's locked."

"That's unusual. Think they knew we were coming?"

"Car's still in the drive. I'll check around back. You, wait here."

The short woman disappeared while the taller one knocked again. She could hear her partner knocking on the backdoor so she walked over to the window. She peered through a gap in the drawn drapes but couldn't see any movement. Shattering glass brought her to attention and she stepped back, looking first toward one side of the house and then the other. Frantic footsteps echoed inside and she placed a hand on her taser, eyes trained on the door

As it opened, she pulled out her taser. Then stopped. Her partner stood in the open door, looking confused.

"What happened?" she asked.

Her partner looked around and seeing her in front of the window, asked her own question.

"What are you doing over there?"

"Being discrete," the tall one replied, putting the taser back on safety. "I take it, that was you breaking and entering."

"They're not here," was all her partner said.

"So what do we do now?"

The short one shrugged. "Call it in and wait."

"Damn, there goes any chance of a promotion."

MONIKA

Monika heard noises filter in from outside the cathedral but she ignored them as she laid the copy of her eulogy on the podium in front of her. While she organised herself, straightening the papers that insisted on curling back upon themselves, the mourners also settled. As a hush filled the cathedral, Monika looked out over the attendees. A few last minute coughs circulated, then the cathedral fell silent. She welcomed them, making eye contact with various individuals so as to command the attention of everyone. She began with her brief description of their relationship and moved on to the main part of her address, extolling the former Premier's dedication to her community, and there were murmurs of agreement. Heads nodded as she mentioned how Dorothy Anderson was looking forward to the upcoming elections, but as she began listing those projects that Dorothy had hoped to pursue if elected, the sound of a siren interrupted her well-rehearsed speech. She waited for the sound to cease then restarted her sentence but the sound of car doors slamming distracted her again. The audience shuffled in their seats and Monika waited until she had their attention once more.

"As I was saying Dorothy Anderson was looking forward to recon—"

The doors at the back of the cathedral opened and the audience was torn between turning to see who had come and giving Monika their undivided attention. Vexed at the interruption, Monika realised she'd lost her place and glanced down at her written speech. That lapse in concentration severed her connection with her audience. They glanced towards the commotion. Monika picked up where she left off, this time reading from her script but she'd lost her audience. All eyes shifted in the direction of boots striding up the centre aisle. A procession of brown uniformed women marched in and there at the back was Davina. The presence of security guards aroused curiosity but the sight of Davina created a rippling effect as she passed each pew. Hushed whispers and shifting bodies gave way to open discussions. Monika searched out Steph who seemed equally confused, then looked at Evelyn's pew. Gloria turned to look at the guards but as Catherine started to do the same, Monika saw Evelyn place her hand firmly on Catherine's while keeping her eyes fixed on Monika. Catherine settled back into her seat and Monika took the cue and began again.

"As I was saying Dorothy Anderson's death—"

She stopped as Davina told everyone to remain seated, then standing in front of Evelyn, she leaned over and said something. This time, the message was Evelyn's ears only. Evelyn listened, nodded, then placing both hands on her walking stick, stood up. Davina offered Evelyn her arm as other guards headed towards Monika.

"What's the meaning of this?" she asked as they walked up to the podium.

One guard flicked off the microphone and the other grabbed onto her.

"There's been an incident of the greatest concern. We need you to come with us."

"Leave? Now? In the middle of—"

"Please, Ms Thomas."

"But—" She looked at Steph as they led her away from the pulpit and down the aisle.

"It's for your own safety."

CHAPTER 18
THE OLD ONE'S CABIN

SEPTEMBER 2069

The girl leant forward.

"So you're saying that some dissidents were picked up before the bulletin interrupted the memorial service?"

"That's correct. It wasn't the broadcast that sparked the roundup. During the Catalyst for Change demonstration, Davina had netted several members of the Subversive elite. One in particular had disclosed that someone high up in the Subversive's organisation was part of Evelyn's inner circle. Arresting the woman Davina thought was their leader, along with other individuals of interest, led her to believe she'd nipped their rebellion in the bud but then the bulletin broke into their broadcast of the service. The thought that she'd been outsmarted by amateurs enraged Davina. She couldn't stop the broadcast but she could counteract their attempt at undermining Evelyn. She turned their broadcast from an indictment of Evelyn into a threat against her and the stability she'd created. There was no danger to anyone in that cathedral but Davina made sure the press interpreted it that way. And there was another advantage that she hadn't considered.

"What was that?"

"With everyone talking about the threat to Evelyn, no one asked about those who'd disappeared. You see Davina and Evelyn had discussed not only who had penetrated Evelyn's inner circle but who stood in the way of Evelyn's plans for her chosen successor."

"Did that include dissidents outside Melbourne like Sofia? Did she disappear along with the others?"

No, once the trial was over, the only drama Warragul had to look forward to was the newly revised Hamlet."

DR HARRIS

FRIDAY 10 DECEMBER 2049 - NOON

"Well, today's our lucky day. It looks like we're going to be playing to a full house all weekend. Got permission to do a preview tonight."

The van rocked as Bertha climbed back in. Beaming from ear to ear, she slapped Bonnie's knee.

"Seems everyone's in town for a trial. They're pretty rare in these parts. Trials, I mean. Well, maybe people too," she laughed at her own attempt at humour. "Too bad we missed it. They said it was quite a show. Turned out bad for the accused cause she got banished but good for us because everyone's hanging 'round town. Lots of excitement."

She smiled broadly as she pressed the start button.

"Now, they said we'd find your friend Sofia at the Arts Centre which means I get paid and you can get on with your business."

Bertha's mood had certainly brightened since they arrived in Warragul but getting on with business carried a different meaning for Bertha than it did for Bonnie. Since hearing the traders talking about lancers flooding out of Melbourne, her mind had been on only one thing, and that was heading back towards San Remo so she could look for Josh.

"So what kind of trial was it?" asked Bonnie as she looked out the window for signs pointing back towards Melbourne.

"Murder," said the woman, smiling like a Cheshire cat. "Couldn't be better if I'd thought of it myself."

Glancing over at Bonnie, she added, "You know that Hamlet, or rather Hamletta, as we like to refer to her now, is about a murder, right?"

"Yes, fortunately, I went to school before the Desolation."

Bonnie had almost said, "Don't be ridiculous. Who hasn't heard of Hamlet?" but then realised it was a valid question. Since the Selection, school curricula avoided literature that featured men in leading roles. Men hadn't only disappeared from the physical world, literature had erased them as well.

"How long have you been portraying Hamlet as a female," she asked.

"Oh, this Hamletta thing is new. Outside Melbourne, we performed Shakespeare in the original with females taking the male roles, of course. Nothing new in that. In Shakespeare's time, young boys played women's roles; now, older women play men's. Can't do that in the Greater Melbourne Republic though." Bertha emphasised the word Greater. "There we stuck to modern plays to avoid controversy. Censorship," she hissed, wrinkling up her nose. "Kills the soul, but I suppose for the young ones, what they don't know, they won't miss."

Bertha spotted an old electric pull out of a parking spot and pulled into it.

"Busy as market day, it is. Now, from here, we walk."

Bonnie surveyed the area. It was a spot of green that encircled a building, small by Melbourne standards but bigger than anything else around it. Across the road, there were shops but many of them were boarded up. Most of the people milled around on the green where a few enterprising vendors had set up booths selling food and drinks. Bertha was right. It looked and felt like a market.

"What did you say happened to the murderer?" she asked as they walked towards the wide path that led through the green.

"Ran her out of town." Bertha was picking up her pace.

"Her?"

"Yeah, murderer was a woman. Killed her partner."

They passed a bench where young girls were passing around sandwiches and drinks. Casually Bonnie looked in their direction and noticed a girl whose long brown hair toppled over her shoulders. The hair, the figure, even the stance was familiar from the back and Bonnie caught herself from calling out. The last thing she wanted to do was call attention to herself, or the girl for that matter. As they passed the group, however, she looked back as the girl looked up. There was a similar shock of recognition, then a slight shake of the head and Bonnie understood. She kept walking but an idea was already taking shape in her head.

Bertha was still talking as Bonnie caught back up to her.

"They have a rough kind of justice out here. Branding is old fashioned 'cause if you're later proved innocent, well, there's no going back, is there?"

She looked at Bonnie, who was already deep in thought. "What's up with you now?"

"Nothing," she replied taking another quick look back. "Just familiarising myself with the place and its people."

"You'll have plenty of time for that. Let's see if we can find Sofia. She's the town mediator, so she'll be around because she's the one who tried and sentenced the accused."

Bertha shoved her way through a crowd standing at the top of the steps. A woman in a plain blue shirt stepped in her way as she reached for the door.

"Cafe's closed today."

"We don't want anything to eat or drink. We're here to see someone."

"And who might that someone be?" asked the woman who remained firmly planted in front of the door.

"Name of Vargas. Sofia Vargas."

"She's not seeing anyone today."

"I don't think you understand," said Bertha. "I've got an important delivery for her."

"Come back tomorrow. Like I said, she's not seeing anyone."

Bertha looked disgruntled, but the woman at the door didn't look like she was going to change her mind, so turning to Bonnie, she said, "Well, looks like we gotta spend more time together."

Bonnie wasn't sure if it was the thought of being locked in the van overnight or the idea that the plan coalescing in her brain might be delayed but she decided to make a pitch of her own.

"Tell her Genesis is here to see her?"

The guard seemed to mull this over carefully so Bonnie restated her case. "I assure you, she wants to know I'm here."

Apparently, the threat of upsetting Sofia by not passing on the message outweighed the threat of being told it was irrelevant because the woman disappeared inside.

Bertha laughed. "You into bible studies now?"

"I told you I was educated –"

"I know, before the Desolation. But not many people admit to reading the Old Testament. No wonder they had to get you out of Melbourne. Every time you open your mouth, it's so you can change your feet."

"Humanities degree," said Bonnie by way of an excuse.

It wasn't that Bonnie was keen to meet Sofia but she needed to get rid of Bertha. Her priority was Josh. The lab could wait. And now that she'd seen Karen, it was a matter of figuring out how to get to the road back towards Melbourne. She was sure that if Karen learned Josh was likely to be part of the mass exodus, then she'd jump at the chance to help.

A young girl tapped on her shoulder. "Can I get past," she asked politely.

Bertha replied, "Cafe's closed." Then sniggered at the way she now patrolled the door.

"I know," the girl said. "I just need to use the toilets."

"That the secret password is it," said Bertha. "If I'd known that, we'd be in and out by now."

The girl ignored her and slipped past. She disappeared behind a door that had once indicated males but had a skirt painted over the traditional panted legs. If boys needed a toilet, they had to go elsewhere. Then, it hit Bonnie. There were no boys anywhere.

Bertha looked through the glass door, placing her hands up to block her reflection. The bangles on her wrist tinkled while her skirts swished as she shifted position.

"How long does it take to deliver a message?"

The girl returned from the toilet and Bertha moved back from the door creating another wave of music. Once the girl was gone Bertha resumed her vigil at the door with Bonnie beside her.

"Excuse me. May I get through."

Bonnie started. She knew that voice. Bertha, however, only knew someone else was looking to get past. Swirling around she faced the girl waiting patiently behind them.

"You know the secret password?"

The girl looked flustered so Bertha stage whispered the response, "It's toilets." Then rocking back on her heels, she added with a flourish, "That's for future reference."

The girl mumbled a thank you and said, "I won't be long."

As Karen pushed past, Bertha said, "This place is busier than popcorn on a hot skillet."

Bonnie, who was paying attention to which door Karen picked, heard Bertha's colloquialism and looked back at the woman who responded by saying, "It's something my father used to say." The look on Bonnie's face made Bertha smile. "He had a lot of sayings like that. Nervous as a long-tailed cat in a room full of rocking chairs. That was a personal favourite." Then her face brightened, "oh, and—"

Bonnie cut her off, saying, "I need to go too."

"I thought you went back at the truck stop."

"Don't worry, I won't be long."

As Bonnie walked inside, Bertha called after her, "My father used to say he had to walk the dog."

Opening the door to the former men's toilet, Bonnie was confronted by urinals that had been turned into plant stands. The large fronds of the ferns, in the dim light filtering through the window, partially obscured the white porcelain of sinks and bowls. Within its walls, the sound of the festivities was hushed, and Bonnie felt like she was back in the seclusion of the Women's Peace Garden. There was no sign of Karen but Bonnie was sure this was the door Karen had entered so she walked further into the room allowing herself to be swallowed up in its mystical greenness.

Behind her, the door banged shut and Bonnie jumped.

"I don't have much time."

Bonnie whipped around and saw Karen leaning against the door to hold it shut.

"I'm supposed to be a wilding girl so don't call me Karen. Lives, not just my own, depend on me not being recognised."

Bonnie nodded, but before she could speak, Karen's face registered an even greater concern.

"Please tell me Josh isn't with you. Warragul's not safe—"

Bonnie wanted to ask why, but time was short, so she got right to the point.

"No, he's not here and at the moment, I'm not sure where he is."

"But I thought Patricia was taking you someplace safe. You were supposed to stay together."

Karen kept her voice low but the anger came through loud and clear. Bonnie was taken aback but managed to say, "There was a fire."

"A fire? When? Where?"

"You haven't heard?"

"Who's going to tell a wilding girl anything about Melbourne? Besides, there's enough of our own drama. So what happened?"

"We went to a deserted apartment building in the old CBD but while Patricia and I went to find a way out of Melbourne the whole area caught fire."

"And Josh—"

"I don't know. I tried to get back to the building but they drugged me and when I woke up, I was half way here. That woman I'm with has instructions to deliver me to a Sofia Vargas."

"How's Sofia involved?"

"It doesn't matter because I'm not staying. This morning I heard that there are lines of lancers streaming out of Melbourne and heading for a place called San Remo. I think Josh might be in that group."

"But you said the building was on fire."

"Josh is alive, Karen—" she stopped seeing the look from Karren. "Sorry, I won't --. Anyway, Josh is alive. I can feel it."

Bonnie could see the conflict registering in Karen's face and pushed harder.

"That's why I need your help. I need to get out of here so I can find Josh."

"I don't know." Karen faced her, but her eyes had a faraway look, "Helen and that trader told me--. Their eyes reconnected, but Karen's demeanour had shifted. "look, I have to stay undercover."

"I thought you wanted to be with Josh." Bonnie was restraining her voice but the more Karen hesitated, the angrier she felt. "Wasn't that what you two planned? To run away. Without even consulting me, the two of you were just going to skip across the border. Well, now you're here, and Josh is out there with a bunch of lancers, and he needs us to find him."

Karen was pushing herself up against the door, shaking her head.

"I can't."

"Are you listening? Hundreds of lancers are streaming out of the city. We need to go and find Josh."

"I can't leave here and I can't—"

Bonnie knew something was holding the girl back.

"You can't what?"

"I can't face a swarm of lancers."

The girl looked ready to burst into tears.

"I can't do that. Not even for Josh. I'm sorry."

Before Bonnie could respond, Karen fled the room.

For a moment, Bonnie stared at the door, then turned back to look at her lush green surroundings. What was that all about? The door squeaked open and Bonnie spun around expecting to see Karen but it was a stranger. Feeling confused and crestfallen, she washed her hands in the sink and then joined Bertha back at the door.

Bertha took one look at her and started to say something, but then the blue-shirted woman returned.

"Sofia said she'll see you now."

Bonnie was watching Karen walk towards the other girls.

What had changed? The old Karen was always so bubbly, so full of mischief. She wouldn't have shied away. Then Bonnie thought of that last night in Melbourne when they were hiding in the morgue. Patricia had forced Bonnie to face what had been done to Zane. Maybe Karen was right to be afraid.

"You coming?"

The blue-shirted woman was heading down the hall, and Bertha was hissing and motioning for her to follow. If Karen wouldn't help then Bonnie figured she'd have to find another way.

She followed Bertha's swishing skirts and found herself in front of a set of double doors. The woman opened one, indicating that they should enter. The room contained three conference tables set up in a U-configuration, and there, at the far end, sat a grey-haired woman with her back to them.

"Go on in."

For the first time, Bonnie saw Bertha look uneasy. She hesitated, looking from Bonnie to the woman holding the door, then she puffed up her chest, and skirts tinkling, she walked into the room.

Once the door clicked behind them, she said meekly, "I hate to interrupt you, Ms Vargas."

The woman stood up and turned to face them. Bonnie felt like she was staring in a mirror. The grey-haired woman's eyes reflected the same anguish she was feeling.

"Who are you?"

Bertha spoke up, "A mutual friend asked me to deliver this woman to you, no questions asked. She said you'd pay me 60 chits."

"I take it you're not Genesis."

"Oh no, that's not me. This here's," she pointed to Bonnie, hesitating, "the one I've been asked to deliver from Melbourne."

Sofia and Bonnie studied each other. Bonnie saw a woman whose hopes had been irretrievably crushed and wondered what that woman saw in return. They were similar in age and height but those were only physical features. What connected them emotionally was deeper.

The woman looked back at Bertha and then reached for a piece of paper on the table.

"I'm sure she said 40 chits."

"Yes," stammered Bertha, "you might be right. It was late and I was tired," Bertha was talking rapidly, her eyes on Sofia's hands. "On the other hand getting out of Melbourne—"

The woman had finished writing and held out the paper.

"Give this to the woman outside and she'll organise your payment."

Bertha took the paper, scanned it and then, turning to Bonnie, said, "Well, this is goodbye then."

It was an awkward moment when Bonnie thought the woman might hug her, but instead, she folded the paper in half and left, bells jingling and skirts rustling.

For a minute the two women, Bonnie and Sofia, faced each other. Bonnie wasn't sure what to say. The word Genesis had gotten her this far, but beyond that, she wasn't sure what was expected of her. It was Sofia who broke the silence.

"You could've picked a better day but I've been expecting you."

"How could you know I was coming when I didn't know myself."

"A mutual friend," she said mimicking Bertha, "I was told that at some point you would be heading out this way. We've been storing your goods out of town so tomorrow, I'll get someone to take you to the site. I don't suppose you could tell me what this is all about." Then she quickly rejected the idea, saying, "No, on second thought, I don't want to know."

"You've been storing goods and waiting for me but you don't know what any of this is all about?"

"We operate on trust out here. Sometimes the less we know, the better. What I do know is that we were asked to find a place, somewhere out of the way, that would suit a lab."

Bonnie now understood Karen's conflict. This woman, and who knew how many others, were taking a big risk without even knowing what they were risking everything for. She thought back to Geraldine, Patricia and Carla. So many people had pinned their hopes on this lab and on Bonnie but without Josh, she asked herself, what was it all for? Carla had asked if she would continue looking for a cure even if it was too late to save Josh. At the time it hadn't felt like a real choice. Josh was safe, and she had clues about the disease, but that choice was becoming agonisingly real.

When Bonnie didn't respond, Sofia said, "Look you don't have to tell me anything. I don't suppose you have a place to stay?"

Bonnie shook her head. Then, risking a half smile, she said, "I'm kinda new in town. No money. No I.D. Any suggestions?"

"I can think of one. But only one. Follow me."

"Can I ask where we're going?"

"For now, we'll go to my place. It's not far from here and I could use the company."

"But surely you have duties. I mean with you being the colony's mediator and this business with the trial?"

"The trial's over, and as for my position as mediator, that is too. I've resigned. Effective immediately."

CHAPTER 19
THE OLD ONE'S CABIN

SEPTEMBER 2069

"Sofia quit? But who could replace her?"

The Old One chuckled.

"No one is irreplaceable. Before the ink dried on her resignation, there were candidates lining up to take her place, but things were moving ahead quickly now, so pay attention."

MONIKA

FRIDAY 10 DECEMBER 2049 - 1:00 P.M.

When Davina Warren entered the cathedral surrounded by a contingent of her guards, Monika wasn't the only one thrown off-kilter. The reporters who'd been lounging around outside, looked equally bewildered as they were herded inside. That was distracting, but what Monika found truly disconcerting was Davina announcing in a voice that required no microphone that everyone was to remain seated.

Incredulous at the interruption to her eulogy, Monika looked towards Evelyn for an explanation but the stateswoman's face remained blank. Even as Evelyn's head of security leaned in to talk to her and uniformed officers lined up beside the pews, Evelyn remained calm. Then as attendees turned to each other, seeking some explanation, Monika watched Davina escort Evelyn from her pew. The reporters, initially taken aback by the change in plans, swung into action. They snapped pictures of Evelyn being escorted down the aisle, looking dignified as ever, then retrained their lenses onto Monika. There were no flashes going off, no reporters yelling 'look this way' but Monika knew they had captured the moment when she was brusquely pulled from the pulpit. Her papers with Dorothy's eulogy floated to the floor as she was shoved in the direction of the aisle.

Furious, as much at herself as the guards, she shook their hands off, then head held high, proceeded to the aisle. There she joined the other members of the front row who'd been hustled out of the pew. As Evelyn disappeared out the door, Monika felt a firm grip on her elbow and before she could object, found herself being pulled unceremoniously down the aisle. It was as if there were some imminent threat but for the life of her, Monika couldn't figure out what it was.

Once they were outside, the guards let go and returning to the cathedral, closed the doors behind them. Reporters, guards, and mourners confronted each other inside while outside, Monika and the others were left isolated and wondering about what had just happened. Parked at the curb was Evelyn's limo. Were they supposed to climb in? Were they expected to summon their self-drives? Monika nearly panicked. They'd taken Steph's. Was she going to be left behind? Her brain was in turmoil.

She'd spent the last week choreographing every aspect of this service with Evelyn. The flowers, the flag, Evelyn blessing the coffin, they were for show. Behind the scenes, security had been tightened to ensure there weren't any protests. Attendees had been vetted and coached so that there would be no outbursts of emotion. (A few tears were acceptable but no outbreaks of real lament) Even the eulogy had been written to make the deceased sound as vibrant and colourful as dishwater. That was Evelyn's stated objective, so what could be important enough for Davina Warren, of all people, to disrupt it in such a dramatic way?

Looking around for signs of calamity, all Monika saw was the metro police dispersing bystanders. She looked up at the large screens set up to televise the event, they were blank. Nothing was happening outside and there was no way to know what was going on inside. The only explanation was Evelyn's black stretch limo.

As Davina climbed inside, the guard standing next to the back door opened it and indicated that she should get in. Evelyn sat in the far corner, eyes narrowed, lips pressed tight, with her chin resting on her walking stick so that Monika was struck by the resemblance between the woman's profile and that of the lioness' head.

Catherine took the seat opposite Evelyn, facing Monika. She'd regained her composure, but Monika'd seen her rival's face turn ashen as the guards grabbed her by the elbow and pulled her out of the pew. For the briefest of moments, Monika saw something in Catherine. Was it fear or guilt? Whatever had shaken her rival, was now hidden behind her mask of inscrutability. It was a talent that worked for and against Catherine. That cool aloofness that she exhibited in person melted when in front of the cameras, making her, paradoxically, seem open and approachable to the general public but closed and sphinx-like to those who worked with her. It seemed that only the public, the cameras and her wife were capable of drawing warmth from this woman. So what was it that Evelyn saw in her?

And Gloria, poor Gloria, sitting across from Monika. She'd nearly fainted as they pulled her from the pew. Two guards, one on either side, had carried her past the shocked onlookers. Her hands were no longer shaking but she surreptitiously twisted the ring on her finger. Was it Rose, the missing fourth, that Gloria was worried about or was it something more personal? Gloria was the peacekeeper and had been a long-time supporter of Evelyn's. She'd always been the one who acted as a go-between when there was dissension in the ranks. But, she, along with Rose had been truly shaken at the news of Dorothy's death. Was it because of friendship or was there more to that relationship than Monika realised?

And what of Rose? The missing person. The usher had said that Ms Walsh wouldn't be coming so whatever happened, there'd been time to change the seating arrangements. Once again Monika thought of the woman being escorted away.

That's when it occurred to Monika that the disruption to the service might have more to do with who was not there than who was. She replayed the faces she'd made eye contact with. Steph's pew was missing Catherine's wife, but now that she thought about it, neither was Geraldine Williams, Catherine's mother. Had she been invited? Was she the woman stopped and removed? Was that why Catherine looked scared? Continuing with her mental list, Monika checked off the individuals in attendance and realised who else was missing. Joan. Where was Joan Symonds, editor-in-chief of the DailyNewsFeed? If she was the mystery woman, then she was the one who needed to be concerned.

The limo, speeding down a side street, hit a speed bump that bounced them off their seats. Monika recalled a similar ride in this same limo. That time, she'd been sitting next to her father, the Prime Minister while her fiance, Tom, sat across from her. They were at a rally when someone threw a beer bottle. It exploded as it hit the stage and from everywhere and nowhere, security officers appeared and hustled all of them into this car. Originally made for the American President's visit, its windows were bullet-proof and the chassis was reinforced steel that could withstand a bomb blast. Her father often quipped that it was a tank disguised as a car but that didn't stop him from appropriating it for himself once the visit was over.

Thinking of Tom, her fiancé and her father's most senior advisor, Monika realised who else was missing. She hadn't seen Jennifer Connors in the cathedral. Had Monika failed to see the woman who served as chief advisor to both her and Catherine? That was a real possibility because Jenny had a talent for remaining inconspicuous even when she was standing in plain sight.

The limo drove through the quiet leafy suburb of Kew and pulled up in front of Evelyn's house. Built as a single-story structure with a smooth facade of sandstone and timber, it lacked the grandeur of Evelyn's former home in Toorak. Monika thought it ironic that the old house in Toorak served as the Infrastructure Minister's residence because rather than symbolising the future, it epitomised the past.

Well, won't be home for long, she thought. After the election, Catherine can move in because I'll be moving to Government House.

As for this modern house that Evelyn occupied, it would have its own history. It would always be the residence of the Greater Republic of Melbourne's first Premier and after she passed away, it would become a library dedicated to preserving her memory. It was fitting that the house Evelyn called home epitomised the 21st century because, love her or hate her, she was the one who'd kept it alive.

Davina helped the elderly Perkins out of the car and shut the door.

It was a clear signal for the other occupants to remain where they were. Out of earshot, Davina bent down to speak into Evelyn's ear. They conversed for a minute, then as Evelyn went inside, Monika thought they might be taken to their own homes, but instead, Davina returned and ordered everyone to come inside.

Unlike their exit from the cathedral, this time they were calmly ushered through the marble foyer and into the formal sitting room by Evelyn's housekeeper. The oversized entry doors opened to reveal soaring ceilings that gave the foyer a sense of grandeur that led into the formal sitting room with its wall of windows that looked out on the expansive gardens. Monika had been to this house so many times that she knew it as well as her own. During the early days of the Transition, she'd even lived here. Like so many women of her generation, the world she knew had been shattered and this house had been her sanctuary and Evelyn her family. But today instead of feeling warm and welcoming, it felt foreign and intimidating.

The presence of Davina standing in the doorway instructing a guard only added to Monika's unease. Things had changed between her and Evelyn and as she took a seat in her favourite winged back chair, she wondered when things had started falling apart. Evelyn introducing Catherine into the inner circle had widened the wedge but now that she was back in her old haunt, she realised the distance between them had been growing for some time. It dated back to the growing faction within the NOP itself. Outwardly, Monika had remained in Evelyn's camp supporting the increased restrictions on males, but inwardly, she had concerns, and privately, she'd shared them with Dorothy and Steph. They all shared a common interest in 'boys'. Not that Monika preferred young males. It was that they were the only males available. Dorothy, recognising her desires, had invited Monika to some of her less outrageous parties and encouraged her heterosexuality. This did not go unnoticed by her mentor and Evelyn had even warned her about public displays of affection towards the opposite sex. 'Matched' relationships, according to Evelyn, were essential to the stability of the Republic.

Unfortunately, sexual preferences weren't as easy for Monika to switch as political agendas. By way of compromise, Monika retained discreet relationships with 'toy' boys and had, at Evelyn's urging, announced her engagement. Her choice of partner, Stephanie Steele, however, hadn't met with Evelyn's approval. Aside from her predilection for male company, Steph needed the cheap, expendable labour they provided. The question foremost in Monika's mind at this moment, however, was not whether Evelyn approved or disapproved of Steph. It was whether Evelyn knew that she'd quizzed both Joan and Steph about the night Dorothy Anderson was murdered. And worse yet, did Evelyn know that Steph proposed that Monika split from the NOP?

At the sound of Davina's voice, Monika started from her reverie.

"Evelyn would like to speak to you in her study."

Standing slowly, she straightened her back, raised her chin defiantly and walked past the guard who stood ready to escort her. As she turned her back on the others, she heard Davina say to Gloria, "Ms Fenton, you're free to go. One of my officers will make sure you get home safely."

Catherine asked, "And what about me? Am I free to go?"

Monika paused to hear the answer, but the guard opened the door to Evelyn's study, and she had no choice but to step inside.

Unlike the sitting room, Evelyn's study had an intimate, enclosed feel. The ceilings were lower and the walls were lined with bookshelves except for the one behind Evelyn's desk. That was filled with photos. Every aspect of the room had been designed so that visitors focused on the massive desk and its diminutive occupant.

Monika waited uneasily by the door as it closed noiselessly behind her. She was loath to approach without some signal from the grand old lady and so she stood observing the woman who studiously ignored her. It was a game Monika recognised. Evelyn employed it to put her opponents off-guard. So what was Evelyn after this time?

Without looking up, Evelyn motioned for Monika to take a seat. Dutifully she sat and waited while Evelyn continued to read the single sheet of paper in front of her. The minutes ticked by and the silence was starting to wear on her. She squirmed in the chair and Evelyn immediately looked up, pinning her in place with her stare. In her head, Monika could hear Steph's voice saying, "Why didn't you just demand to know what she wanted?" It was hard to explain to her fiancé how she felt in Evelyn's presence.

"I suppose you want to know what's going on."

Several responses jostled inside Monika's head, but before she could respond, Evelyn spoke again.

"It seems that I was right about someone in our group talking out of turn."

There was a warning in the directness of Evelyn's tone and it sent the obedient Monika scurrying for answers to questions that had yet to be raised.

"I don't know what anyone's said but I can assure you—"

"I thought I told you to keep an eye on Jenny Connors."

The accusation Evelyn thrust at her, stopped her in her tracks, and she stuttered, "I..I have been but you asked me to assign her to Catherine. Why aren't you asking Catherine what her staffer has been up to?"

"When's the last time you talked to Ms Connors?"

"A couple of days ago, I suppose." Monika wasn't sure what transgression Jenny was being accused of but gathering her thoughts, she explained, "Evelyn, we've all been focused on the fires. I assumed Jenny was assisting Catherine so, no, I haven't spoken to her in days. Has she said something to the press? Is that what all this is about?"

Evelyn glared for an uncomfortable length of time. It was a trick her mentor employed to elicit confessions but now Monika was outraged and refused to succumb. If Jenny had leaked anything confidential then it came from Catherine. She was the one who should be under interrogation and Monika was about to point that out when Evelyn humphed. She picked up the paper she'd been reading and held it out so Monika had to stand up and step forward to retrieve it.

As she absorbed its contents, Evelyn said, "That was broadcast live on every station. They broke into the memorial service."

Monika hurriedly scanned the rest of the document. It asked what Evelyn was hiding and why she lied about the details of Dorothy Anderson's murder. Monika replayed the scene by her pool when she'd asked these same questions of Steph. The image of her houseboy, Daniel, standing behind her as he delivered the drinks recalled Steph's question about whether he could be trusted. She looked at Evelyn for some sign that she was being accused of leaking information but Evelyn wasn't accusing her. She was asking about Jenny. Relieved and wary, Monika decided to shift the conversation from the source of the leak to the way it was delivered.

"How did they manage to break into the broadcast?"

"The same way we sent out that message from Catalyst for Change to spark that demonstration. Only they hacked into the Emergency warning system. They used our ploy against us."

"But Jenny isn't involved in systems security. That's under –"

Evelyn banged the table with her fist.

"What Jenny is involved in is much bigger than some publicity stunt. Davina has elicited information from one of those dissidents we picked up. It seems she didn't have names but she knew that several of their leadership were high up in my government."

"Is that why Rose wasn't at the service?"

"Rose has never fully supported my policies. Davina has detained her for questioning but she also sent out officers to pick up other likely suspects. Everyone was at home except Jenny and as you probably noticed, she wasn't at the service either."

Monika started putting together a series of missing persons. First, it was that girl who announced the closure of the lab. Then it was Dr Harris' son, followed by his mother. What they all had in common was proximity to Jenny and now Jenny was missing. Was that what Evelyn was concerned about or like Evelyn's explanation of Dorothy's murder, was something crucial being left out? She reread the bulletin looking for clues.

Evelyn dismissed it as propaganda, but what if the Subversives had something truly damaging? Once again, she thought of Joan and wondered if her reporter had uncovered something more damaging than Evelyn covering up Dorothy's indiscretions.

"So what do we do now? How do you want to address this in the press?"

"A flat-out denial, of course."

Monika placed the paper back on Evelyn's desk, her mind already calculating how she could turn this day to her advantage when Evelyn spoke.

"But someone's going to have to take the fall I'm afraid."

"What do you mean?"

"We'll publicly announce that Jenny Connors, as a disgruntled dissident working within our ranks, was responsible for this salacious piece of gossip. We'll state that it was meant to undermine the stability of this government in order to further her own deviant cause. Unfortunately, someone in government, her superior, for example, will also need to take responsibility."

Monika, who earlier had felt Evelyn deserting her, now felt vindicated. Of course, the inexperienced Catherine, whose mother ran Gentec and was disgruntled about her lab being shut down, was the perfect scapegoat. As for admonishing Monika for not keeping a closer eye on Jenny, Evelyn was giving her another one of her lessons. Well, point taken. Which explained why Evelyn called her into her office. As leader of the NOP, it was Monika's job to administer the punishment. Whether Evelyn wanted Monika to kick Catherine out of the party or merely relegate her to the back bench was a decision Evelyn would make, but either way, Monika would enjoy delivering the message.

Putting on her business face, she asked, "So you want me to tell Catherine she's moving to the back bench?"

"Not Catherine."

Monika felt the earth shift under her.

"Jenny was only assigned to Catherine temporarily," said Evelyn. "No, Monika dear, I'm asking you for your public resignation."

The revelation caught Monika unaware.

"Me? But I've toed the line on everything you asked. I was next in line after Dorothy. You can't just—"

"I am. But because you have been loyal and hard-working and because I see you as a kind of daughter to me, I'm going to tell you why you're going to let Catherine run in your place on the NOP ticket."

Evelyn stood and walked slowly around the desk. She leaned against it as she faced Monika.

"It's the company you keep, male and female. Oh, I know some of it is my fault. I indulged you by turning a blind eye to those boys you kept. I understood that it was a failure of your generation. I was also aware that Dorothy wooed you. Did you think I didn't know that she was planning to reverse my restrictions once she came into office? And as for your darling friend Steph, she needs boys as slave labour to increase her profits. If she hasn't already poisoned your mind, she will in time. As long as there are boys, they will be exploited and there will be dissidents demanding we spend resources on finding a cure. No, Monika, I can't let these narrow worldviews undermine all my hard work. The world I have striven to create, a world in which women control their own destinies, has no place for males—not as workers, not as playthings and certainly not as citizens. As long as there's a male alive, they're a threat."

As Evelyn spoke, her demeanour, while remaining outwardly calm, had an undercurrent that became more and more virulent. Monika'd seen Evelyn frustrated. She'd even seen bursts of anger but she'd never seen such hostile determination. There was a hint of madness in the woman's words that terrified Monika.

Looking even older than her 80 years, Evelyn waved her hand and said, "Now get out. Davina will see that you get home and I expect your letter of resignation by tomorrow morning."

Holding back her rage, Monika stood up. Whatever warmth she'd once felt for Evelyn was gone.

"And if I don't resign?"

Returning to her place behind the desk, Evelyn picked up her stick and banged it sharply on the floor three times. The door opened and Evelyn said to the guard, "Take Ms Thomas home and ask Davina to show Ms Williams in."

CHAPTER 20
PATRICIA

FRIDAY 10 DECEMBER 2049 - 1:00 P.M.

Expectations are funny things, thought Patricia. *You only consider them when they fall short.*

And to say that the four musketeer's childhood clubhouse failed to meet Patricia's expectations was an understatement.

Penny seemed to be of the same opinion.

"This is it?"

Patricia stared at the hand-drawn map in Penny's hand and then at the stop light on the corner and the bus stop.

"This is it alright."

"I've been to some shitholes but nothing like this."

Patricia had her doubts, too, but they were out of options. It was only a matter of time before someone figured out that the body in the self-drive wasn't her and as the adrenalin wore off, the excruciating pain of her burns was likely to rival the pain in her heart. The only thing driving her now was survival and a burning desire for revenge.

Penny wavered and Patricia figured her friend was desperately searching her brain for an alternative. That was understandable. The place looked like it had been abandoned even before the Desolation.

As if to confirm that suspicion, or perhaps to procrastinate a little longer, Penny fingered the torn and peeling edges of a poster plastered to the weathered plywood. Like an archaeologist, she carefully teased off a piece of the top layer.

"We don't have time for that," said Patricia.

Penny ignored her and teased off another strip. The more Penny exposed the layer underneath, the more Patricia too became interested. Pain and anxiety took a back seat to curiosity, or maybe they were both delaying that moment when they had to face the deserted interior of this building.

"What do you think this place used to be," asked Penny, wiping a scrap of paper she'd removed against her pants.

"Who knows? A shop of some kind, I suppose."

Having gotten a foothold, so to speak, Penny pulled away a larger strip of paper exposing more of the layer underneath. The top layer promoting the Transition era slogan, Stability to Rebuild, was reluctantly giving way to the poster from the past.

Patricia's excitement grew as Penny uncovered more and more of the forgotten era. The bland top layer had preserved the vibrant colours underneath. A shadowy hand on a blue windshield.

Patricia, recognising the image exclaimed, "I remember that album. The band was called 9-inch something."

Inspired, Penny pulled away another strip of paper exposing the word Year and the letter Z.

"Now, I remember. Nine Inch Nails and the album was—"

"I wasn't into bands," said Penny.

While Patricia struggled to remember the name of the album, Penny moved towards the padlocked door to study a phrase that had been stencilled onto it. The once red paint had faded to an almost illegible pink and Penny wiped at the surface.

She studied it for a moment.

"When All Hope Is Lost. Pray to—"

"Zero," said Patricia. "Year Zero."

Penny gave her a quizzical look.

"Pray to Year Zero?"

"No, the album was Year Zero."

Joining Penny at the door, she read the stencil and her exuberance over the past evaporated.

"It says, pray to the dead."

It was a saying that had been plastered all over town at the height of the pandemic and it wasn't that long ago that she and her mother had talked about what it might have meant. After today's explosion, however, the phrase took on new meaning. She ran her fingers over the rough wood with its fading red paint. She needed time to process but not now. Not here in public view.

As if sensing Patricia's grief welling up, Penny said, "We need to get off the street before someone notices your hands. How do we get into this dump?"

"Karen said that the entrance was around the back."

Penny took her friend's arm and pulled her away from the door.

As they walked down the side of the building they passed a window that sat barely above ground level. Patricia imagined Karen and her friends discovering this place. They must have dashed down this shadowy passageway, excited at the prospect of claiming a space that belonged only to them. Which one of them, she wondered, had been game enough to explore this derelict building first? Had it been Josh, the quiet sensitive reader in the group. Or perhaps it had been the boy Zane. Karen said he was braver than the rest of them. Or was it Benny? She hadn't met the boy who started this chain of events but she didn't think so. Perhaps it had been Karen. The one with the deep blue eyes that reminded Patricia of someone else who had those same blue eyes. Was Karen the real leader of their group? Girls had a habit of taking the lead these days but when these four were kids, things had been different. Before Selection, there was still that sense that boys were the adventurers and girls were the followers.

Like her memories, Patricia picked her way around bits of trash, mindful that it was important for them to maintain their silence. Out front, they'd been indiscreet, but that slogan reminded her of the danger they were in, so when Penny accidentally kicked a can, she shushed her as if they were thieves executing a break-in. This reversal of roles did not go unnoticed by either of them. At some point, the balance in their relationship had shifted. Instead of Penny taking the lead, it was Patricia calling the shots.

When they found the steps leading down Patricia halted and studied the back of the building. Up a set of stairs, there was a back door, but it was barred and locked. The only viable option was the door at the bottom of the cement steps that led down to a basement. Penny looked doubtful, but Patricia figured they'd come this far, so she decided to take the plunge. Shielding her red and swollen hand, she used her shoulder to shove against the door. Unlatched it swung inward slightly until it caught on some debris. Something inside scuttled and Penny had heard it too. It was followed by a whimper soft as a kitten mewling. Bolstering her courage, Patricia took a step back, then, using her foot, landed a hard kick square at the centre. The door flew open.

Patricia had no idea what she expected to find but it certainly wasn't what she saw half hidden in the dim light. Stepping forward, she moved towards the couch, but before she cleared the door, she heard Penny yell, "Look out!".

The warning came too late. Something heavy hit her shoulders and Patricia crashed to the floor.

CHAPTER 21
INVERLOCH

FRIDAY 10 DECEMBER 2049 - 1:00 P.M.

"What do you mean he's not going to die?" Jack was still hostile, but Benny's disclosure distracted him from throwing that first punch. "Everyone dies."

"But not like us," insisted Benny. Jack hesitated but Benny could see that the wiry lancer was still less intent on understanding than sorting things out physically, so he moved closer to Steve. He stood shoulder to shoulder with his companion and used his hand to call attention to Steve's face and then his own, but Jack continued to look confused. Exasperated, Benny said, "Can't you see the difference? Look at him. He's not 18 or 19. He's older than that."

Benny paused expectantly. Jack wasn't backing down, but he was considering the possibility, so Benny gave another shove.

"You see it, now, don't you? He's 25, Jack. Think what that means."

Steve and Jack were still eyeing each other like tom cats with their backs arched, and their fur fluffed out, but Benny could feel a shift. What he needed to get through to Jack was what Steve had come to represent. Steve was protective, informative, and a tutor. More importantly, he represented what males no longer had, a father figure.

Travelling with Steve had opened Benny's eyes. He'd taught Benny not only how to survive but how to live. In Melbourne, life had been comfortable, and he'd learned to manipulate the system, but if Monika had taught him anything, it was that his life was not under his control. And Inverloch, even though the rules and the daily routines differed, there was security in the sense that it was a world Benny understood. But that was the problem. His life was too predictable, too secure and so were the lives of all males. Lancers, studs, grunts, floorboys, and even the no-gos all lived lives that were predetermined by others. Whether it was Melbourne's Selection test or Inverloch's initiation ceremony, boy's lives were determined for them. And why? Because it didn't matter what route they took, they were all destined to die by the time they were 20. That was fact. But StevSteve'sstence proved that the impossible was possible and that breaking free, while scary, was also addictive.

Steve had freed himself from bondage and that changed his perspective. True, he was going to die but the difference was that he didn't know how or when. He might die here in a fight between himself and Jack or he might live to 100. Fate could step in at any moment and it was that sense of uncertainty that Benny longed to feel for himself. Even living it vicariously through Steve was better than facing the inevitable pointlessness of his existence. The question was how to get this through to Jack.

"Steve says there are others like him, men who live normal life spans. He says they're held in a prison on French Island."

Benny saw a flicker of interest.

"This true Steve?" Jack wasn't convinced but he was listening.

For his part, Steve was still tense but he acknowledged Jack's query.

"Yeah, it's true. I escaped with another survivor, my mate Matt. He didn't make it but I was rescued by the Subversives. You, Bulldog and that girl Cherry were supposed to take me to Warragul for safekeeping."

"And that's why the Melbourne government wants him," said Benny. "It's not because he murdered the Premier. It's because he's a survivor. And it also explains why he couldn't be the murderer. See, he was busy escaping from French Island on Saturday night, and that's when she was murdered in her yacht on the Mornington Peninsula."

Jack turned to Benny. "What do you mean Saturday night? They said she was murdered on Sunday."

"But that's just it," replied Benny. "I overheard Evelyn Perkins herself say that the Premier wasn't murdered on Sunday night. She was murdered on Saturday night and they—"

He stopped because all of a sudden, everything fell into place. Steve changing the subject when he talked about his escape. The concern about running into anyone from Melbourne. His eagerness to get out of Inverloch. He glanced over at Steve and instantly confirmed his suspicion. Evelyn Perkins hadn't only changed the date the Premier was murdered, she'd changed the location. The Premier was murdered on the beach at French Island.

Recovering his composure Benny said, "So it couldn't have been him." He glanced from the lancer to Steve. At least one of them was falling for his story.

"And how do you know all this?" asked Jack.

Benny felt the colour rising up his neck, partly because he had to expose himself and partly because he needed to lie to keep from exposing his friend.

"I was Monika Thomas' personal stud. I overheard a meeting they had on Sunday morning when Evelyn Perkins told her that the Premier had been murdered. Steve was in the hands of the smugglers by then so if you don't believe me then go ask them."

Scratching his chin, Jack considered Benny's account. Then, turning to Steve, he said, "If what this kid says is true, I guess that gets you off the hook, but to be straight, I'm not convinced you two haven't cooked up this story. And if it's true that you got some kind of immunity then I reckon the head woman'll want to meet you.

Jack stood his ground but Benny could see he was thinking. Finally, the lancer spoke, "I'll take your story at face value for now. But I tell you this, if I find that you had anything to do with Cherry's abduction, it won't matter if the head woman wants to know about your immunity or if she wants to punish you for the crime of killing a woman. By the time I finish with you, there won't be anything left."

Steve hesitated. Benny could see that something was troubling his friend, and for a moment, he wondered if Steve was going to confess, but instead, Steve said, "If you want to get Cherry back, you're going to have to go up against the Republic. Do you think you can do that by yourself? Even if you convince your mates here to join you or those lancers gathering at San Remo, you don't stand a chance."

"Spoken like someone trying to protect himself."

"Maybe," said Steve. "Or maybe someone with a better plan."

"I'm listening."

"The prison on French Island has a group of men older than me. I've only been there for the last five years but there are others who've been there since the Desolation. They're at least forty-five. Hell, some of them are over sixty. And you think your head lady wants to know about immunity? Well, so do the researchers at the prison. They say they're looking for a cure but then why're they holding us prisoner? I can't tell you what, if anything, French Island has to do with Cherry but I can tell you that someone pretty important wants to make sure that no one knows about the survivors on that island."

Anger gave way to incredulity and Jack said, "Why would the government want to hide the fact that it was possible to survive?"

"Because they want you to accept that you're inferior. I think that whoever is in charge of that prison doesn't want you to find out because if you did, you wouldn't slink off to the wilds. You'd demand to know about a cure. You might even stand up and fight for your right to live."

Before Jack had arrived, Steve had been looking at Benny with a mixture of sympathy and compassion but now he was fired up and that righteous indignation was invigorating. It spread to Benny and he could see that it was starting to infect Jack as well. The fear. The injustice. The realisation that he could, no, that they, as a group, could do something about it, took shape in his head as Steve continued.

"You should be storming that prison and releasing those men. And while you're at it, you should find out what those women in white coats, the ones that run that place, have been up to. They're the ones who have the answers to the questions you should be asking."

With each statement, Steve was moving forward, pressing Jack back.

"Instead of running off to some trumped-up lancer council in San Remo, you should be filling up boatloads of lancers and heading to French Island."

This last statement hit a nerve and the lancer stood his ground. Concern marked his features.

"What do you mean, trumped-up council?"

"Isn't it obvious? Who is your leader?"

"What do you mean? We don't have a leader. Why would we—"

"So who called this council? Who printed those flyers that are showing up everywhere?"

"Do you think we're incapable of organising—"

Jack was firing up again but so was Steve.

"When's the last time a council was held?"

Those words were a bucket of cold water on Jack's fire. He shook his head as if trying to shake off its effect.

"This is the first time, isn't it?"

The truth of what Steve was saying was starting to get through to Jack.

"Yeah, I can see it clearly now," said Steve. "I'll bet you all got excited about the idea of a lancer council. Get together. Compare notes. Maybe party a bit. Think about it. Head to San Remo and you're doing exactly what they want you to do."

Benny saw Jack connecting the dots. Suddenly, it didn't matter, at least not to Benny, whether Steve killed the Premier or not, the real crime was what was happening to them. That's what had been bothering Steve about the flyer and its message. As for this place, Inverloch, with its head woman controlling everything, there was something still in the shadows. They had their rules but all women had their rules. No there was something else. And this business of Cherry's abduction. Did it matter if her abduction was related to Steve's escape or not? What really mattered was whether they accepted their lot in life or, as Steve suggested, they fight back.

Jack must have been thinking along the same lines because he said, "You think they're herding us into San Remo."

"Like sheep to the slaughter," said Steve.

Jack looked out at the water as if searching for something, then with sudden clarity, he said, "San Remo's this narrow inlet with a bridge to Phillip Island. They herd us onto the island.—"

"Burn your boats," added Steve.

Then Benny completed the image by saying, "It's another prison."

Jack had grasped the situation but he still struggled to accept it.

"But why bother? We're as good as dead."

"That's a very good question but the answer lies on French Island, not San Remo."

CHAPTER 22
THE OLD ONE'S CABIN

SEPTEMBER 2069

The Old One barely finished the sentence when the cough returned with a vengeance. Doubled over, the elder fought to catch a breath and the girl panicked. There was no cough syrup left so she rushed into the bedroom and searched for the puffer. Not finding it on the table, she dropped to the floor. Frantically, she searched around the side table and under the bed.

She felt around between the bed and table, and at last, her fingers felt the small, cylindrical object she needed. Grasping it with her fingers, she rushed back to where the Old One sat coughing uncontrollably and shoved the inhaler up to lips that had gone blue.

The jagged gasps slowed, and the Old One leaned back in the wheelchair, pushing the puffer away.

"A glass of water is all I need now."

As the girl returned with the water she wondered about French Island. As far as she knew, it was nothing more than a large empty land mass off the coast of Victoria. She'd heard Tanya ask Jocelyn about it but Philippa caught her eavesdropping and pulled her away before she heard Jocelyn's answer. As for Patricia Bishop, the reporter, never mentioned going there in her book on the war years.

The Old One held the glass out.

"It's getting late and there's still more you need to hear from me before you leave Warragul and put your mind in the hands of those--. Never mind. Sit."

EVELYN

FRIDAY 10 DECEMBER 2049 - 6:00 P.M.

Davina stepped into the room and looked at the chair that had recently witnessed Monika's demise. Over the years, it had witnessed a number of disappointed occupants. In Evelyn's former residence, the house in Toorak, the last remaining male leaders had sat in that chair as Evelyn told them, one by one that going to the bunker was not a matter of choice. Nor were they given the opportunity to say good bye to their families. They were shuffled in, one by one, given their directive and taken away. Councillors who were too vocal in their dissent, newsfeed editors that didn't comply, anyone who needed to be pulled into line, was introduced to the chair. It witnessed ultimatums and directives as well as praise and sometimes it witnessed the last time the person who sat there was seen.

"Do I need to allocate more security?" asked Davina.

"On Monika?"

Evelyn considered the question. She fingered a large manila envelope and said, "No, I think she'll be fine once she gets her anger under control. Her ego's wounded because I've chosen to back Catherine but if there's one thing I know about Monika, it's that for all her outward confidence, she's a follower. She'll fall back into line if for no other reason than to trip up Catherine."

Then looking up, she said with greater interest, "And speaking of Catherine, how did you go removing that little stumbling block?"

"I'm told she climbed in the car, meek as a lamb."

"Good then see that Catherine gets home safely."

"And if she says she needs to search for her wife?"

"Tell her that when the guards went round to check, they saw her wife leaving with a bag. Offer your assistance but I don't think it will take much convincing for her to think her wife's left her. Monika's fiance is more of a challenge."

Davina detected that look in Evelyn's eye that indicated she had a new task in mind.

"Stephanie Steele will need to be dealt with using a carrot rather than a stick."

That was the way they communicated. Evelyn spoke her thoughts out loud and Davina listened.

"I don't suppose you've been able to infiltrate her household?"

Davina stepped farther into the room.

"Not as yet."

"That is unfortunate because Monika will run to her for guidance and we need to nip that dependency in the bud."

Sensing a new assignment, Davina took the chair and moved it closer to the desk. She didn't ask permission. She didn't need to. Others might be brought into Evelyn'Unlike Monika, she knew exactly where she stood with Evelyn.

Evelyn's sphere, used, then discarded but their relationship was much closer.

"Do you want her brought in for questioning?"

"No I don't think that would help our cause. She's too prominent and has too many supporters in the business sector. No, we need to either discredit her or bring her into our sphere of influence."

Davina picked up the letter opener that sat on the desk and fingered it. She read the date she'd had engraved on it. 01/27/2032.

"You know she's opposed to eliminating males. Aside from her personal preferences, she needs the cheap labour."

"Which is why we must find a way to give her what she wants without compromising our long term objectives."

Davina considered the word compromise as she pressed the sharp tip of the sword shaped opener against the soft mound of flesh on her palm. Exerting enough pressure to dent but not penetrate she watched as her skin yielded under pressure.

"Are you thinking of letting her keep the boys registered to her work sites?"

Evelyn looked across the desk and seemed to take an equal interest in the actions of the letter opener.

Then she replied, "The colonies supply us with food do they not?"

"That they do."

"Then I'm afraid we are in the same boat as Stephanie. Until we can produce machinery that reduces the labour load, we need boys in the country working on farms. Sometimes it's good to have something in common with your enemy, is it not?"

Davina released the pressure on the opener. Her flesh sprung back but the letter opener left a mark. She balanced the tip against the index finger of her other hand.

"Would you like me to offer some kind of peace offering?"

"I think we need to make a concession of some sort. Something where both parties benefit." She paused, then quickly added, "What's of the utmost importance, is that we stick to the requirement that all males get tested. That way the special ones, the element x ones, can be located and eliminated from the gene pool."

Davina stared at Evelyn over the top of the letter opener.

"And how do we control the fertilisation process in the colonies to ensure that no undesirables slip through."

Davina spat out the word 'undesirables' as she tossed the letter opener back on the desk.

Evelyn noted the action, ignored it and continued unfazed.

"We sterilise those who don't qualify and contain those who do. Our breeding stock only needs to be large enough to maintain genetic diversity."

"And where do we contain our breeding stock so they don't escape back into the general population?"

"I was thinking we might utilise the facilities on French Island."

At the mention of the internment camp Davina hoped Evelyn hadn't picked up on her discomfort but soon realised she had.

"I'm sure enough time has passed that you no longer harbour resentments about our last experiment."

"It's not that," said Davina, perhaps a bit to quickly so she paused before adding, "That escape last week is what concerns me. If it happened once, --"

"It could happen again." Evelyn finished the sentence, then sighed. "The men in that camp were trained in the military. The boys we'll be sending there will be less, shall we say, proficient."

"One of our escapees was untrained."

"Yes, but he escaped with the help of a trained SAS individual. I think we can ensure that doesn't happen again."

Davina didn't need Evelyn to spell it out.

"You want the current camp wiped out."

"Yes, I think it's time to start over, don't you?"

"And the researchers?"

"I'm afraid there's going to be another fire," said Evelyn.

A smile, barely perceptible, played on Davina's lips.

"I think that can be arranged. "

Evelyn nodded and leaned back in her chair.

"As for Stephanie and her compatriots, they can have their supply of workers for say the next decade. That should give them time to clear the areas slated for demolition but going forward I want women picking up the slack. That's my compromise. Can you make sure she receives it?"

"I can give her your offer but what if she doesn't accept?"

"Stephanie is a reasonable woman. Tell her that if she doesn't agree, then there may be more unfortunate fires. Only they won't be in areas that she wants demolished."

Davina stood up but as she walked towards the door, Evelyn asked, "And speaking of bringing everyone into line, how are we going with the Eastern colonies?"

"A number of lancer colonies have joined the San Remo enclave."

"But not all."

"Lancer colonies are no longer a threat and most of the wilding communities have agreed to our offer of protection. It's colonies like Warragul and Inverloch that we need to bring to heel but we'rworking on it."

"Perhaps we need to use the same tactic that we plan to use on Stephanie."

"You want to start fires in the farming regions. That's a bit dangerous, especially at this time of year."

"No, I'm thinking of starting a different kind of fire. I think it's time for the lancers to retaliate against the wilding women attacking their colonies."

It took Davina a moment to comprehend what Evelyn was suggesting.

"You're referring to Bunyip."

"Evelyn dumped the contents of the envelope on her desk. A jumble of dog tags and I.D.s spilled out.

"Perhaps it's time a few lancers headed somewhere other than San Remo. Didn't saere was a boy from Inverloch asking about your daughter?"

"You want me to make sure he goes to Bunyip."

It was a statement.

"Fear is a great incentive but like fire, it must be fed."

"That will likely work with Warragul but Inverloch is different."

Evelyn swiped the dog tags into the bin.

"I'll deal with Inverloch personally."

CHAPTER 23
JOSH

FRIDAY 10 DECEMBER 2049 - 3:00 P.M.

"How long we gonna keep goin'?"

The kid had a point. They'd been walking for hours and the heat and fatigue were getting to Josh as well.

"We'll find a spot," he said begrudging the energy required to respond.

"I gotta rest," whinged the boy as he whipped off another layer.

Josh wasn't sure how many layers the boy wore but he had been stripping pieces off every kilometre or so as the heat increased. Not that anything the kid wore was a whole garment. As for how many layers were left, that was impossible to tell. No matter how many were discarded, there still seemed to be plenty left. Josh guessed that in Melbourne the boy kept everything he owned on his back, picking up bits and pieces like a hermit crab, as he wound his way through the urban laneways. Out here on the highway, however, as the afternoon sun bore down, the burden of all those layers was harder to bear. And why not? There were no high rises blocking the sun. No tunnels to crawl in, to escape the heat. No breeze. No clouds. Just a searing white light that sucked up the sweat before it could cool the skin.

The boy pulled a bit of clothing up to cover his head and Josh felt a twinge of envy. Smelly and wretched as the kid's rags were, they provided protection from the sun whereas Josh's clothes; clean, well-made and lightweight, did little in that regard. He'd wrapped his windbreaker around his head to act as a sunshade but that left his arms exposed and they were now turning an ugly shade of red. And his t-shirt, soaked in sweat, proved irresistible to a hoard of flies that gathered on his back and buzzed incessantly while his sneakers transmitted the heat the road had absorbed. The overall effect was that of being slow-roasted in an oven. The kid was right, they needed to rest, but not out in the open.

Josh scoured their surroundings. The nearby fields of brown grass offered no shelter so shading his eyes, he scanned the horizon. About half a kilometre away, a line of trees stood on one side of the road as if waiting for the traffic to clear so they could cross. Except there was no traffic.

"There's shade ahead," he said. "Think you can make it?"

The kid stood beside him and stared in disbelief.

"I don't know."

"C'mon," said Josh, "we gotta keep moving," then realised he was trying to convince himself as much as the kid.

Shifting his pack he plodded forward, emptying his mind of everything except the will to get there. Rags, too, must have focused all his attention on placing one foot in front of the other because he ceased his grumbling and followed.

It was a short distance compared to how far they'd come and yet with each step, it seemed impossibly far away. By the time they'd covered about half the distance, Josh's body was crying out in protest and his pack felt like it was cutting into his shoulders. When they were close enough to smell the gum leaves, his mouth was hanging open from exhaustion. His tongue, dry from breathing in the hot air, scraped the inside of his parched mouth but he refused to stop and drink. Counting each step, even though he had no idea how many were required, helped him focus on his goal and his concentration became so intense that he wasn't even sure the boy was still tagging along behind him. A hint of a breeze spurred him on. There was one and only one objective and that was to get to the sanctuary of those overarching trees. So intent, was Josh on getting there that he almost didn't notice that he'd arrived. It was only when he realised that the quality of the light had changed and that the temperature had dropped that he stopped. Exhausted, he let the pack slip from his shoulders. Then as the boy joined him, he dropped to all fours.

When he and Karen had talked of running away to the Colony, he had no sense of how far away it was. It was a spot on a map with distances that meant nothing to him. Nor had their plans gotten far enough along to address issues of transportation. The vastness of Melbourne hadn't sunk in, never mind the expanse beyond its borders. Riding the train from the inner suburbs to the outer reaches of Melbourne had taken him and Rags hours. The walk from there to Warragul was likely to take days. And then there was the heat. He'd lived in a house where the temperature was controlled. Even on the warmest days when the reverse cycle air con failed to maintain a constant coolness, the leafy suburb he lived in had never reached these extremes.

Rags fell down next to him. Overhead, little green birds twittered and flitted from branch to branch. It was the first sign of life Josh had noticed, aside from the flies, since they left the train in Pakenham and started walking the M1. Come to think of it, it was the first sign of life he'd noticed since Patricia took him and his mother to the apartment in the old CBD. That area had appeared as devoid of life as this stretch of road until the fire forced its inhabitants to scurry from their nooks and crannies. Fingering the brown grass in front of him, he wondered what creatures would be flushed out if he were to set it alight.

"Where do you think they took everyone?"

"Don't know but one thing's for sure," Josh said sitting back on his heels and pulling a bottled water out of the pack, "They sure didn't bring them out here."

Rags held out his hand.

"I thought you said there was lancers out this way. How come we haven't come across any?"

Josh handed the bottle to Rags. Rags was the name he'd come up with for his companion because when he'd asked the kid for his name, the boy had said "Dunno. No one ever called me by a name. Not as I can remember, anyways."

Josh plumped the pack as best he could and rolled over onto his back, resting his head on it like a pillow. Rags took a long sip then said thoughtfully, "And if they were taking the lancers out of the city, why haven't we seen any sign of them?"

He wiped the lip of the bottle with his hand and gave it back to Josh.

"I don't know," replied Josh using his shirt to re-wipe the bottle. "Maybe they took them someplace farther away."

They passed the bottle a couple more times till there was only a bit left.

"You finish it," said Josh.

The boy downed the last few drops, banging the bottom to make sure he'd gotten every bit. Meanwhile, Josh stared at the leaves overhead and wondered what Karen was up to at this moment.

The boy rolled over onto his belly and crossed his arms to make his own pillow. Josh glanced over at him. The kid couldn't be more than 11 or 12. At the same age, Josh had been living at home with his mother and attending school. He'd been hanging out with his friends and although they'd sat the Selection test, the impact of that test hadn't been unknown. What he had known at that age was that he was already in love with Karen.

Rags, on the other hand, had been dumped. Not only by his mother but by society. While Josh had heard of 'lost boys' who lived on the streets, he'd never met one before. Setting thoughts of Karen aside, he said, "We'll walk a bit further and then call it a day. What d'you say to that?"

"Let's rest a bit longer," said the boy yawning. "My feet are killing me."

Lifting his head, Josh glanced at the boy's feet and noticed how red and swollen they looked. On the smooth city pavement, running barefoot had toughened up the soles of the boy's feet but his city callouses were no match for a hike on a burning highway.

"Next sign of a town, we'll detour and see if we can find you some shoes."

"Don't need 'em."

"But your feet are raw."

"They'll toughen up. Got any more food?"

"Just a protein bar that's about 10 years out of date."

"That'll do."

Josh hadn't asked the boy how he managed to live on the streets or even how long he'd been doing it rough. One minute the kid was 11 and the next he sounded like he was 50. Sitting up, Josh found the cellophane-wrapped bar and tossed it to Rags.

"If we find any abandoned houses, we can at least find you some clothes."

"These'll do."

The boy also sat up. Legs crossed he attacked the protein bar the way a dog might attack a bone.

"How'd you learn to get around so well," asked Josh. "I mean with the fire and the smoke, why didn't you panic like the others?"

Josh knew that by 'others', he was referring to himself because if it hadn't been for Rags, he would have either perished in the bfire or been captured.

The boy wasn't getting anywhere gnawing on the protein bar and decided to attack it from another angle. He grabbed the bar with two hands and tried to break off a piece as he replied, "Like them lancers, you mean?"

"Yeah, that's what I'm asking."

"You learn as you go. Like when I lived with some boys along the river. One night these rounders came."

"Rounders?" said Josh, not recognising the term.

"Yeah, women who round up boys livin' on the street. They take them to the labour camps. Ain't no way I was goin' there. I hid in a drain pipe til they left. After that, I stayed by meself. I learned they weren't interested in one boy. Groups was what they wanted. Pays better."

The bar refused to break. Frustrated the kid said, "Got any more water or somethin' I can soak this bar in?"

"We've only got one bottle left and that's got to last us until we get to Warragul."

"Warragul again." Rags tossed the bar away. "What's with you and this Warragul?"

Shocked more at the blasé way Rags tossed away the protein bar than his whinge about Warragul, Josh said, "Hey, that's all the food we've got."

"It may have been food at some point but it ain't food no more."

Josh considered retrieving the discarded bar but it was covered in dirt. He watched as ants scurried to claim it as there own. They sampled it with their feelers, then they too decided it was no longer edible and went on their way.

Having given up on food, Rags turned his attention to the area beyond the trees. The remains of a fence indicated that this area had once been inhabited.

"Hey, what's that?"

Josh looked in the direction Rags was pointing. "What? I don't see anything."

"There, that board lyin' on the ground. It looks like a sign maybe."

Josh stood up and that's when he spotted it as well.

"Don't know," he said, but it had piqued his curiosity too so he ambled over to where the board lay face down on the ground. Bending over, he reached to turn it over but Rags grabbed him and pulled him back.

"Not with your hands, stupid. Anythin' could be under there."

As Josh stood mystified, Rags looked around then spotting what he needed, grabbed a fallen branch.

"Let me show you."

Josh stood back as Rags moved a rock, then eased the branch over the rock and under the sign. Rags may not have gone to school but he understood how levers worked.

Watching with good-natured amusement, Josh walked over to help but jumped back as something scaley shot out from under the sign.

The kid laughed as a large lizard scuttled into the nearby scrub. "It's OK," he said, "Nothin' more than a blue tongue. Ain't poisonous but if it latches onto your finger, you'll never get it off. Now, help me turn this over."

The kid dished out the command like a foreman and Josh wondered again about the kid's life on the streets.

"Well?" asked Rags once they had the sign face up.

"It used to say Bunyip Native Sanctuary but someone's scratched out the word 'Native'," said Josh pointing at the red line drawn through the word. "And written 'lancer' instead."

Rags repeated the name, "Bunyip Lancer Sanctuary." Then pointing at the arrow on the bottom of the sign, he asked, "Think it means there's a road up ahead?"

"It's worth a look," replied Josh.

"So what are we waiting for? Let's go."

The kid was right. They needed a safe place to spend the night and what could be safer for a couple of boys on the run than a lancer community? And they could certainly do with some decent food and fresh water. Maybe even some clothes for Rags. And a shower. They could both use a shower. The more he thought of the plusses, the more he picked up on Rag's enthusiasm. If the kid, with his keen ability to survive, wasn't hesitating, then why should he?

Josh retrieved his pack, then took another look at the sign. What caught his eye wasn't the sign but its posts. They were jagged where they'd split but otherwise, they didn't look rotten.

Not that it mattered, how or why the sign had been knocked over. The main thing was that it told them there was a lancer colony nearby and thanks to Rags, they knew about it. All Josh had to do was catch up with the kid who was skipping down the road.

They found the entrance to the turnoff but only because they'd known to look for it. It was nothing more than a dirt road but it was one that was frequently used and not only by hikers such as themselves.

Rags pointed at the ruts in the dirt and said, "Looks like truck tracks. Think they bought some of us here."

Josh also studied the tracks. They hadn't seen any trucks on the M1 but that didn't mean that they hadn't come this way either last night or earlier this morning. Certainly, relocating lancers to the wilds made sense because their homes in the old CBD were now gone. And taking them to lancer communities sounded more compasionate than dumping them in the wilds.

"Damn. We coulda hitched a ride," said Rags kicking the dirt.

Josh thought about that. If they'd known that lancers were being taken to the border would they have been so keen to evade them? Then he remembered how the soldiers scanned everyone and reminded himself that he was on a wanted list.

Rag's pace slowed as the road wandered deeper into the bush. They had no idea how far the community was from the M1 and that had a sobering effect on both of them. That, and the silence. There were the usual sounds of birds and insects but what was missing was the sound of other humans. Still, walking was easier in the cool shade and on soft earth. And they had the expectation of a community of boys to revive their spirits.

Josh wondered how the lancers were likely to greet them. Would they welcome them or would they take one look at his clothes and know he was not one of them. If roles were reversed, like they were back in Melbourne, Josh knew that seeing someone like Rags in his neighbourhood would have been cause for concern. Instead of offering the kid assistance, Josh admitted to himself that he'd probably ignored the kid or worse he might have called the police.

Watching the kid leading the way, Josh thought about the kids life. Rags had evaded 'rounders' who would have sold him to the labour camps and had seen 'brownies' drag boys into buildings. He'd seen another kid jump to his death. Josh and his friends had played at being chased. They'd pretended to foil the plots of evil villains and were always victorious in their battles. They had dreamed of being heros but Rags made Josh realise that real-life heroism wasn't about glory. It was about survival. Josh had felt sorry for himself because the female students treated him, like any other no-go, with disdain but at least his life had been safe and comfortable. His thoughts turned to Zane. He turned his childhood heroism into something that was real. Zane had worked with the Subversives to save kids like Rags but he hadn't died heroically. It was almost comic. A comic-tragedy. Zane died because he'd been mistaken for Benny because he was caught riding the bike

Benny's mistress, (there was an outdated term) had gave him. And why did she want Benny dead? Was it really because Benny'd overheard some secret or was it because he'd had the effrontery to run away?

"I see it!"

Rags' exclamation startled Josh. Looking in the direction Rags pointed, he saw the tip of a tin roof. They were close now and Josh was relieved to think they would soon be in the company of others, introducing themselves, exchanging stories of their escape—

Rags noticed it too. Something was wrong. They were close enough that they should hear voices but there was nothing. Rags disappeared into a clump of bushes, leaving Josh standing alone on the road. He waited but Rags didn't return but he also didn't call out.

Confused Josh headed in the same direction only now he was paying close attention. There was a bend in the road next to the bushes Rags had scuttled through. Suddenly, Rags called out and Josh responded.

He dashed around the bend and stopped. He was in a deserted parking lot facing an entry gate that stood open. Walking through, he found himself looking at a variety of wooden buildings of various sizes and shapes. But the place was deserted.

"Rags!"

At first, there was no response, then he heard Rags say softly, "In here."

His voice came from inside the building they'd spotted with the peaked tin roof. It looked like a large house with a wide porch and a screen door. Above the door, a hand painted sign said Cafe but it didn't look like any Josh had seen before. The building, like the others in the clearing, looked hastily put together using odd bits of wood and corrugated iron.

As he walked towards the door, he heard a buzzing noise that intensified as he got closer. But when he opened the door, a sickening sweet odour overwhelmed him and he gagged. Holding his hand over his nose, he swallowed it down and waited for his eyes to adjust to the dim light. There in the centre of the room, stood Rags. He was staring at what appeared to be a pile of old clothes stacked up against the back wall. The pile was alive with flies.

Josh walked over to Rags and that's when he realised that it wasn't a pile of clothes.

Turning aside, he vomited.

"Oh my god!"

Wiping his mouth, Josh straightened up and looked in the direction of this new voice.

CHAPTER 24
DR HARRIS

FRIDAY 10 DECEMBER 2049 - 5:00 P.M.

Sofia suggested they take a walk, away from prying eyes and interested ears. Setting a brisk pace, she led Bonnie out the back door of the Arts Centre, where a tearful Kerry held the door open then closed it behind them. The crowd Sofia was avoiding was what was left of those who'd come for the trial. By Melbourne standards, it wasn't much of a gathering but as Sofia pointed out, most of the town people had dispersed. Undoubtedly, Bertha, the theatre company's owner, expected them to come back later. At least she seemed pleased with how the day had turned out. She'd gotten paid for delivering Bonnie and received permission to stage a preview performance on the steps of the Arts Centre this evening, to give her new lead a chance to rehearse with the troop. Bonnie, on the other hand, was in a town somewhere to the east of where she wanted to be, dependent on a woman she hardly knew. The only thing they seemed to have in common was that they'd both been sacked. Okay, Sofia had resigned, but the result was the same.

They walked through a car park to a road. Looking to her right, Bonnie noticed the roundabout she and Bertha had passed earlier and tried to remember their route through town. It would take her to Melbourne but would it take her to the road heading south? The ones with lancers fleeing Melbourne's fires.

Sofia, intent on her destination, kept walking which meant Bonnie had to run to catch up. She might not be planning to stay in Warragul but until she found how to get out of here, she needed this woman.

They crossed the road and headed down a quiet street, with dried grass on one side and empty parking spots on the other. It retained that post-pandemic feel that Melbourne had swept aside and Bonnie wondered why Karen and Josh wanted to come here in the first place it was at best, unimpressive. Passing a large but otherwise, nondescript building, Sofia turned left. On the other hand, did it matter as long as the place offered them sanctuary?

By now, the noises from the Art's Centre had disappeared but Sofia kept up her pace. This was becoming a workout but Bonnie didn't want to ask the former mediator to slow down because the woman probably needed to work off the pressure of the trial. Bertha had said it was a murder trial and that the accused was female. It must have been difficult, sentencing a woman for merely killing a boy. Especially if the boy was in his cusp years. Then she remembered seeing Zane's body in the morgue. It didn't matter that Zane only had another year and a bit to live, he deserved that year. Josh had said Warragul was a free colony that gave boys the same freedoms as girls so it was only fair that male or female, the murderer should stand trial. If it had been Josh, instead of Zane, she would certainly have cried out for vengeance.

Passing a roundabout, they turned right and walked along a tree-lined street. This was more like her neighbourhood, except instead of comfortable suburban houses there were more undistinguished buildings. This town had no quaint features like the rural towns Bonnie'd visited before the pandemic. It lacked the grace and cultural history of a Bendigo but then there'd been no gold fields on this side of Victoria either. Nor did it have that sense of being stuck in the past like Clunes with its main street that hadn't changed since the eighteen hundreds. This area to the east of Melbourne had developed differently. It was stuck in the past but that past had been unremarkable. Maybe that's why Geraldine thought it was suitable for a backup lab. Who would think to look for her here?

As they came to another roundabout Bonnie recognised the building Bertha had stopped at when they arrived in town. It was the police station and the thought occurred to Bonnie that if she could get away from Sofia, she could go inside and ask for directions. That was if they didn't have a list of Melbourne's most wanted list. She'd never before wondered if the colonies had extradition agreements with the Republic. She decided the police station was a last resort.

The next block contained a shopping mall. Its big blue sign hovered over doors that had once been glass but now consisted of plywood boards. That had happened to the malls in Melbourne as well. Some of the stores facing out reopened during the Transition but the inner spaces remained closed and barricaded like huge man-made caverns. Rumour had it that the Melbourne police regularly raided these areas for lancers and Bonnie wondered if they were heading into Warragul's lancer end of town. Sofia said she was going to take Bonnie to her place but surely the town mediator lived in a more fashionable part of town. Before Bonnie could ask, Sofia broke the silence.

"I think we've come far enough."

Not that she stopped walking or even slowed down.

"Do you have a phone on you?"

"No, I left mine back in Melbourne."

"That's good. We assume all phones are being tracked and monitored. Especially, if they're from Melbourne."

Before meeting the reporter Patricia, Bonnie'd never given her phone much thought. The idea that it was communicating where she was, who she was talking to and what she was saying, had never crossed her mind. It was a device for communicating but now she understood it was communicating more than she imagined. Still, if she and Josh still had theirs, they could contact each other. She'd know he was alive and where to find him.

"If you don't use phones, how do you communicate?"

"We tend to talk to each other in person like we're doing now. But you're right we use phones when we have to. We just don't trust them.

And sometimes we use them because we know they'll be tracked. Your transport is being tracked as we speak."

"My transport?"

Bonnie's face must have signalled her confusion because Sofia smiled and continued. "If we knew you were coming, we might have organised things differently, or maybe not. Things have a way of playing out the way they're supposed to."

They had reached the end of the road they were on. It fed into what looked like a main road. On the opposite side was a large red brick building and Bonnie wondered why she hadn't noticed it until now. The sign was faded but the purple was still visible as were the white letters. For some reason, it seemed out of place or perhaps just out of time. It was the Warragul Train Station. In Melbourne, trams and trains became erratic during the Desolation but transport was one of Evelyn Perkins' main objectives. They were necessary to finish clearing out the dead and essential for bringing in food to sustain the living. The same didn't appear to be the case in Warragul. The train sitting on the tracks was rusted and its windows had been graffitied over.

Following Sofia into the roundabout, Bonnie automatically looked to her right even though there was no sign of traffic. It was a habit but in this case, it served her well because she spotted a different kind of sign. It had been defaced but she could make out the letters Melbo. Close enough she thought. It had probably even displayed the kilometres but half the sign had been ripped off so that information was gone. Not that it mattered. Bonnie knew from the sign at the truck stop that she was at least 100 kilometres from Melbourne. Distance aside, the sign gave her the information she needed. It was a road back to Melbourne and with any luck, it intersected the road south. And the road south was all she cared about because the traders said boys from Melbourne were on the road heading south.

Sofia, however, was still talking about communication.

"I know you must be eager to let your colleagues know that you've arrived safely but I think it would be safer to wait until you've left town."

"Isn't the lab here in Warragul?"

"Hardly," said Sofia as she turned right and led the way towards a small park next to the station.

"Don't worry, you'll be safe at my place for a couple of days, then Jackson will be back and she'll take you to your lab."

"Did you say that the trader's name is Jackson?"

"Yes," replied Sofia now turning right to follow a different main road. "You met her at the morgue. She drove like a demon that night to get Helen and that girl out of Melbourne."

And left my son behind, thought Bonnie. Out loud she said, "So is she on another rescue mission?"

If Sofia noticed the sarcasm it didn't register in her face or her stride.

"She left town so May, our police Commissioner wouldn't suspect her of going after Jocelyn."

"And who's Jocelyn?"

Bonnie was breathing heavily and struggled to get the words out.

"She's the woman we banished today. And much as we love her, we can't risk our operations to save her."

Bonnie stopped. She was out of breath and confused.

"This woman you banished is a friend of yours but you're not going to try to save her?"

"Sorry," said Sofia, "you aren't from here and I'm jumping around. First, it's illegal to help someone who's been banished that's why they're branded with a mark denoting their crime."

"That's barbaric."

Sofia ignored the remark.

"The punishment for aiding someone banished is having all your goods confiscated. We can't afford for Jackson to lose her truck because it's necessary for our operations and now for getting you to your lab. Secondly, we don't know where they've taken Jocelyn. The location is deliberately kept secret so no one can come to the rescue."

All this secrecy and spying was tiring. Bonnie was used to ferreting out information but the secrets she unearthed were in nature. There the rules were constant. Humans with their conflicting wants and needs weren't so straightforward but there was one constant Bonnie understood. You don't desert the ones you love.

They returned to walking.

"So if your friend is left to fend for herself?"

"We were going to wait a day or so, then one at a time, go for walks or in Jackson's case, drives. Surreptitiously, of course. But now we can't risk that."

"Why?"

Sofia looked surprised.

"Because of you. We can't take any risks until you're settled in your lab."

"But your friend, what about her?"

They veered off the main road and onto a side street.

"We have to hope she can survive for now."

"But surely Jocelyn is more important to you than some stranger?"

"We all love Jocelyn but we knew what we were signing up for. Well, Jackson and I did. We decided to keep Jocelyn out of it because of her involvement with the boy Reg."

"And who's Reg."

"The boy she murdered."

They crossed through another roundabout. This town seemed to be full of them. But Bonnie was starting to put the pieces together. This Jocelyn had murdered Reg and was now being set on a road to somewhere with a brand that said no one was to help her and the ones willing to try couldn't because of this lab. The lab she had no intention of going to.

Bonnie didn't like the idea that she was responsible for someone else's life, even if she didn't know the person.

"I don't see why this lab has priority over your friend's life."

Sofia looked at her. They were about the same height and although the woman appeared older, Bonnie learned long ago that age had become difficult to gauge since the Desolation. At the beginning of the Transition, women in their thirties, like Bonnie, found their hair turning prematurely grey and most had wrinkles, especially around the eyes. But more than that, there was a hardness in their features. For Josh's sake, Bonnie refused to let that hardness into her life but for many women that hardness was the scar tissue that killed all feeling. But the hardness Bonnie saw in Sofia's eyes was different. It was more like Geraldine's, the hardness of tempered steel. She'd seen that same look in Evelyn Perkins' eyes too, when she gave her Stability to Rebuild speech. It was hardness with a purpose and in the face of that hardness, Bonnie felt that she was letting down the team.

"You know better than I what you plan to do with that lab," said Sofia, "but I assure you, I will not let anything stand in the way of duty. My husband died doing his duty. My oldest son died doing his and I'd like to believe my youngest was the same. Friends and family are important but duty comes first."

If Sofia had stabbed her with a knife, Bonnie couldn't have been more surprised. Beneath that calm exterior was a woman dedicated to her work. She didn't know what the lab was for and yet she was committed to the task of setting it up and getting Bonnie to it, even if it cost her friend's life.

"There might be another solution," said Bonnie.

Her voice sounded small.

"You could show me how to get there. Surely there's a map in this town. I could walk or hitch a ride."

"Let's keep moving," said Sofia as she led the way down another side street. Bonnie was finding it difficult to keep track of all the twists and turns and wondered if she'd be able to find her way back to the train station and the road to Melbourne. Sofia, however, knew where she was going and how to get there.

"I appreciate your offer and I know it comes from a good place."

Sofia was picking up the pace again.

"But where we're taking you requires passing through the wilds. The main roads are safe enough but the back roads are treacherous and you're far too valuable a resource."

Why does everyone talk about me as if I'm a thing, thought Bonnie. She felt like screaming, I'm not a resource, I'm a mother. Instead, she took a few deep breaths and hoped they were getting close to their destination.

"There are lancers and pirates on the backroads and while there are traders on the main roads, a lot of them trade in information as much as anything. If they knew how valuable you were, they'd be likely to drive you back to Melbourne. I understand that you don't want to be a burden and I can see that you're eager to get to your lab but, trust me, you're better off staying with me until Jackson gets back."

Ahead Bonnie could see a major roundabout with a garden in the center. It looked vaguely familiar but all these roundabouts looked the same so she couldn't be sure.

"A few days ago," continued Sofia, "a trader was killed. I don't say this to scare you, but whoever attacked her dumped her truck on the road leading south out of Melbourne, not far from your lab site."

"Did you say her truck was found on the road leading south?"

"Don't worry. The lab site is about a kilometre off the road and Lang Lang has been deserted for years. No one goes there anymore."

Sofia continued talking but Bonnie had heard all she needed to know. The lab was near the road heading south and Jackson was going to take her there. She half expected to see a rainbow up ahead. All she had to do was wait. She was so consumed with the thought that she would soon be near the road where she hoped to find Josh, that she hardly noticed they'd come full circle. They were back at the Art's Centre where they'd started from but now it looked completely different. Bertha and her troop were busy converting the area that had witnessed the trial into a stage for their new production, Hamletta.

CHAPTER 25
CATHERINE

FRIDAY 10 DECEMBER 2049 - 8:00 P.M.

Catherine says if it's a boy, we have to get rid of him but I'd rather leave than consider any option that means giving up my child.

Where the hell was Thom and why had she left her baby journal open on the couch? They used to talk not leave messages lying around. Notes on tables. Comments in journals. There was so much good news Catherine wanted to share but instead of a contrite Thomasina, what she found waiting for her was these scribbles.

It was after 6pm and it had been a long day. Coming home to an empty house yet again was the last thing Catherine wanted. Yes, she was late and yes, she probably should have called to say she was going to be late but that was how it was when you have an important job. And after this morning's argument and Thomasina's refusal to attend the memorial service, she was justifiably irked. Sure, there was the whole last trimester hormonal thing but this morning's confrontation was pushing the boundaries of their relationship and besides her wife should be by her side not out, God only knew where.

Looking at the front window she saw her reflection and thought something was wrong. Then it dawned on her. Why were the curtains still open? Thom always closed them once it got dark. And why was the TV on? Muted, its images flashed across the screen as silent and uncommunicative as the house. Words scrolled along the bottom. Something about rioting. More words. What were words if there was no communication? She ignored them and let the journal topple to the floor.

At this hour the kitchen should smell of dinner and Thomasina should be patiently waiting for her arrival. A little remorse wouldn't hurt either. If she apologised, Catherine was more than willing to forgive and move on. That's the way it was supposed to be. Her job was demanding, especially now and she thought Thomasina understood that. She should be here pouring her a glass of wine and asking for details on what happened. After all the drama of the interrupted service and then the tension as they waited to learn its cause, was it too much to come home to a wife who fussed over her as she related the events of the day? Because that's what she wanted to do this evening. Talk about her day. Instead of solace though, she faced silence. She looked at the journal lying face down on the floor, turned and walked into the kitchen.

There was no meal waiting on the counter. She checked the microwave. There was nothing there either. No consideration whatsoever. Opening the fridge, she looked at the fresh ingredients sitting on the shelves and wondered what Thomasina had been up to all day. Seeing a bottle of wine, she grabbed it and slammed the door. Then busied herself looking through the cupboards for the wine glasses. She found them on a rack suspended from one of the shelves. When had that been installed? Opening the bottle and grabbing a glass she retired to the breakfast table and looked at the darkening sky.

The day had gotten off to a bad start. Like this evening she'd come home to an empty house. Instead of waking Thomasina with her good news, she'd found a note. Nick! She splashed wine into her glass. Why Thomasina and her mother felt compelled to look after him and coddle him was beyond her. He went missing. So what? Boys that age, even younger, went missing all the time and it was usually a relief to their family when they did. If they weren't acting out, they were sullen and despondent. Evelyn was right. Males, especially those who had little more than a year left to live, were a drain on society. Looking after them was worse than futile. It was ridiculous.

Why couldn't Thomasina see that? That's what made this morning's argument so ridiculous. OK, maybe she shouldn't have said that Thom's mother should have gotten rid of Nick the day she gave birth to him. Back then who knew what the future held? The Desolation was petering out and everyone thought the next generation would be fine. They certainly looked healthy. She took a sip of wine. But by the time she and Thom were at university, it was obvious what was going on. Boys were doomed and without a cure in sight they became—

Became what? She asked herself. Nothing, she muttered. They became less than nothing. The boys she and Thom grew up with were dead. It didn't take long for everyone to accept males dying. No, not acceptance. It was a deliberate turning away from the inevitability of it. Women, young and old, were sick and tired of death and she and Thom weren't exempt. No one wanted to deal with death any more. They wanted to live. She swirled the wine in her glass. To celebrate life. Wasn't that why they'd lost interest in boys?

When we first started dating, thought Catherine, I was the one who said that the best way to embrace life was to turn away from the dying and Thomasina had agreed. We had so much in common back then.

Lifting the glass, she drank half of it, gulping it down like water.

Not that they were like those couples who strove to be identical in every way. They were complementary. She was decisive, competitive and the first to spot an opportunity. Thom said she liked that about her. She said she didn't mind staying in the background. And she liked being the wife of an up-and-coming politician. Liked the nice house. The car. The extra stipend.

Catherine finished the wine in the glass and refilled it.

But Thom had changed. It started with the pregnancy. There was that outburst over the eggs being destroyed. If she'd had her way they'd have implanted all of them. And that argument at Monika Thomas' engagement party and always requests about Nick. She used her influence to get him a job at Steele Construction but he complained. And then announcing he was joining a stud farm. What a joke.

She took another gulp of wine and looked at the label. It was a viognier from that new winery in the Heathcote area. Hadn't they been saving that for a special occasion?

Catherine put up with these things because her wife was sensitive. It was part of her creative nature. But when her sensitivities got in the way of their future, she had to draw the line. If only Thom could see Evelyn's vision the way she could.

Condensation puddled at the base of her glass and Catherine wiped it with her hand.

There had been a time. Catherine downed the contents of her glass.

When Evelyn pointed out that society needed a new structure, they embraced that change. When Evelyn pointed out that this new society also needed to maintain continuity with the past, they were ready to support whatever Evelyn proposed because more than anything they wanted stability and a path laid out for them to follow. That path Evelyn said was linked to the concept of the nuclear family. It made sense, at least to Catherine. Thom had been less sure because of the whole job situation. Thom was an artist and said that the government placed no value on art. Catherine said that would have to come later. And they both benefited when the NOP gave her a choice position on the back bench. There were inequities in their careers but Catherine vowed to make changes.

Taking another drink, Catherine saw that she was the one making all the concessions. Even putting up with the stigma of having in-laws who kept a lancer at home.

Shadows ate away at the garden. And Catherine drained her glass.

"So if we have a boy, you think we should dump him. Just toss him away at birth as if he was a mistake that had to be erased."

Thom's words piqued her the way picadors' lances enraged a bull. Each word was a sharp barb aimed with precision. She felt like reaching out and smashing them. Squishing them on the table the way you'd squish a fly. She'd been tired and Evelyn's conversation had made her realise the impact of raising a boy in these changing times.

"Which is why we need to get the gender test done. The sooner we know we're having a baby girl the better."

She had planned to make it a simple request. Instead of firing it across the table, she should have said something about how gender testing would allow them to announce to the world that they were having a girl. Then once they had the results of the test, if it was a girl, they wouldn't have needed to talk about alternatives.

She emptied the last of the wine into her glass.

It was because of Nick. She should have known Thomasina would read that into what she'd said about gender testing. That's why Thom had stood up from the table saying, "Better for who? Better for the baby? Better for the world? Or better for you? That's it, isn't it? You think that if we raise a baby boy it will affect your political future."

That's when things escalated out of control. If Thom hadn't made that accusation about her political future, she might not have responded the way she did.

The world outside was black so instead of looking out on her garden with its green grass and flowers she saw her reflection. It looked distorted and ugly. She heard her voice saying, "That's right Thom I am thinking about my future but it's your future as well. I wish you could for once take a look at the practical side. I know you're an artist and you like to see the sensitive side of things but I need to take care of you. This house. You think if I lost my status in the party we'd be allowed to live in this house? Do you think if we had a baby boy we'd be allowed to live in this nice neighbourhood? Our future rests on us having a girl."

"Future," Thom had flung that word. Knives. They'd escalated from throwing barbs. It was time for the muleta, that sword hidden behind the red cape.

"I thought we were going to change the future. Build a better, more equitable world."

"Yes, a more equitable world but one that doesn't cling to the past. The way forward requires making sacrifices."

They were both standing and Catherine had the strange feeling that she was standing in the park, confronting her mother again. Why was it so hard for those around her to see that she was building something?

Something for all of them. At least she'd attempted to diffuse the anger between them.

"It's getting late and we need to get dressed," she'd said. She even explained how important the day was. "Our arrivals at the service are timed so that we arrive in a certain sequence. We're seated next to Evelyn so I have to arrive before Monika."

But what had Thom done? She'd manoeuvred Catherine into position only to deliver the final blow. She refused to go! And now she was gone and hadn't even left a note.

Gulping a mouthful of wine, she let it sit in her mouth, absorbing its slightly bitter taste, then swallowed. Thom had probably run home to her mother. Well she, Catherine, had more important things to think about than a silly argument with Thom. What Evelyn spoke to her about after the memorial service. Now that's what mattered.

The Subversives had hacked into the public address system, interrupting the service but instead of garnering sympathy for their cause, they'd shown how desperate they were to disrupt the stability of the Republic. The accusations were aimed specifically at Evelyn. Evelyn Perkins of all people. But Evelyn was quick to point out that an attack on one was an attack on all.

Catherine tipped the bottle but there was no wine left in it. Her glass was empty and she had no idea where Thomasina kept the other bottles or even if there were any more. Anger, like the wine, was gone leaving only a bad taste in her mouth.

Besides, it was time to sleep. Thom could wake her when she came home and then she would tell her the good news. Everything would go back to normal when Thom learned that Evelyn had asked her to run for Premier in the February elections. Tomorrow, they would announce the date but tonight she needed to get some rest.

Standing up she stumbled then steadied herself against the table. Making her way to the front room, she stopped to watch the images flashing across the TV screen. She looked around for the remote and seeing it on the coffee table stumbled towards it. She stubbed her toe on something and looked down to see what it was. It took a moment to register that it was Thomasina's journal. With a flick of her foot, she kicked it out of her way.

CHAPTER 26
DR HARRIS

FRIDAY 10 DECEMBER 2049 - 8:00 P.M.

From the Arts Centre, a cheer rose.

"Sounds like the play's beginning," said Sofia as she stood up. Indoors, the kettle was whistling in conjunction with the crowd on the other side of the green.

It was a warm night and Sofia had suggested they have a cuppa on the porch. She offered Bonnie the porch swing taking the straight-backed chair that set next to the door.

"How do you like your tea?"

"Milk and one," replied Bonnie.

The tranquillity of Warragul made the conflagration in Melbourne feel like a distant nightmare. Even Karen's surprising refusal to help locate Josh felt like a minor setback.

As Sofia re-emerged with a couple of mugs, another burst of cheers and clapping erupted.

"Perhaps Hamletta has made her appearance," said Bonnie.

She tried to remember Hamlet's opening line. It was something, not as famous as 'to be or not to be', but equally enigmatic. Then she remembered. The words, "a little more than kin and less than kind."

"I suppose In Hamletta, Claudius has been renamed to Claudia," she said as Sofia handed her one of the mugs.

"Hmm, the uncle become stepfather is aunt become stepmother."

"I'm guessing it's aunt become guardian if the play's to be accepted in the Republic of Melbourne."

"Yes, they have that requirement don't they?"

"It was part of Evelyn Perkins' plan to create a new kind of nuclear family. Women with children could only receive a living stipend if they had a working guardian as part of the household."

"Do you have children Dr Harris," asked Sofia.

"I have a son."

"So do you have a guardian back in Melbourne?"

"No," replied Bonnie. "I was spared that requirement on two counts. First of all my son was in the first Selection group and secondly, applied and received an exemption under the Pre-Pandemic Essential Worker Act. For that, I have my boss Dr Williams to thank."

"It must have been a difficult transition. Personally, I wouldn't want to be told to share my life with someone else."

"It's only become a requirement in the last five years and it's only necessary if you want to receive a child care stipend."

"And did you receive a childcare stipend with your exemption?"

Bonnie smiled, but it was a wry one. "I have a son."

"I'll take that as a no."

"I receive, or should I say, I used to receive, a good stipend along with my government house so I could afford to keep my son. And like you, I didn't want to introduce someone else into our house."

As Bonnie stopped to take a sip of tea, she thought of Karen. She knew the girl didn't get along with her guardian. Josh had told her as much but never explained why. Like Hamlet, maybe she resented her mother remarrying or maybe she didn't trust the woman because she worked for the government. Still, it had allowed them to keep their house and gave them a comfortable life. The same couldn't be said of Zane or Benny's mothers. With no guardian and no stipend to pay for their children's upkeep, they were reduced to poverty. Ironically Zane was killed because he was mistaken for Benny but for all Bonnie knew, Benny was dead now too. Her one hope was that Josh had survived.

Getting back to the subject of Hamlet, she said, "How do you think they'll handle Ophelia in this new version?"

"My guess is that she'll be made to represent the pre-Desolation female; jilted by Hamlet, controlled by her father and her brother, they'll kill her off but maybe change her last words."

"Or maybe not. Doesn't she bless the souls of the dead before she dies herself?"

"So she ends up representing the old social structure because to be politically correct, that's what must die. On the other hand, there's the ghost of Hamlet's father or I should say mother, who—"

Sofia suddenly stood up. "Someone's headed this way."

No, I think the line's, "Who's there?"

"Not the play," said Sofia, walking over to the edge of the porch to get a better look.

Bonnie looked in the same direction and realised that Sofia was right. Someone was rushing towards them. She was too far away and the clothing was different but Bonnie's heart quickened. Perhaps Karen had changed her mind. Joining Sofia at the railing that separated the small porch from the green, Bonnie struggled to make out the features of the girl who rushed in their direction. Whoever it was, they were running, stopping to catch their breath, then picking up the pace again. As the figure came closer Bonnie thought it couldn't be Karen. This person was barefooted. Her white feet contrasted with the dark path. But couldn't Karen have discarded her shoes? She searched for something to indicate that it was Karen. The height was right but the hair was wrong. The closer the girl got, the more it became obvious that it wasn't her. But even as her hopes were crashing, she could feel Sofia's rising. The girl, so close in age and with a build so like Karen's, had stopped again and was bent over, catching her breath but Sofia could no longer contain herself. Eager as a dog to greet its master, she ran out to meet the girl. Bonnie watched as the two greeted each other.

"Catch your breath girl," Sofia said as she helped the girl up the step.

In the dim light from the cottage window, Bonnie saw the girl's dress was torn along the hem, and the dirt-stained feet that moved towards the first step missed and Sofia caught her.

"Come sit down."

The girl's cheeks were flushed the dust and grime streaked with trails of tears.

"Bonnie, can you get Philippa a glass of water?"

Bonnie had been so mesmerised by the presence of the girl that she was startled at Sofia's command. It was as if she'd been watching a play, waiting for the next line or action.

"Of course," she responded and ducked into the cottage. The girl's ragged breaths and sobs urging her on as she heard the girl force her words out between ragged breaths.

"I got here as quick as I could. It's awful. Truly awful."

There was the sound of the porch swing squeaking as a weight settled onto it.

Inside Bonnie searched for a glass but not finding one, filled a mug with water. As she returned she heard the girl saying, "There were bodies stacked up. It smelled awful and the flies. The flies were everywhere."

Bonnie held out the mug and Sofia snatched it from her hand and held it up to the girl's lips, encouraging her to drink.

Once the girl had swallowed a few sips, Sofia said, "Back up and tell me where you saw these bodies."

The girl gulped more water, then pushing the mug away, replied, "Out near the sanctuary in Bunyip."

"The lancer colony?"

More tears were welling up in the girl's eyes. If she was even aware of Bonnie, she didn't show it but Bonnie was eager to learn more.

"Sofia, there were dozens of them. Stacked one on top of the other."

"It wasn't the collapse was it?"

Now the tears were streaming freely and the girl delivered the rest of her message, in between sobs.

"I don't think they collapsed. Because, because, oh god. Sofia, they were all stacked up one on top of the other, like, like—"

Sofia forced the mug up to the girl's lips again. Her voice was soothing but practical.

"It happens in lancer colonies that so many collapse around the same time that, they, they don't have the strength to bury their dead. Maybe they were going to burn them."

Automatically the girl replied.

"No, Sofia you didn't see it. It was like they all died at once. The younger ones along with the older ones."

"Did it look like the place had been attacked?"

"No. That's the strange bit. They were in the Cafe and the chairs and tables were still in place. There were plates that still had food on them. It was like they'd sat down to dinner, then everyone died and then someone stacked them all up. Why would they do that?"

Sofia squeezed in next to the girl with her arm around her shoulder. She leaned her head in close to the girl's ear.

"It's OK. I'll get hold of May tomorrow and she can look into it."

"No!"

The girl was suddenly animated.

"You can't send May out there."

Sofia straightened up. Bonnie could see the look of concern.

"Philippa, what aren't you telling me?"

"I can't give you any more information because if you knew then you'd be an accessory and you'd lose everything."

"Philippa, I'm going to ask you again, "What were you doing out near Bunyip?"

"I told you—"

"Is that where May took Jocelyn?"

Bonnie started to make the connection. May was the name of the Police Commissioner who'd taken away the murderess.

"I knew they were taking Jocelyn as far as Drouin and that they planned to leave her on the road that goes to Longwarry. I'm from that area so I thought once they dropped her off I could find her and take her someplace safe. There's no way she could walk to Melbourne. Not in her condition."

Sofia was all business now.

"Where is she now?"

"I can't involve you."

"You already have. Where is she?"

The girl choked back her sobs. "There's a farmhouse not far from the sanctuary. I left her in Longwarry while I went to the sanctuary to get some food and supplies. I couldn't bring them from here. Some of the boys I grew up with went there. I thought they'd help."

Bonnie watched the way Sofia stood. What had the girl done that was so awful, she wondered.

"I'm going to call Juanita and she's going to take you home."

"No, no, I need—"

"But first I want you to tell me how to find this farmhouse."

"No Sofia." The girl's voice was pleading. "You'll lose everything. I only came here to tell you about Bunyip and—"

"And what," asked Sofia.

"I need to get food but I can get that from Heart House and it won't take much to get the farm going again and then we can look after ourselves."

"But surely there's plenty of food stocked at the lancer colony."

"No, we need different food because the boy said we shouldn't take anything from the sanctuary in case it's contaminated."

"I thought you said all the boys were dead."

"That was the lancers. These boys were from Melbourne. They were headed this way but I told them Warragul wasn't safe but one of the boys said he needed to find someone here so he was coming anyway. He only agreed to stay with Jocelyn while I came for help."

"He didn't happen to tell you his name did he," asked Bonnie.

"He didn't tell me his name but he asked if I knew a girl named Karen."

"Josh."

The word hadn't come from Bonnie, although the thought was in her head. All three women looked over at another girl standing on the steps.

Karen?

CHAPTER 27
THE OLD ONE'S CABIN

SEPTEMBER 2069

The room fell silent leaving the girl to think her own thoughts and draw her own conclusions.

"We'll finish in the morning," said the Old One backing the wheelchair away from the fire.

The girl was eager to know what happened next but the Old One was right, it was getting late and they were both tired. She told the Old One to wait by the fire while she warmed the bed with a hot water bottle.

As she filled the kettle, she pictured herself going to a play in Melbourne. It would be so much grander than the performances they staged at the Arts Centre because the actors and the scenery would be at a higher standard. Things had changed since Dr Harris and Sofia listened to Hamletta. Theatre companies had gone back to Shakespeare. They probably even stocked his plays in the Melbourne libraries now. As the Old One pointed out, there were advantages to growing up in Warragul. The library had remained open and none of its books had been censored. She could still remember discovering the Complete Works Of Shakespeare. It was a thick book, with a leathery cover that felt like," she stopped in mid-thought. That book under the bed felt the same. Was it a book saved from Melbourne's censors? Or was it something that Tanya didn't want her to read, like that copy of The Three Musketeers, that she found? Or maybe, it wasn't hidden at all. Maybe it had been left behind by a previous occupant of this room.

The kettle screamed and she filled the hot water bottle. Looking over her shoulder she confirmed that the Old One was still occupied in front of the fire. There was only one way to answer her question.

"I'll warm the bed a minute then come and get you."

There was a wave of the hand and the girl disappeared into the Old One's bedroom. She placed the hot water bottle between the sheets and dropped to the floor. It didn't take long to find what she was looking for.

Using her fingertips she slid the book towards herself. It was a thick black book with a hardcover. She snuck another look towards the main room. The Old One sat in the same position facing the fire. There was nothing on the cover. That was disappointing. Rifling through the pages she saw that it was handwritten. Most of it was a combination of tiny cursive text and neatly printed tables. Neither could be deciphered in the poor light so she turned back to the beginning. There on the first page, written in bold black script were the words French Island Research. Underneath was the number 20 but the remainder of the line was smudged and unreadable. Another disappointment.

She flipped to the back but those pages were empty so she flicked through until she found the last one that had been written on. There in neat print was the date February 8 2049 and under it was a single line that said:

We found the key. It's on the x-chromosome.

"How long does it take to heat my sheets," called the Old One.

"It's ready. I'll come and get you now."

Shutting the book, the girl slid it back in place.

STEVE

FRIDAY 10 DECEMBER 2049 - 8 P.M.

The water and sky shared the same shade of ebony, obscuring that line where one ended and the other began. Stars pinned one overhead while their reflections weighed the other down. And there, caught between, sat Steve. Somewhere off to his right lay a large black mound. It attracted and repulsed him in equal measure for it was his home but it had been defiled. Why go back to a place, if what you loved about it, no longer existed?

Sirens wailed in the town of Inverloch. It signalled that the women's area was now closed. Women and children had their place in the centre of town and boys had theirs on the outskirts. Last night, he and the other newcomers, Benny, the Warragul boys and the twins had spent the night imprisoned. This morning, after they'd been told the rules, they were allowed to wander at will but they weren't any freer than they had been when trapped inside the warehouse. Instead of bars on the windows, the rules and the fear of breaking them created invisible shackles.

Fear. This place was segregated by fear and Steve wasn't sure who feared the other more, the women or the lancers. On the surface strict rules kept everything running smoothly but it was a peace built on intimidation rather than mutual respect. Maybe that was how it had to be. Lancers lived their lives knowing every day might be their last and Steve remembered one of the older men at the prison on French Island talking about being sent into a war zone. They were supposed to be a peacekeeping unit but both warring factions refused to abide by the rules.

"A whiff of wrongdoing by either other side was all that it took," said the old soldier, "and retaliation was swift. The ones who wanted war orchestrated it, while the people slaughtering each other forgot why they were fighting in the first place. And there we were caught in the middle. As bullets whizzed past my head and buildings blew apart around me, I also forgot that I was there to maintain the peace. I shot back at whoever shot at me but fear is a funny thing. It doesn't wait for someone to take that first shot. I anticipated death from all sides and soon I became the one who was feared. Fear had turned me from protector into an instrument of death."

Changing tone, the old soldier said, "When we received our orders to come home, I thought I'd been rescued but the fear created by the pandemic was as bad as the fear I'd felt overseas, maybe worse because now it was the unseen enemy and that meant bullets didn't do me much good. Maybe that's why we were all so docile. They said this place was our sanctuary."

Then the soldier had turned to him and said with a touch of sarcasm. "This," he waved his hand, "was never intended to be a sanctuary. It was built to be a prison."

Thinking of the past, his freedom as a boy, his wild teenage years as a stud and then being sent to the prison because he was a survivor, only to escape and wind up here, in Inverloch, he felt like he'd come full circle. There were no guards or fences. He was free to stay or he could leave. Become one with the night and the waves, melt into the darkness and slip away. It wasn't the women of Inverloch that stopped him. It was the island. Physically he'd escaped but there was nowhere to run to because every place was just another form of imprisonment. He might as well be back on French Island.

"Benny said I might find you here."

Steve hadn't heard the Bulldog approach but he accepted his presence as if he'd been expecting him. The lad sat down and Steve felt the heat of his presence.

"Jack told me about your plans to go to French Island. I don't think there's many here that will want to join you."

Steve sighed. He hadn't expected anything different.

"I raised it with some of the older blokes and they didn't sound too keen. It'd be different if you weren't so new."

"You tried," said Steve.

"Don't get me wrong, it's not a definite no. They just don't understand so I was thinkin' you could talk to them yourself. Explain what they would be fighting for?"

"Maybe I should have printed up flyers," said Steve sarcastically.

"That's a bit unfair mate. Lancers have a bond. It's not a personal one but we know we share the same fate and the way Benny tells it, you aren't like the rest of us ."

"I understand Bulldog. I do."

Lights flickered on in the houses in town. It signalled home and peace. Steve could understand why the lancers of Inverloch didn't want to leave. It might be a kind of prison but it was still home. The problem was that it could never be his home. To break the silence or more importantly, to change the subject of home, he said, "It's a shame Jack didn't catch up with those women who abducted Cherry. Do you know what he plans to do next?"

"He thinks she's been taken to Melbourne but even if he could get there, he doesn't know his way around. It's about as hopeful as your idea to free the prisoners on French Island." Then he quickly added. "No offence."

"None taken. But why would the kidnappers take her to Melbourne?"

"Cause that's where she's from. She stumbled into Inverloch a few years ago with her twin brother Charley. Looked worse than you lot when they showed up. They were only thirteen, then. She didn't say where they were from but we knew they weren't no wildings. Later, when we got to know her, she said they were running from their mother. Anyway, once they turned sixteen, Charley was told he had to move to the male side of town but Cherry refused to be separated from him. She and Jack were already tight at this point so he says to meet him on the road to Warragul and he'll show her this disserted cabin he knows. He has connections and says he can get her a job at the big co-op outside town."

"So how did she wind up back here with you and Jack?"

"You mean Venus Bay, where we picked you two up?" said Bulldog.

"I guess I'm asking if she was one of these smugglers."

"Nah, politics's not her thing. She got fired from the co-op and they moved her into town but she ran away. Got to the cabin and Charley wasn't there but someone had been fixin' the place up. Well, she figured maybe he was headin' back here 'cause it's the only place he knows so she hitches a ride with this trader who comes here regularly but of course Charley's not here. Jack says we'll head back up to Warragul with the trader but she says she's got to do a pickup in Venus Bay. She makes a deal with us. If we help with the pickup, she'll help find Charley."

"So that's why Cherry met us at the jetty?"

"Too right."

"And now you figure her mother found out where she and Charley were hiding and came for her."

"Most likely pirates. We knew there was a bounty for them two. Jack went to San Remo to put out the word and that's how he got to talkin' to the Warragul police. Turns out that trader's truck ended up 5k outside San Remo with the body of the trader in the back."

"So the trader was the same one who organised the pickup ?"

"Same. Her name was Lauren. She ran from Venus Bay up to Warragul cartin' fish and bringin' back goods. Ain't no way she was killed by lancers but you can't tell that to the good women of Warragul."

BENNY

Benny sat motionless. On the green, the noises from dinner had died away and the evening siren had sounded. From his vantage point on the hill, he could see Steve talking with Bulldog down by the pier. He imagined Steve convincing the stocky lancer of the need to go to French Island but Benny wasn't so sure he wanted to stick with Steve. The man he knew or thought he knew, had another side. Why hadn't he told him what happened that night?

In the half-light, he saw a darker shadow eclipse his own. Looking up he saw that Jack was standing behind him. He was also watching the two down at the pier.

"Your friend wants to create an army and storm French Island."

Benny dug his fingers into the sand. The warmth was quickly fading and he shivered.

"It's a fool's errand," said Jack. "The kind that's likely to get a bunch of lancers killed."

He sat down next to Benny.

"Our lives are short enough without tossing what's left away but then I suppose you'll follow him like you did back at Venus Bay."

Benny gritted his teeth. If Jack had asked him that question at the start of this day, he would have said, yes. He would have supported anything Steve said. But that was before he realised that Steve hadn't trusted him enough to tell him what happened on French Island.

Down at the pier, Steve was shaking hands with Bulldog.

"Looks like they've made a deal, doesn't it? Course, it's not like either of them needed to consult us."

Jack's words stung the way the truth had a habit of doing.

"They could be talking about meeting for breakfast, for all we know," replied Benny but his heart and voice conveyed his disappointment. That was the other reason Benny was cool on Steve's idea to go to French Island. They should never have stopped in this town. He felt like he'd found his tribe. He could see himself settling into life here with the boys from Warragul. Even the twins. But that wasn't enough for Steve. And Jack was right. Steve hadn't bothered to ask Benny what he wanted.

"While I was in San Remo, I saw all these boys heading south. Something's going on and your friend may be right that San Remo's a trap but if that's the case, then Inverloch isn't all that safe either."

"Maybe no place is safe," said Benny.

"Maybe yes. Maybe no."

Benny glanced over at the scrawny teen.

"You got a plan of your own."

"I ain't got a plan so much as a need."

"You referring to Cherry?"

"You mightn't understand but she's everything to me."

Benny thought about that and said, "Yeah. I get that."

Jack wrapped his arms around his knees and stared out into the night. As they sat there looking into the expanse of water that had captured the stars and now made them dance to its own rhythm, Benny pictured Monika that morning before he made his mistake. Life had been good living in her fancy house but there'd always been that wall between them. He was never more than a toy to her. He pictured his friends the last time they'd all been together. Zane's look when Benny gave him his bike. The way Josh hugged him when they said goodbye but more than anything, he remembered how Karen looked as she dropped him off at the stadium. His fingers longed to touch the strand of hair he felt sure was still in his pocket. They were his real family and like Jack, he wondered where they were and what they were doing. A weight settled in his chest. His friend's plans had got him out of the Republic but they failed to get him to Warragul. Instead, he'd wound up in Inverloch. A place with rules as onerous and controlling as the ones he'd escaped from. And his own plans, plans of travelling with his new companion Steve, well, he wasn't sure that was working out either. The weight pressed harder and he knew what it was. He missed home. He missed his friends but more than anything, he realised, he missed Karen.

CHAPTER 28
THE OLD ONE'S CABIN

SEPTEMBER 2069

It was the morning of her last day and the girl woke early because she had to finish editing her recordings. The set she was taking with her was for the admissions board in Melbourne. She knew what they wanted to hear and she wasn't about to disappoint them. As for the originals, she wasn't sure what to do with them. The version of events the Old One told her, fascinating as it was, could hardly be presented as a historical record.

All night she'd wrestled with questions that had no answers. Was Evelyn Perkins, the Saviour of the Republic only interested in saving the women of the Republic? Had she ordered the arrest of those who threatened her goal to eliminate all males? And now, the really big question. Did the book under the bed prove that there was a lab on French Island? But whose lab and for what purpose?

But the dawn brought with it the need to decide. These questions might not have an answer today but the answers existed. And that's why she put on her runners, finished editing the tapes and started packing. When she came to this cabin in the woods, her only thought had been to finish her assignment and get out of Warragul. The stories changed that. By going to Melbourne, by doing her own research, she would find answers to those questions.

As for the fate of the teens, unlike Dr Harris and Patricia Bishop, they didn't leave a written record of their part in the Great Upheaval and the Truce that ended it so the girl might never know what happened to them or that other person, Steve. She'd seen that name before. It was at the bottom of a letter, hidden inside that book, The Three Musketeers that Tanya took away from her. Was it the same Steve or some other Steve from a pre-pandemic past?

"Are you going to pack that history book of yours?"

The girl looked up to see the Old One sitting in the wheelchair.

"How did you get out of bed on your own?"

"I'm feeling stronger this morning. And how about you?"

Rolling over to the table, the Old One picked up one of the tapes the girl had set aside, then looked at the ones the girl was holding.

"I thought we were going to continue recording?"

The girl placed the revised tapes in her bag and zipped it shut.

"These are the ones I need to satisfy the board in Melbourne."

"And how about you? Are you satisfied?"

The girl wanted to say no. She wanted to say that there was so much more that she wanted to know like how Dr Harris got to her lab and how Patricia wound up as a war correspondent. She wanted to know why Sofia disappeared from history and how Jocelyn survived. She wanted to know what had happened to Karen, Josh and Benny but before she could blurt out her questions, there was a knock at the door.

The Old One placed the tapes down and the girl stared at her bag, She wanted to say that she'd changed her mind. That she still had so many questions that she could only find the answers to here in Warragul but the second knock was more insistent.

"We're coming." Said the Old One rolling towards the door.

She'd made her decision. All her life she'd asked questions and she wasn't going to stop. She'd keep asking those questions until she found her answers. She picked up her bag and faced the door expecting to see Philippa or Juanita. Instead, she saw her advisor Tanya.

"I thought I'd make sure you caught your ride to Melbourne. Did you finish your assignment?"

This was the moment she'd fought for and now she was waving. Stay or go, there was no turning back.

She looked to the Old One but the chair was already rolling away. She looked at her advisor. For so many years they'd fought a silent war. The girl looking for answers. Tanya keeping secrets. Well, maybe it was time to call a truce.

Picking up her recorder, the girl shoved it in her carry bag. What this interview had taught her was that the past was never certain. She couldn't know it any more than she could control it but she could control her future. Maybe that lay in Melbourne or maybe it lay somewhere else but she certainly wasn't going to find it in Warragul.

"All done," she said, as she took hold of her other bag and headed for the door.

"Aren't you forgetting something," asked Tanya pointing towards the tapes on the table.

"No, I'm not taking them with me. They just contain some old stories that won't be of much use to, probably, anyone."

These last words tumbled out but she saw something in Tanya's eyes. Her advisor wasn't looking at her though. The look was between Tanya and the Old One. Confused she looked from one to the other but the moment was gone. Tanya picked up the last bag and the girl watched as she headed out the door.

Turning towards the Old One, she said, "Thank you again."

There was no response. The Old One wasn't even looking in her direction.

"Let's go," called Tanya.

As the door closed the Old One waited until the steps had been absorbed by the surrounding bushland, then picked up the tapes, placed them in the box and packed the other items on top. Perhaps it was best if Sara didn't know the rest. Isn't that why they'd brought her here in the first place?

ABOUT THE AUTHOR

Just who do you think you are?

Alyce Elmore got tired of being asked that question, deciding instead to write about it. Her short stories, audio dramas and novels search for answers by scavenging through time and place, exploring the real and the fantastic, and along the way encountering the outrageous and the mundane. She has lived in major cities around the world, journeyed through jungles, hiked in the mountains, and currently resides in an off-grid shed in the middle of nowhere. To date, she has no answers, just lots of clues, but she invites her readers to hitch a ride anyway because a search for the unknowable is in itself an enjoyable quest.

Visit her website at www.alyceelmore.com

facebook.com/alyce.elmoreauthor